AF207352

Coffin Drop

J. Van Dyke

squeek-by
Graphics
Publications

ISBN 0-9642734-0-3

Format and Design by Squeek-by Graphics
9571 Joy Road
Plymouth, MI 48170-5026

Cover Art by Anna Willis

Printed in the United States of America

For John and our friends at Nature's Last Stand
who supplied the patience, inspiration, support, and friendship

🐎 1

"Don't do it, Tim!" Continuing his pursuit, David dodged around startled shoppers, vaulted a low wall, and landed awkwardly on a set of stone steps. He bounced off a brick wall and raced down the stairs, thrusting people out of his way as if they were lifeless barriers to his desperation. He burst into the open esplanade and saw the cigarette lighter strike into flame. "Tim, no!"

Before the shout died, Tim's fuel-soaked clothes roared into a flash fire. David charged through an instant of stunned silence toward a pillar of fire wearing grey cords and scuffed running shoes. He leapt forward, driving his shoulder into the flames at the height of his friend's waistline. His momentum lifted the blazing body over a low wall into a shallow fountain. Water hissed around their tangled bodies. Pain jarred through him when he hit the concrete bottom on his side. He gulped in a breath of thick, chlorine-scented air, wrapped his arms around Tim's thin body, and rolled over and over, back and forth, until he felt soaked and cold.

When David sat up, clasping a limp, drenched weight against his chest, a gawking, one-faced crowd pressed toward the fountain in a staring wall of rounded eyes. A policeman swam through the parting crowd beside the ashen face of a Sanford Security guard. Somewhere in the parking lot a siren wailed. When the policeman reached the edge of the fountain, David relaxed his arms, letting

1

Tim roll toward the uniformed men.

Stunned, David looked at what he held in his arms. With no hair to frame it, the face was rimmed with reddened flesh, but the center was unblemished. In reflex, Tim had thrown up his hands and covered his face before the blast of heat engulfed his head. The sudden plunge in the cold water had saved Tim's face but not the flesh on the backs of his hands, arms, and chest, where dark patches showed like splashes of war paint. David's throat clogged from the gagging smell of burned clothes, hair, and flesh. Twisting away from the bundle that the paramedics lifted onto a stretcher, he knelt with his arms wrapped around his waist. The horror retched out of him in nauseating waves.

A week later, the dramatic moment was a forgotten event in Ann Arbor, Michigan. Tim Hubbard occupied a private room at the University Hospital burn center. David Breton sat in a metallic-grey sports car beside a gravel road and stared down a sloping hillside at a cluster of barns, outbuildings, and houses.

Trees and grasses blushed with the vibrant green of spring growth and angled sunlight warmed the facade of the old, three story mansion, but David was unmoved by the beauty of the farm. Since his mother's marriage four years ago, he felt he was little more than a lodger in his stepfather's home. The alienation had increased last winter until he now felt he was an unwanted intruder in a family that was not his. He was especially reluctant to go home today and had asked Karen to pull off the road.

Turning from the farm, he looked across the car at her soft face with its impish nose and dark, bottomless eyes. When he had come to Michigan five years ago, he had loved Karen with an undeclared adolescent crush. Two years ago, when Paul, a tall, dark, and handsome medical student, entered Karen's life, David experienced intense jealousy that turned to envy, and, finally, to friendship. Karen was now a senior at the University of Michigan, Paul an intern at University Hospital. They were the only people who treated him as more than a shallow teenager. The only friends he allowed to know him.

He looked away from Karen, back toward the farm below him.

"I keep thinking I should have let him die. It's what he wanted."

"No, it isn't," Karen answered flatly. "When a person really wants to kill himself, he doesn't do it in front of a crowd."

David wanted to say that Tim would because he always wanted an audience, but he knew the answer had to come from Tim, who wasn't saying anything right now. David had acted. He couldn't feel right about it. If he hadn't acted, he wouldn't feel right about that. "I'm still not ready to talk about it."

"Remember me when you do feel like talking about it." Karen looked past him at the horse and rider working in the main dressage ring. "Is that Vulcan?"

"Mom's been riding him. Maybe it will be good for Hugh — if it doesn't make him bitter. He drinks when he's bitter."

Sharon pressed her leg against Vulcan's sleek, mahogany flank, added a touch of spur. The stallion's hind leg crossed under him in a two-track that maintained the even, two-beat cadence of the trot while he moved diagonally across the ring, his neck and body curved, just perceptively, in the direction of his movement. With crested neck arched, red-lined nostrils flared, he snorted rhythmically and worked the two bits in his foaming mouth. When she reached the center line, Sharon reversed the horse's flexion with a smooth change of aids and moved him away from her right leg, back toward the track she had left.

"He's lazy on the right hind. Use the whip."

Sharon frowned and used more right spur, emphasizing it with a smack, just behind her leg, from a long training whip. The horse snorted and stepped farther under his body, crossing his right hind leg in front of his left.

"Good. Collect the trot at H, then extend from M to F. Collect at F."

Sharon vibrated the curb rein unnoticeably and sent the stallion forward with her seat and legs. Push, push, push. Sometimes she thought her back would give out.

"Stop making faces. You're working too hard. It should be easy, pleasant."

When she collected the stallion, Sharon felt him spring

beneath her — light, bouncing, evenly cadenced, his body shortened and rounded from head to tail. The corner from H to C was too deep. She held hard with her outside leg to keep his haunches from spinning out.

"Hold him, damn it! That's a grand prix horse, not a training level colt. Look where you're going. Balance him through the corner. Right leg! Right leg!"

The corner from C to M was good, even beat, smooth bend, no loss of impulsion. Just before M, she opened her seat, stretched her back, felt him surge into her hands.

Loosening the coil of collected power, Vulcan lengthened his stride, his back, his neck. His forehand lifted, allowing hind hooves to reach beyond the imprints of fore hooves. His forelegs snapped out in front of him, pausing at full extension while powerful haunches propelled him forward like an express locomotive.

"Stay with him. Don't throw him away. He'll break. Hold him and push."

Sharon felt a loss of contact with the horse's energy. She regained control before he broke into a canter, but his rhythm stuttered until he found his even, balanced cadence again. Then she was at F, holding him between hands and legs, back into the lightness of collection.

"Do it again from K to H and don't lose him. Keep him in your hands. Push, hold, push, hold, shape the arc of energy. If you break the circuit, he'll fall apart. You're the conductor from his generating haunches to his receptive mouth."

With her eyes looking ahead, she rounded the end of the ring and drove him into extension again. This time she held his power in her hands while it thrust him forward. The animal's entire muscular structure lengthened until he was reaching, flying. It was work. It was concentration. It was fantastic. She was part of this animal. They moved together, communicating by movements so subtle they were reflexes, unconscious and instinctive. The transition from thrusting power back to floating grace was smooth and within one stride. Vulcan was collected again, using his power for slow elevated motion with precision and balance.

"Good girl. Medium walk at C, free rein at R. Let him relax and praise him. My God! He's magnificent."

Sharon settled into the saddle, dropping the horse to a walk. She held Vulcan on the bit while she rounded the corner. Then, letting the reins slip through her fingers, she pushed him into long, swinging strides. His neck reached out and down, stretching muscles that had held him arched and balanced.

Sharon relaxed when she looked down the ring. Hugh was smiling. Sea-green eyes brightened a gaunt face that was starting to fill in again. Strong, broad shoulders thrust the wheelchair forward, keeping it parallel to her while she walked the horse toward the opening at the A end of the ring. She suppressed the pain that burrowed in her chest when she approached the rolling chair with its swivel base for teaching and ground training horses.

Once outside the low fence of the dressage arena, Sharon slipped her feet from the stirrups and halted beside the wheel chair to let Hugh scratch the horse's head. When she dismounted, she lowered herself to the grass, but landing was still a jolt. Vulcan was 17 hands tall, five feet, eight inches at the withers, two inches taller than she was. She handed the reins to Matt Stone, Eminence Farms' head stableman. When he led the horse away, she pulled off her black gloves, set both hands on the arms of the wheel chair, and leaned forward to kiss Hugh.

She straightened, laughing at his surprised look. "He's magnificent because you are. He's your horse."

"Not any more."

"He still is and always will be. I may be on his back, but you trained him. It's your hands and voice he responds to best." She walked beside the chair while he wheeled it toward the barn. Hugh insisted on moving himself to the point where he ignored the machine's electric drive, only using it when he needed his arms and hands for something else.

Although Hugh had lost the use of his legs, he refused to give up the strength of his arms and upper body. Or his conditioning. His pride rejected sympathy or help and castigated him with self-pity, which was unlike the Hugh Jamison she had married four years ago. He had the pride then, but it was a winning pride that had never known failure.

Hugh Jamison had not actually been given everything he wanted, but he never had to work hard to get it. Born with wealth, intelligence, good looks, and a determined, energetic nature, he had been athletic and adventurous all his life. He had risked injury and stressed himself in numerous ways: football, Karate, skydiving, ski jumping, mountain climbing, a Green Beret officer in Viet Nam, and his main interest and later profession — training and competing with open jumpers, dressage, and combined training horses.

Hugh had jumped a horse over seven feet, ridden cross-country courses at speeds that horrified Sharon. She watched him with her heart stuck in her throat, gasping whenever he fell or the horse missed his striding and crashed through or onto what looked like a logjam of multicolored poles, barrels, wooden walls, or gates. He always stood up with a curse or a grimace to check his horse. If the animal was uninjured, he remounted to jump the reconstructed obstacle.

In the past four years, Sharon had lived through so many flash panics that when the police arrived at the house last November to say Hugh was on his way to the hospital, she was unable to grasp it. He was not even on a horse, just hiking up to an old cabin on the back of the farm. The police called it a hunting accident, a shotgun blast from behind, too low to kill, high enough to lodge buckshot in his spine. Hugh dragged himself or rolled to where a neighbor was cutting firewood. The hunter was never found.

Sharon refused to believe it was an accident and, although he flatly refused to talk about it with her, she suspected Hugh felt the same. She doubted even the police believed it. There was no evidence to support further investigation so they called it an accident.

As far as Sharon knew, Hugh's decision to go to the cabin had been spur of the moment. He said he heard shooting and hoped to run poachers off his land. No one else had heard shooting.

At the brick mansion house, Sharon jogged up the stone steps beside the wheel chair ramp. She crossed the porch to open a wide door, holding it while Hugh bumped the chair over the threshold. In the entry hall she stopped at a long table beside the staircase and picked up a bundle of mail. Hugh turned into his office, where

Leon would shift him from the large outdoor wheel chair to a lighter, indoor one.

Leon Williams was hired as a private attendant, but he was more than that to Hugh. They had known each other as boys, teens, and young men. Leon's parents had taken care of the Jamison house and grounds since before Hugh had been born. They had stayed on after his widowed mother's death three years ago with no objections from Sharon, who was more interested in horses, dogs, and art than housekeeping chores.

Two years before Hugh's entrance to the University of Michigan in Ann Arbor, Leon had gone to the U of M on a football scholarship, as many blacks did, and then, unlike most sport scholars, graduated with a 3.5 average and a degree in pre-med. As a paramedic, Leon had gone to Viet Nam before Hugh. He was shot in the knee and spent the next six years in and out of surgery and therapy until he learned more than enough to be a competent attendant for Hugh.

While Sharon sorted the mail, a brown and white mop of dog trotted up to her. He reared up on his hind legs and, with his forepaws resting on her thigh, looked at her with dark eyes. The dog waved a feathery tail until she dropped a hand to scratch behind his ears. When he continued to paw at her leg, she pushed him down, then crouched to face him.

"I'm glad to see you, Sigmund, but I don't want you clawing at my breeches." She accepted a quick, pink-tongued kiss on the chin before giving him a last pat.

When she looked back at the mail, one of the letters caught her attention. She ripped it open, frowned while she read it, then picked up the stack of mail and took it into Hugh's office.

Hugh sat in the small wheel chair with his hand wrapped around a glass that was half-filled with light amber scotch and two slivers of ice. She tried not to scowl at the drink when she handed him the mail. At least he waited until afternoon now.

When he had first come home from the hospital, Hugh started drinking scotch as a replacement for brunch. By dinner time, he made little sense and ate less. No one was able to tell him anything or do anything with him, except Leon. At least once a day Hugh spun off into a tantrum of cursing and insisted he could walk as well as ever. In a surge of fury, he would launch himself out of the wheel chair and crash to the floor when his useless legs failed to support him.

The winter had been hell until Leon, a confirmed teetotaler, tempered Hugh's drinking. Leon made him accept the truth and helped him design the big wheel chair so he could be with his horses again. After they purchased a gentle Percheron gelding and cart, Hugh started driving the big, black horse on the farm roads. By early spring, when the last patches of snow melted and the mud dried up, he was working with several horses.

Two weeks ago, Hugh took Vulcan out of early retirement. In a major retraction of his winter decree that no one would ride the stallion again, he allowed Sharon to ride him. Vulcan was the only horse Hugh had trained to grand prix level. Emotionally, he had not wanted to see Vulcan under another rider. Practically, he had been unable to let such a magnificent animal waste his abilities and serve no purpose beyond breeding. Now, he wanted to teach Sharon to ride the horse, insisting it was only for appreciation of the art of dressage and enjoyment of a quality performance.

Hugh took a swallow of the scotch before nodding at the open, typed letter in her hand. "Your face doesn't look pleased."

"An understatement at best. It's from Haskill Academy."

"What's David doing now?"

"He's not going."

"Where have you been taking him every morning?" His question had an accusing bite to it.

"I've been taking him to school, and Arlene Metzger has been picking him up at school. But he has not been attending classes as often as three days out of the week. He had notes, forged I imagine, for the first few times. Then he said he forgot to get notes."

"If it's a scheme to get a car, he's on the wrong road. He can drive to school when he's a senior and not before. There is no way I will change my mind."

"This week he told them I didn't know and he didn't care. That doesn't surprise me. Tim was the only one at Haskill David cared about."

Sharon stared across the office at framed pictures of Hugh,

herself, and David leaping cross-country fences, riding in dressage tests, and clearing brightly painted stadium jumps. Horses and eventing filled so much of their recent lives she sometimes wondered what else they had in common. Three people with a compulsive interest in horses that buried conflicts with its intensity. Before Hugh's accident, the frictions had been below the surface. Now, they were boiling up like lava in the mouth of a volcano.

"Is he home?" Hugh asked.

"I don't know."

"Tell him I have no intention of spending over three thousand a year on a school he doesn't go to."

"That's what he wants. Public school has more appeal."

"I didn't say he would go to public school. I'll spend eight thousand and send him to a good boarding school."

"That's not an answer. You don't try to understand David. You tell him what you would do and expect him to do the same, even if he sees it differently."

"How can I understand him?" He thumped his empty glass onto the desk. "He's nothing like I am. You lived with his father for thirteen years and never understood him. The damn kid's just like him."

"So you shut him out because he reminds you of Marc Breton." She pivoted toward the door. Anger festered in her as it always did when she crashed into the barrier of Hugh's jealousy. She wanted to explain Marc to him, but he would never listen. She controlled her anger and softened her voice, removing any trace of defensiveness. "At least when I lived with Marc, David had a father."

"I've tried."

When she turned back, her face was burning, but she battled down her anger and answered softly, "Not lately."

"You're right. I've let David think he's God Almighty because I wasn't up to coping with him."

"That's not the way I meant it. You used to relate to David."

"Not very well." He gave her a discouraged frown. "I can make David behave, but he'll never accept me as a father."

"Because you were foolish enough to insult his real father."

"Sharon, I despise Marc Breton. David knows it. There is no reason to pretend otherwise."

"You don't have to hate David because he's like his father."

"I don't hate David." Hugh sat back in the chair and stared at her from troubled eyes. He calmed his voice and added. "It's the other way around, and it isn't all for no reason. I've put the screws to David a few times. He was spoiled enough to resent it."

"David could understand your hate of Marc because of me. When you cut Marc for other reasons, such as his relation with David, you lost his respect."

"There's only one way David respected me. On a horse I was a worthy challenge, someone to learn from and eventually defeat. Last fall someone called off the contest and I became unimportant as a rival."

"Let him ride Vulcan. Let him—"

"No."

"I think he'd regain respect for you if he could feel what you've accomplished with that horse."

"David is a good rider, but he can still learn from Casey. I gave him a horse that can teach him more than I can because, right now, David doesn't want to learn from me. When lessons turned into ego battles, I stopped teaching him."

"He does seem to think he knows it all right now." Sharon looked at the letter crumpled in her hand. "I don't know what to say to him any more."

"He doesn't listen, so what difference does it make? David doesn't want to go to school, but he has to go to school. Inform him that if he doesn't like Haskill, we'll send him to a boarding school. He will not go to West Ridge High."

"The high school isn't that bad. And Haskill isn't without problems. We both know Tim took drugs. I'm not naive enough to believe David hasn't."

"The problems are on a smaller scale and better monitored. You know damn well David would be in the thick of it."

"But he's good friends with Leon's Bruce. He has no one at Haskill any more."

"Bruce is two years younger than David. Leon would rather he didn't share some of David's interests."

"Leon never felt that way before."

"David respected Bruce's older brother. But Rob's too busy at the University to have much time for David, who definitely thinks he knows it all." Hugh gave her a patronizing look that said he knew what he was talking about and had stopped listening. "Sharon, he can't blast his way to success on his charms."

"His father did."

"If you call it success." Hugh scoffed and refilled his glass.

"I used to. He was a famous soccer player in Europe."

"Fame is a fickle mistress. You can be ten feet off the ground one day and flat on your ass the next with no more fast cars or rich women. That will be the end of Marc Breton's success story. He just better not come here looking for handouts."

"I can't see Marc doing that. He would never stoop to begging. He might try to work a con on someone, but not on me." She twisted her face and looked thoughtful. "Marc never conned someone who didn't deserve it."

"He'll need money sooner or later. I doubt if he's invested one cent in anything lasting."

"I wouldn't know about that. I never had anything to do with money, beyond spending what he gave me." She stepped behind him and worked her fingers into the hard, tight muscles beside his neck.

"With Marc, life was fast-paced." She kept her voice even, wondering how much she could explain before emotions dragged them into an argument and he slammed his shell closed. "It was always one con after another, always a risk to gamble on. If Marc couldn't charm his opposition, he could outwit it or trick it. He could fight. He could persuade. He could smell out suckers and bleed them. Marc could bankrupt swindlers, then turn them over to the police flat-broke with an airtight case against them."

The muscles beneath her hands grew tighter, but he was silent, letting her say more than he ever had before. "He outswindled the swindlers, outrobbed the robbers, and outspent the rich. Marc did everything wrong better than his competition while balancing on the edge of the law. He was a rogue. And although he went after the bastards, he was out for himself. How can I tell that to a seventeen year old boy who worships his father and blames me for taking him away from him?"

"Because the son of a bitch did it to you." The muscles became rocks and his hands tightened on the chair arms.

"I won't believe that." She kept her hands on his shoulders, hoping her touch could keep his irritation in check. "At least not with the malice you see in it."

"Why won't you admit he took you for every penny you had?" She stepped aside when the chair rolled back and spun so he could face her.

"Marc Breton was a handsome, charming, fun-loving man. I fell for him like a witless baboon and helped him spend my mother's money as fast as we could get it out of the Chase Manhattan Bank. We had a hell of a lot of fun doing it." She sat on the edge of his desk and gave him a chagrined look. "In his defense, he told me what he was doing. And when it was gone, he didn't dump me. He just looked somewhere else for fun money."

"He told you?"

"He told me right off that he conned the rich. I was too full of rebellious independence to realize I was one of the rich and ripe for conning, which he could have done with a lot less compassion." She smacked her hands down on her thighs and shook her head. "Young, foolish, and gullible. He told me that, too. I figured he was there to take care of me and protect me from the world's evils."

"You should have come back sooner." Hugh's anger cooled to grumbling resentment.

"I had an infatuation to burn out on that man. And I had no reason to come back." She rubbed her hand through his dusky blond hair and looked into his green eyes. "My father was disgustingly proper and disapproved of me. You wrote me one pompous, condemning letter, then married Midge Paxton, who always rode on her crotch with her little round buns thrust out. She was a terrible rider, who only won ribbons because her father bought model hunters and hired a full time, professional trainer." Sharon chuckled. "I always wondered if she was as stiff-backed in bed as she was on a horse."

Hugh caught her wrist, pulling her into his lap. "You're showing your bitchiness again. The truth is she screwed as badly as she rode. However, the problem was in her head, not her back. You know I only married her because you were shacked up with Breton."

"I didn't know I'd be welcomed back. I wasn't even sure of that when I heard you were divorced." She wrinkled her nose and teased him, cajoling him out of his sulk. "You always were a double-standard, proper bastard. I was sure you'd written me off as morally unsuitable. The old damaged goods syndrome."

Hugh laughed with a spontaneity she had not seen in a long time. "I tried that until you came home and showed me how enjoyable liberated morality can be."

"It's more fun to enjoy life than worry about how it looks to everyone else." She wondered if his conceding smile would vanish if he realized who had taught her to know her own center and reject guilt imposed by others. "I want to get out of riding clothes and take a long bath so I can think things out before I talk to David." She gave him a quick kiss and stood up.

"Sure. I have some paperwork to catch up on." He held her with a firm hold on her hand. "If you want, I'll talk to David. I can't convince him of anything, but he does know where the free lodging comes from and when he's pushed me too far."

"That's one of the things I need to think out."

2

While she soaked in a tub of hot water, Sharon found she wasn't thinking about David, but about his father. Whenever she thought about Marc, she was surprised to find her memories strong and vivid, as if it had started a few months ago, not eighteen years ago. Today, they were so clear she could remember every detail of the drive along the Appian Way to her hillside apartment outside of Rome.

The apartment was in a building of white stucco with a wall around the grounds and black, iron gates. Tall cypress trees framed a gate house where a little, white-haired man opened the gate for her tiny, red Fiat. The big wall and the little man made her feel safe in her second floor apartment, which had a minuscule kitchen, modern dining/sitting room, and a studio bedroom with a balcony. She felt grown-up in her first independent home and enjoyed the balcony, where she could breathe the fragrance of cascading flower gardens and gaze beyond their brilliant colors to twisting, hillside streets that sketched irregular lines toward the sprawl of the Eternal City.

She came to the oppressive heat of Rome from a school in the cool silence of the Swiss Alps, and she left the balcony door open at night to catch any wisp of breeze that drifted up the hillside. At first, the sounds of traffic moving in and out of Rome kept her awake and made her wonder if there were several sets of Italians, who constantly changed places.

14

Two weeks later, when she thought she had adjusted to every possible street noise, she was awakened by a hideous screech that ended in a loud thump. The rude bleating of a siren broke the silence and crescendoed into a burst of frenzied Italian voices trying to shout over a background cacophony of car horns and more sirens. Sharon threw aside the bed sheet and strode toward her balcony to close out the hubbub of noise. Before she reached the door, she saw a bulky darkness flip over the iron railing and roll across the wood decking into the shadow of the building. Her throat clogged, choking off the start of a scream.

She listened intently and stared at the pocket of darkness, trying to see through curtains that framed the open door and undulated in a quickening breeze. Stillness convinced her that imagination had amplified something as simple as shadows cast by tree branches in the lights of passing cars. The fear relaxed, but her heart was still thudding and her hand shook when she snatched a robe off the back of a chair and pulled it on.

Tense, but less frightened, she moved toward a reading lamp on a round, marble-topped table. When she reached for the dimmer switch on the lamp's base, a strong arm slid around her and pressed her back against a broad chest. Her gasp was stifled by a large, left hand. The tips of long fingers pressed firmly but not painfully into her face. When she struggled against the hold, her assailant made no harsh move, only held her in firm restraint. When she stood still, the grip softened, but did not release her.

"My apology for barging in. I'll be glad to explain if you'll give me the chance." A right hand closed over the hand she set on the lamp's switch. He let her turn it but pulled her hand away before the light was bright enough to spill onto the balcony.

"We were introduced yesterday after the soccer game." The voice was familiar — deep, with a hint of a roll, the accent more British than Italian. "You may not recognize me in street clothes without the dirt, sweat, and blood, but I'm hoping you will."

The hand left her mouth and he turned her to face him. "I'm Marc Breton."

She flinched when his hands caught her arms, but they were more protective than threatening. His touch distracted her, and it took a moment to recognize him without the smears of dirt, bleeding lower lip, and sweat-matted hair. His rugged face was clean-shaven, wide mouth twisted in a teasing smile, black hair a riot of loose curls. She did not remember the short, jagged scar that made his left eyebrow stutter. Nor did she remember that his wedge nose took a slight jog to the right, just below the bridge. She did remember his eyes — bright, violet-blue with curled black lashes. Celtic eyes that blazed with arresting intensity.

"You made the winning goal." She stammered out the first thought she could verbalize.

"Yes, I did." He dropped his hands and stepped back.

After he closed the balcony door, Marc walked into the sitting room. He stopped and cocked his head when he heard the buzz of a doorbell in the apartment next to hers.

"Damn." He turned back to meet her eyes. "Don't ask any questions, just tell them you don't know what they're talking about. And don't let them in."

Marc pulled the bedroom door closed and took off his shoes. He kicked them under the bed while he peeled off his shirt. When he opened his belt and dropped his jeans, Sharon forced out a shocked protest. "What are you doing?"

"Creating an alibi." He tossed his clothes on a chair before he slipped into her bed with nothing on but very brief briefs and a wrist watch. As an afterthought, he slid off the watch and set it next to hers on the night table. "Would you expect a pretty American girl to let a fleeing burglar jump into her bed?"

"No."

"See? A perfect alibi. If they insist on forcing their way in, they will find sleepy lovers, who are confused by the ruckus and indignant about infringement on their privacy."

"I'm not getting in that bed with you," she answered with genuine indignation.

"You're going to answer the door. You already look as if you just got out of bed."

Sharon took a quick glance at the dressing table mirror. Her long hair was pushed out of order by sleeping and wisped around her face. She started to fix it with her fingers and then stopped when he objected.

"What did you burgle?"

"It's a long story. That may or may not be the police."

"What if I tell them the truth?"

"They'll try to arrest me, but so would the other side. Since I have a strong desire for freedom and abhor being on the receiving end of brutality, police or otherwise, I'll put up one hell of a fight, which will cause considerable damage and danger. Since I'm innocent of crime and you didn't give me a chance to explain, you'll feel like hell for sending me off for abuse. They're terrible hosts. I've been their guest before."

"The police or the other side?"

"Both."

"Maybe I won't feel bad." She pursed her lips and glowered at him with a scolding look.

"You will because you don't believe in the use of violence or brutality. Besides, your friend Roland will vouch for me."

"Then start explaining. I'm a law-abiding person when it comes to thieves."

"It isn't what it appears—" The doorbell cut him off. "I don't have time. You have to trust me." He gave her a plaintive look before he shrugged himself under the sheet, snuggling his head into the pillow. He looked as if he had been asleep for a while.

When the doorbell continued to buzz with irritating insistence, Sharon adjusted her robe, strode through the sitting room, and opened the door on its chain. She saw halves of two men in street clothes, the arm of a third behind them.

"Who is it?" A torrent of Italian answered her. She shook her head and said, "*Non capisco.* American? *Ou Francais?*"

One of the men stepped closer and answered in harshly accented English, "Let us in, signorina. We must search your flat."

Blunt-nailed fingers pressed a battered wallet with a badge and greasy card in it against the crack of the door. Sharon hesitated. Then, reluctant to argue with their authority, she sighed and opened the door.

"Why do you need to search my apartment?"

"A man has stolen something and run over the wall. Some witnesses saw him climb to a balcony, yours or one near. He is dangerous."

"I heard a crash. I thought there was an accident."

"Yes, yes, but it is no matter. Two police cars were chasing the man. The fools collided when he jumped onto a car's roof then went over the wall like an acrobat in a circus."

Sharon saw the other men move around the room toward the kitchen. They were wary and held their right hands under their coats. She was beginning to feel that Marc had been right. This was turning into an unpleasant, even dangerous situation. "What did he steal?"

"That is not important." The man in front of her shrugged his shoulders and reached inside his coat. When he pulled out a short-snouted gun, Sharon pulled in a breath and backed toward the bedroom door.

"The man is a thief and armed."

His words frightened her. She knew Marc had no weapon, unless it was ingeniously concealed. These men were both armed and dangerous. When the man started toward the bedroom, she said, "I can't help you. Put away that gun and get out of here."

"Are you alone?" He stopped in front of her, reached out with his left arm, and caught her wrist with the cold pincers of an artificial hand.

In spite of her efforts for control, she trembled and her voice failed. "Yes— well, I—"

A snide comment was made in Italian, and the man who had searched the kitchen answered with coarse laughter. The man holding Sharon moved closer to her. His hold was painful, his breath heavy with tobacco and sour wine. When she drew back, he laughed and pushed her aside, moving toward the bedroom door.

Sharon had no idea if Marc was still there, but she knew she did not want these men to find him. With nothing else to say she blurted out. "You can't walk into my bedroom like that. It's my apartment, and I want you to get out."

"Honeybee?" The loud voice from the bedroom had a drunken slur in an unmistakable redneck drawl. "Y'all got trouble in there?"

"The police thought they saw an armed man on my balcony. I told them we didn't see anybody."

"There ain't nobody in here. Now you c'mon back here, girl.

Tell them po'leese they ain't got no right to bust in here and spoil our l'il ole party." There were a few thumps before he continued. "Jest as soon as I find my damn pants, I'll come out there and tell them they can't mess with citizens of the U.S. of A. and get away with it. I'll complain to my damn embassy if they don't get their asses outta here. Shee-it, girl, what did you do with my goddamn skivvies?"

While Marc ranted like an angry moonshiner, Sharon herded the uninterested men out the door. She thumped it closed and locked it and bolted it and refastened it with the night chain before she leaned against it with her heart thumping in her chest. When she tried to analyze what had happened, she could not believe it. She had deceived the police and locked them out while a man she hardly knew was in her bed hiding from them. But her instincts supported her actions. Those men were much more terrifying than Marc Breton.

Sharon was unsure of how she felt about Marc, but the longer she thought about it, the more she wanted to choke him for his audacity. Her conscience had prompted her to turn him over to the police. Her feelings had rebelled at the thought, especially when she faced those rude, frightening men.

She had been frightened and insulted and found the whole thing outrageous and hard to accept. But somehow, what galled her the most was the way Marc had called her honeybee and talked as if she were his plaything for the night. Granted, it had gotten them out of a bad situation, but he could have used a different approach and given her credit for intelligence and good taste.

Deciding that from now on she was making some of the rules and he had a lot of explaining to do, she clenched her fists at her sides and marched to the bedroom, where she thrust open the door. She slammed it behind her and took long, strong strides toward the bed. She stopped with fists on her hips. Her glare demanded a response.

"That was a damn fool thing to do." He was sitting up with his arms folded across his chest, glowering at her with his brows lowered.

"What?" The accusation stunned her. She felt he had made

the errors, not she.

"It was stupid to let them in. Lord, girl, you're the most trusting fool in the world."

"I don't believe you. Those were policemen. You're telling me not to trust them. At the same time you expect me to trust you."

"Someone needs to protect you. I'll do the best I can, but if you don't do what I tell you, I make no guarantees."

"What's wrong with trusting the police?"

"They weren't the police. Their credentials were phonier than fourteen dollar bills."

"You said they were the police."

"I said they may be the police. However, the police are still outside arguing about their damn accident." Marc gestured toward the raised voices in the street below the balcony. "I didn't think they would continue to chase me with the police outside, but they took the chance."

"Are you sure you're sane? I can't make sense out of any of it." When he laughed, she shook her head in disbelief. "Why did you let them know you were here?"

"I convinced them someone else was here. They were commenting about the embarrassed American trying to hide her lover, so I played the part. They are looking for a European, not an American redneck."

"You speak Italian?"

"Certainly. And French, German, Dutch, Russian, Spanish, English, American, some Polish, and Hillbilly."

"Where do you come from?"

"Everywhere." When she scoffed, he shrugged and explained. "My mother was an Irish-American girl from Boston. My father was a Franco-Italian Welshman born in Australia. I was born near London. I've lived in so many places I can't remember them all. If I have to name a place I spent more than one straight year in, I would have to say Washington, D.C. between the ages of eight and eleven, while my mother was married to an Air Force colonel. The most frequented place would be Monte Carlo. I kept bouncing back and forth between my mother in the states and my father in Europe. The marriage only lasted about six months after I was born."

"How old are you?"

"If you want the vital statistics straight from the soccer articles, I'm twenty-four years old, five feet ten inches tall, one hundred and seventy pounds, have all my own teeth, which is a bloody miracle, and am a leading scorer in my league. I gave it to you in American, but if you'd like British or metric?"

"They said you stole something."

"I did." He settled back against the headboard and crossed his ankles.

"Then you are a thief."

"Depends on the viewpoint. I stole what they didn't want to tell the police I stole." He shrugged and added. "I mugged a pusher and stole his grass."

She felt a smile quiver on her lips and break into a grin. "You're still a thief."

"But I have my code of ethics. One of them is that I don't believe in honor among thieves. I never trust any of them. I can't see what I did as illegal. I committed a crime against a criminal, which, to me, cancels it out. Honest people should pay cops to protect honest people, not pushers."

"I guess there's logic there somewhere. Who were those men?"

"They work for the pusher's supplier." He gave her a long look while he seemed to be making an important decision. "Sharon, the less you know about it the better. Take my word for it — I'm on the right side."

"What is the right side?"

"The side against drugs."

"Do you do that often?"

"No, it's risky. Some pushers are quick, some of them have guns."

"These men had guns."

"You better believe it. Mostly, I play soccer. When I need extra funds, I con the rich or rob the robbers, which is basically the same thing. It keeps me comfortable. My father was a thief, strictly high class. He was one of Europe's finest."

"What does that mean?" She wrinkled her nose.

"He was sophisticated enough to operate under the noses of his wealthy victims. Dad was good, but even the good ones can't always win. They kept putting him in jail." He made a sour face. "The roller coaster ride from caviar to prison slop can be hard to take. He died of stomach cancer a month before he was due for parole. I decided that no matter how good I am, the law has better resources. Since I don't want to end up a grey man in prison, I do my best to stay on the right side of the law."

He reached forward and patted the edge of the bed. "Why don't you sit down? You look like a lawyer sizing me up to see what you can get out of me."

"Why don't you get out of here so I can go back to bed?"

"I can't."

"What do you mean you can't?"

"They're combing the streets for me."

"You could get out of my bed."

"Don't play the innocent virgin. We both know better."

"How do you know better?" A flash of indignation heated her face.

"I'm not without resources. I promise I won't rape you. It would be an ungracious way to say thank you."

She stopped arguing and sat facing him on the edge of the bed. "It just isn't a situation I feel comfortable about. You're practically nude. I'm in my nightgown. I hardly know you."

"I just told you my life story." He caught her hand and traced a line across her palm. "And I see here that you are rebelling against 'all that establishment crap', which you believe is 'outdated hypocrisy that preaches peace while arming itself to kill'"

"How do you know that?" She frowned at the tone that gently mocked her ideals, but she didn't pull her hand away from his touch or look away from his eyes.

"I could say I have fantastic powers that enable me to read people like billboards." He teased, then turned serious, as if he sensed he was raising her hackles again. "The truth is I know Roland Townsend, the charming gay artist who introduced us yesterday. He has many of the same ideals. He also told me a lot about you."

"Is he really gay?"

"Uh-huh."

"I guess I can forget about romancing Roland."

He released her hand and leaned back, opening a space between them that both relaxed and disappointed her. "He showed me where you live, which was fortunate when I needed a place of sanctuary."

"It's a novel way to get into a girl's bed. Does it always work?"

"It's worked every time I've tried it." He winked and started to laugh.

Something about his expression was familiar and it took her a moment to place it. "Roland's painted you, hasn't he?"

"Several times, which is why I know so much about him. His brush doesn't work unless his mouth is running. He says the only thing women want from men is babies, so they can control them by wrapping the umbilical cord around their testicles."

"That does sound like Roland, and you have it right about me. I'm a rich bitch trying to purge myself of the guilt my wealth gives me."

"Where did you get that line?"

"From Phil, one of my hip friends, who always thought he knew where everyone was coming from. When I met him, I abandoned everything I'd been programmed to do since they sent out my engraved birth announcements until the party at the hunt club when my father announced my engagement to Hugh Jamison, a suitor I found companionable and attractive, but not very exciting. I panicked, flunked out of Smith College, joined the peace movement, and gave myself to love. It seemed so clear, so perfect — love, flowers, and marijuana. It was the way to world unity. 'Make love, not war.' I was in love with the simplicity of the ideal. I left school and took a wild trip that landed four of us in jail for vagrancy and use of marijuana. Unfortunately, we'd been making love not money. Daddy bailed me out and took me home. I had the feeling he wanted to put Phil in front of a firing squad and turn me over his knee like a toddler, but he had more sense than that. I have to give him credit for trying to understand what I was feeling."

"Did he succeed?"

"Just about the time I thought we had made a breakthrough in father-daughter communication, he sent me to a nondenominational convent in Switzerland. Only the religion was money, the doctrine snobbery. It was only endurable because of its skiing and riding instruction. When they let me out last month, I cashed in my plane ticket and tapped into the interest on a trust fund from my mother. I came to Rome to paint and be free. That's my life story."

"Why so cynical?"

"I see a lot of things I don't want to be, but I can't find what I am."

"Maybe you spend too much time worrying about it. Is it necessary to fit into a group philosophy?"

"Everyone has to belong somewhere."

"You only have to belong to yourself. Don't try to wear anyone else's beliefs. They fit like hand-me-downs and chafe in vital places."

Sharon felt her apprehension melt away. "You have an uncanny way of getting to the inside of me. Maybe I don't know my own beliefs and that's what scares me into following causes."

"You know them. But they're so familiar you don't think they're remarkable. There's a great deal of security in parroting others. It keeps your vulnerable self-esteem off the firing line."

Marc set his hand on her face and trailed his fingers down her cheek to her chin "You're not sure about me, are you?"

"It's a little too bizarre to take in stride."

"It's too real." His answer surprised her. She started to argue, but he stopped her with a gesture. "You can't hide behind your facade. Tonight was no game. You felt real fear, real danger. You made a decision that mattered. You stood up to criminals and probably saved my life."

The meaning of his words hit her like a mallet in the chest. "Would they really have killed you?"

"I don't know, and I don't want to find out." His smile eased her tension. "We made a good team."

"Does that make it a relationship?" She quipped.

"Such a relationship deserves to seek deeper rewards. Please accept my invitation to share my bed as a sincere compliment to you."

"May I remind you that it's my bed, not yours."

He moved closer and slid his hands up her arms until they caressed her shoulders. "But I'm the one who's in it."

"And you want me to be your honeybee for the night?" She wanted to sound disapproving, but her voice caught in the back of her throat.

"I could pick from a swarm of them at the party I stole the grass for."

"You still have the grass?" Sharon found it easier to make decisions like this while enclosed in the velvety closeness of a marijuana high.

"I don't use it."

"Then why did you steal it?"

"I had to steal something more than the information he passed me. The mugging protected him and gave me an excuse if they caught me. I thought I'd take it to Roland's party and see if you were there or if Roland could arrange another meeting for us. As it stands, I'd rather Roland didn't learn about what happened with the pusher." His fingers tightened on her chin while he held her gaze with a strong stare. "Roland is hooked on more than grass. It makes him manipulable. Do you understand what I'm saying?"

"I think so." She studied his face and saw a clear warning. "You mean you don't trust him and I shouldn't either."

"The only thing I want people to know about me is that I'm a soccer player, reckless playboy, and con man. Unfortunately, you got into the middle of something else."

"What is the something else?"

"You don't need to know."

"Why tell me at all?"

"I want to keep knowing you, and I don't want you for a sex object." He wrinkled his nose at her. "You seem very upset about that."

"It's shallow and degrading."

"With whom have you been having sex?" He twisted his face and huffed sarcastically.

"Nobody lately. It was a very strict school." His hand slid to the back of her neck, making her look into hypnotic blue eyes. She sighed. "It's been a very long winter."

Now, almost twenty years later, Sharon could still think about him and feel the swelling thrill that meant Marc and only Marc. She shuddered, forcing away the ache of empty desire and took a long look in her dressing table mirror. The years and three pregnancies had been kind to her. Bathed, dressed in dark-green slacks and a print blouse, with short, honey-gold hair brushed until it was light and softly feathered into place, she believed she looked closer to thirty than forty. Her complexion was smooth, which she credited to her rebellion against cosmetics back when she joined the hippy generation and spurned the use of things unnatural. Now, either from habit or inherent perversity, she continued to face the world with as few artificial aids as possible.

She had added a few pounds since those days in Rome, but she was not dissatisfied. She rode almost every day and ran or swam three or four times a week. She was firmly muscled and still had what Marc, in his blunt way, would call an ideal figure—"Two mouthfuls of breasts, two handfuls of bottom, and enough action to keep me humping."

She smiled at the memory of his rolling, bawdy chuckle and caught a candid glimpse of her face in the mirror. Dark eyes, lashes and brows, small nose, and wide, slightly crooked mouth. There was a glow on her face, a sparkle in her eyes, a wry look of mischief in her expression. She had been thinking of Marc too much today. It always stirred up her emotions with a nostalgia that forgot there had been more than one side to Marc Breton.

It had been that same year, in the autumn. She sat in a sidewalk cafe, sipping at a glass of wine while she sketched a twilight street of tall, purple-shadowed buildings. The darkening structures leaned toward each other like brooding ogres, who watched scurrying man-forms ebb and flow at their feet in the golden glow of artificial light.

With a diabolic smirk twisting her smile, she sketched macabre faces on the buildings with fine, barely discernible lines and shadings. It suited her mood as well as the ambience of the time and place. This was an area of Rome she had never been to before — off the tourist and commercial paths, teeming with the business of vice and no-questions-asked liaisons. She was here because of a feeling she had about Marc, who had been giving her vague answers to pointed questions.

While Marc was at soccer practice, she had done some snooping in the wallet he left in the apartment. The address of the hotel beside this cafe had been scribbled on a piece of restaurant check, along with today's date and the note, "from 7 until after 2." This morning Marc had told her he was going to Naples and would be home late. Suspicion gnawed a hole in common sense until she felt justified sitting here waiting to see what the note meant.

When the sky darkened, she closed her sketchbook and put away her pencils. She picked up her wine glass and drank the last swallow of dry, red wine. The waiter caught her eye and she signaled for another glass. While she waited for the wine, she picked through the lightweight coins in her purse and stacked them on the table like a city of ultramodern skyscrapers.

Eying the piles of coins, she judged that the whole mess added up to less than two American dollars. Marc laughed at her unconscious habit of converting everything to dollars, but she needed a standard for comparison, a connection to her roots. Marc was different. He thought and operated as a native anywhere he went. Sharon had pinned a myriad of backgrounds on Marc, and then let each one slip away or shift into something totally incongruent.

After the waiter brought wine and swept the coins away, she leaned back, nibbling on a bread stick. She thought about how long she would wait. Probably no longer than it took to finish this glass of wine. It was possible the note was meaningless and Marc really was in Naples. His vagueness could well have been caused by irritation. Not being European, she often nagged Marc about parts of him that were, such as his insistence that, as a man, he should know everything about her dealings while his business was no concern of hers.

While she mellowed from the wine, her suspicions turned to reproval of her own insecurity. Maybe she found it easier to see misgivings in Marc than accept them in herself. Leaning back in the chair, she watched the changing traffic patterns and sipped at the wine with a new appreciation of its quality.

A new, bright red car jolted her out of complacency when it

squealed around the corner and zipped toward her. It cut across two lanes of indignant, horn-blaring traffic and backed neatly into a parking space about fifty meters short of her. It was a Porshe — black vinyl top down, black leather seats. When she glanced at the driver, her heart froze, then pounded in the empty cavern of her chest. Heat pulsed inside her, raced up her neck, and flamed on her face.

The driver was Marc, the passenger a plump, ash blonde woman encased in a silvery dress that hugged full curves. It was high on the bottom, showing a lot of heavy thigh, and low on the top, showing fleshy mounds of lifted breasts, bared down to a hair's breadth from the nipples. The woman's short, blunt fingers flashed with gem-sparks when she held her hand out so Marc could help her from the low car.

When the couple walked toward the hotel entrance just past the cafe, Sharon stood up so fast she knocked the chair into an empty table. A wave of rage made everything around her lose focus while Marc and the woman stood out in sharp detail. The woman was drunk and all over him. Her impatience to get her catch in bed was unmistakable. Sharon was unaware of her movements, but she was closing on them in long strides. She gripped her sketchbook in one tight fist, her canvas tote bag in the other.

"You son of a bitch." She swung the bag at Marc. He jumped back, stiffened, and glared at her with an expression of contempt that could have been carved in stone for all the feeling in it. He looked at the startled woman beside him, shrugged, and muttered what sounded like a confused, embarrassed apology in Italian.

"Get away from her!" Sharon shouted.

He twisted to face her, his eyes flashing a venomous threat that made her falter. "Keep out of my way, you damn fool. You could get me killed."

His hissed words stunned her, left her speechless while he pivoted and calmly, but hastily, strode into the hotel with his arm locked around the swivelling, silver waistline.

Numb, Sharon turned and walked away with stiff, uneven steps. When she reached the street, her feelings came back with pain and fury. She ran to the Metro entrance and clattered down the metal stairway, shoving her way past startled Italians. By the time she scrunched herself into the crowd boarding a train car, the pain was inside where it writhed like a coiling asp.

At her apartment, she slammed the door without thinking of bolting it. Her stomach churning, her diaphragm convulsing with painful sobs, she threw herself across the bed and cried until she was hollow. Feeling weak and empty, she staggered to the bathroom and sat on the toilet with her pounding head in her hands, her elbows digging into her thighs. When nausea overwhelmed her, she vomited into the bidet. The purging left her trembling and drained of feeling.

After a stretch of empty time that was filled with unremembered, desperate thoughts, she roused herself and took a shower. Not knowing what else to do, she put on a light nightgown, flopped onto the bed, and lay sleepless and crazy, terrified that Marc was jilting her because she was pregnant and a burden to him.

The sound of the opening door snapped her attention to the tapering form filling the doorway. She jerked to her feet, swaying unsteadily. Her eyes were hot, her muscles stone. Her voice sounded shattered. "Get out!"

"You almost blew a carefully planned job." The slam of the bedroom door punctuated his accusation. "I could have lost half a million liras right there."

"Is that what a rented cock goes for in this city? Is that what you sell to rich sluts who want to get fucked in cheap hotels?"

His face reddened. His jaw tightened. She ignored all the warning signs. "It isn't worth one damn lire."

Her rage exploded and her hand closed on a small marble sculpture on the dressing table. She hurled it at him, as if the violence of the action could relieve the pressure of her fear. When he dodged the chunk of marble, she yelled, "I hate your fucking arrogance."

The slap made her gasp, but it only increased her rage. She leapt at him with clawing hands. A hard, backhanded blow snapped her head to the side. A heavy gold ring cut into her chin, gouging to the bone.

With the blinding wave of pain, she lost hold of all reason and flew at him in a fit of savage fury. She hardly noticed when his hands grasped her arms. She felt him throw her onto the bed, heard him shout at her to stop and listen to him, but she continued to slam tight fists on his chest, his shoulders, even his face.

When he rolled with her, wrapping his arms around her in restraint, she bit him, sinking her teeth into a bulging pectoral muscle and clamping down like a furious pitbull. He bellowed from the pain, grabbed her by the hair at the back of her head, and twisted her face away from him. She screamed, and he pressed her face into a pillow until she stopped kicking and went limp.

The world was out of focus when he rolled her over, and she felt it was never going to stop fading in and out. By the time his flushed, wary face was clear, she was beginning to think again. She was startled by the blood running from a ragged gash on his chest, disappearing into the thickness of black hair.

Most of her awareness came back, especially the horrible ache of hurt inside her. "Why did you screw that slut, Marc?"

"That slut is worth several fortunes and has a weakness for two things — big men and expensive jewelry. I took care of the first part. Marcel sold her some baubles." He pulled a tissue from the box beside the bed and pressed a wad of it over the cut on her chin "We've been working on it for months. You almost destroyed the entire scam."

"Marcel's jewels are stolen. You said you didn't steal."

"I don't. Marcel doesn't either. He remakes jewelry and fences for the thieves. My father worked with him for years. They had such a good thing going my father stole the same diamonds four times, each time in a different setting from different women."

"Why don't I hate you now?" Tears blurred her vision when she looked at his rough face. "I did earlier."

"I noticed." His answer was a calm statement, said with a thoughtful lift of his hyphenated eyebrow.

"Don't do it again, Marc. It hurts to think of you with someone else. How would you feel if I did it to you?"

"I would make a gelding out of him." He cocked his head and gave her a sly smile. "But then, would it net a possible half million liras?"

"That's awful." She made a sour face.

"To me, there is business, and there is love. I don't confuse them. To you, it is love or guilty. You confuse them."

"We have my money."

"Only the interest for the next fifteen months. It isn't enough."

"We have your soccer money."

"In my league, a pittance."

"We could economize." She almost laughed at his horrified expression. He looked as if she had asked him to run barefoot on a ski run.

"I don't like to economize. It makes no sense to live poor by avoiding an act of sex that was forgotten before the sheet dried. I owed some people some favors, so I helped them." He lifted his right hand and held it in front of her. "She bought me a ring. It's a good bonus."

Sharon made a disagreeing face. "It's ugly."

"It certainly is. However, I can sell it back to Marcel. Pure profit."

"Marc, do you have any morals?"

"Certainly, but they are mine, not anyone else's."

The next afternoon Sharon stared at a newspaper picture for a while before she realized she was staring at the same woman she had seen with Marc. Only in this picture the woman was dressed in a conservative knit suit and posing with policemen.

She plunked the paper down in front of Marc, who was sitting on the couch reading. "My Italian is still bad. What does it say?"

He scanned the article before he said, "The poor woman was robbed last night. Her villa was broken into, her jewelry and other valuables stolen while she was at—" He glanced at the story and chuckled. "—a charity benefit performance at the opera house."

"Why do you keep telling me you don't steal?"

"I was in bed with her across the city. How could I have stolen anything?"

"Don't tell me you weren't in on it."

"I won't tell you that." He kicked his feet onto the low, glass-topped coffee table while he stuck a marker in the book. He set it and the newspaper on the table. "I said I owed some people some favors. I did my part for them. They did theirs."

"You sold her jewelry that had been stolen."

"No." He held his hand up to silence her. "I put her on to Marcel, but she has no idea that I know him. I also cased her villa and set the schedule. If she'd gone home last night, it would have been a disaster."

"Then that wasn't the first time you screwed her?"

"If it makes a difference, the first time was before I met you. It was a long, cautious job."

"Who does she think you are?"

"Marc Breton, a big hunk of soccer player — a little brain, a lot of brawn."

"Isn't it possible she might figure out that you intentionally kept her away from her villa?"

"I doubt it. She's stupid. Besides, she can think what she wants. That hotel has a reputation for catering to such liaisons. I made sure we were noticed, so did you. The staff would be more than happy to testify that I was there with her when she said she was at the opera house."

"Which could implicate you as an accomplice."

Marc gave her a patient, patronizing look. "Do you think she wants her husband to know that? Italian husbands can get very upset over that kind of thing."

"She's married?"

"Certainly. She has a rich, possessive husband." His eyes laughed and he winked. "However, he travels a lot."

"What if he found out?"

"From what I know of him, he would make a gelding out of me, with a dull knife, just before he killed me — slowly, with the same dull knife. He deals in drugs, the sewer pipe of crime. Criminals like that give the craft a bad name."

"Oh my God." Sharon stared at the newspaper picture. "That man standing behind her. He was one of the men looking for you the night you came in the balcony. He was the one who spoke English, the one with the ugly gun."

Marc glanced at the man she pointed out. One eyebrow lifted, and he puckered his lips. "Phew. You didn't tell me he had a steel hand. That's her husband's head butcher. He's known as *l'artiglio*, the claw."

"Who is her husband?"

"He runs the drug syndicate I was dodging when we met. I told you I don't believe in honor among thieves." He reached out and caught her hand. "Several men who have crossed him have been found dead and hard to identify. The claw gets most of the credit."

Sharon shuddered when she remembered the feel of the harsh steel hand, the cruelty in the man's dark face. When she spoke, her voice was muted, her throat dry. "I don't like the games you play or the people you play with. There isn't enough money in the world to repay me for losing you." She felt tears fill her eyes, tried to hold her voice together. "Marc, don't do things like that. Don't help any more criminals."

"I helped them so they could help me." His hand bunched her hair before it slid behind her neck and rubbed gently. "They stole some of her husband's papers as well as photographed some others for me. I couldn't open the safe when I was there. They blew the safe and covered it with a burglary. At most, that information will put him in jail for a long time. At least, it will put a crimp in his operations."

"If you work for the police, why did you run from them?"

"I don't work for the police."

"Who do you work for?"

He gave her a long, contemplative look before he answered, "Myself. I sell information where I want."

"Why?"

"It pays. And it's something I decided to do a long time ago. I had my reasons. I still do."

She knew that was all he would say. He had already said more than usual. "I don't like it. I want you alive."

"I'll stay alive." His hand tugged her onto his lap. "I'm sure he won't find out. However, since I'm finished with the job, I've been thinking of taking a trip to England. There's a league there that interests me."

"Don't you have a contract?"

"Not a binding one. Would you like to go to England? I want the baby born there."

"Sure." After what he had just told her, she wanted to leave

Rome as fast as they could. "Are we going to get married before I have the baby?"

"You just found out about it. There's time to think it over." He slid a hand across her shoulder to her neck. After a gentle caress, he combed his fingers through the length of her hair.

"Time for you to run off with someone else?" When his eyes clouded, she regretted her cutting question. "I'm sorry, but I'm upset."

"I will never desert you. I want to raise our child. I love you and will take care of you, but I won't change what I do. I won't tell you about that part of my life, but I will tell you it's my way of getting back at some of the bastards. Do you want to be legally tied to a man who may make a mistake, fall the wrong way, and go to prison? Who may lose his winning edge and end up in a drawer in a morgue? I play against rough people who like to win as much as I do."

"I want to be married to my child's father. It's one of those programmed feelings that wants the baby to have your name on its birth certificate."

"I'll claim the baby. We'll be common law married. You can call yourself Mrs. Marcus David Breton, and I'll take care of you. But you'll have fewer strings if you ever want to duck legal entanglements."

"Why would I want to do that?"

"I don't know, but I want to leave all the options."

Marc spent her money, seduced her away from her past, and cheated on her until she hated him. At the same time, he was true to his word and loved her with an intense, emotional caring far deeper than his passions and lust. For thirteen years, Marc Breton controlled her like a drug she knew was overpowering her. He could inflame her, start a desire that gnawed inside her until he satisfied her and left her drained, emotionally wrung out, and happy. There had been a time she wanted him so strongly she cared about nothing else.

Sharon knew now that she had been addicted to Marc, wanting the sensual man so much she was unable to leave him until he threatened something deeper than her pride.

And Marc had been right. When she returned to Michigan,

there were no legal strings. She was able to pick up life as Sharon Collingwood, and later as Mrs. Hugh Jamison. Legally, there were no ties with Marc, except for David's birth certificate and his name, David Marcus Breton.

Hugh had once suggested adoption. He probably would have triggered a milder explosion if he had asked David if he could castrate him. Sharon supposed that had been Hugh's first major mistake with David, who could see nothing but hero in his father. Another mistake had been when Hugh called Marc an unprincipled, thieving bum. To David, Marc was a swashbuckling Robin Hood, who could laugh at danger and pull the props out from under the ruthless. David could see no wrong, no weakness in his father.

🐎 3

Sharon left the master bedroom and walked to David's closed door. She waited a few seconds, listening to the muffled sound of rock music, then thudded the side of her fist on the door.

"Who dareth to enter this day?" The voice that shouted over the music was almost as deep and rich as Marc's, but with a harsher American twang and a surliness that irritated her. Lately, David seemed to have the mistaken notion that any parental request was an infringement on his rights as a privileged freeloader. Sharon understood that David had problems and emotional pressures he chose not to discuss with her, but she felt he could occasionally set them aside and contribute some positive energy toward his family.

"It's thy mother." She pushed open the door and walked into a room that looked as if it housed an extended family of hyperactive chimpanzees. Closing the door, she wondered how one human could scatter clothes in so many odd places.

David was sitting on the bed in ripped jeans and a T-shirt from a rock band she had never heard and was grateful she had been spared the experience. He was sketching something on quadrille paper while glancing at a copy of *The Dungeon Master's Guide*. An open Coke can sweated onto the night table, a bag of Doritos gaped open beside him. A half-smoked cigarette smoldered in a full ash tray. David's thick, curling dark hair was oddly uneven after he singed it knocking Tim into the fountain at Briarwood

36

Mall. He was attempting to grow a moustache, which made his upper lip look as if he had rubbed a sooty finger across it.

Last summer and fall David had gone on a shaping-up campaign of swimming, riding, running, weight-lifting, and, when nagged enough, work on the farm. He started to fill in a build that mirrored his father's — wide shoulders, big hands, and a thick neck. Sharon could see vivid resemblances to Marc and knew it added to the estrangement she was feeling toward David. She had enjoyed the reminders when David was a boy, even when he was an impulsive, often brooding, adolescent. It was different now that he was becoming a man and not only wanted to resemble his father but be his father. She was unsure of how much her son knew or understood about Marc, and it frightened her.

David's fitness campaign had deteriorated by Thanksgiving. Cigarettes, liquor, and marijuana had surfaced over Christmas vacation. He destroyed New Year's dinner and a Michigan Rose Bowl game by showing up in time for dessert in a foul-mouthed mood, smelling like liquor and dead reefer smoke. He started a drunk-to-drunk argument with Hugh that Sharon knew would have erupted into blows if Hugh had not been in a wheelchair, or if David had moved close enough for Hugh to grab.

Hugh, who was much stronger than David, told her afterward that if he had gotten his hands on David, he would have knocked the arrogance out of him. The threat startled Sharon, who had never seen her husband as a violent person. Granted, Hugh was hard and unbendable, even strict, as his military father had been, but he had always handled frictions in a firm, controlled manner, absorbing David's tantrums and outbursts like a wall of resilient padding. She had never seen Hugh hit David, or even threaten him with physical punishment, while Marc had done both on a number of occasions. She knew David would never let Hugh fill his father's place, but he had, until last fall, respected Hugh's authority. The only answer that appealed to her was that it was just another rebellious stage, but it was too intense to accept comfortably. Sometimes she wanted to blame both of them. Most of the time she closed her eyes to it.

There had been a few more clashes after the New Year's skirmish, then Hugh backed away from David's goads and stopped trying to hold a tight curb rein. They paid little attention to each other, which seemed to be making it worse, not better, and Sharon felt like a wall between two opposing forces.

David seemed determined to irritate her. He smoked, swore, drank, and disregarded her limits. Instinct told her there was nothing positive in asking Hugh to step in again. She was sure Marc would know how to handle it, which certainly would not be by ignoring it as she was inclined to do. Marc had always known when David really had a problem and needed to talk it out, or when he was being bratty and needed a spanking, while she often frustrated herself over a temperamental act, then walked roughshod over a problem that was life and death to her son. This was one of those times she wished Marc would walk in and take over the way he had for thirteen years.

However, Marc was not available. The problem was growing and her course of passive avoidance was only making her feel more helpless. She decided it would be best to use Marc's tactics and start offensively.

After pushing a stack of CD cases out of the way, she switched off the stereo, and met David's strong blue glare. "Put out the cigarette and dump the ash tray before you set the house on fire."

When he grudgingly snubbed out the smoldering butt, she set her fists on her hips and waited for him to meet her eyes. "Would you please explain why you have been cutting school? Then tell me where you've been when you weren't in school."

Her demands were direct because, when she thought about Marc, she realized he had always been straightforward. He had an uncanny ability to cut through to the nerve center of any problem by refusing to discuss anything but the central issue. David had obeyed Marc and listened to him without protest.

"Sit up and answer me, David." He gave her a thoughtful look before he obeyed with the, "if you're serious," compliance he had always shown when she took a firm stand.

He swung his legs off the side of the bed and straightened until he was almost eye level with her. When she failed to break from his stare, he grabbed the Coke can and took a swallow while he thought about his answer. "I hate that school."

"Why?"

"I hate the phonies who go there. I feel like a hypocrite because you're making me avoid the truth of our social problems, the way the rich always do."

"That's bullshit." She scoffed, then softened her expression. His opinions sounded a lot like the ones she had used against her father when she dropped out of college. "We are sending you to a school where you can get a good education."

"You think that if you don't have to deal with the failures of our Great American Society, you can forget they exist and continue to perpetuate them."

"With less than six weeks left in the school year, it would be foolish to change schools. If you really feel that way, we'll send you somewhere else in the fall. It's something we can work out over the summer. Meanwhile, grit your teeth and go to school with the phonies. It would be a mistake to flunk now, unless you want to go to summer term. Now, where have you been going?"

"No where special." He played with the still smoldering cigarette end before he ground it out again. When he spoke, his voice was soft. "Sometimes I sit by the river and look at the hospital. I don't understand what happened to Tim and I can't find anything that means anything. I want to stop what hurt him, but I don't know how. I really don't care about anything else."

"Is that your trouble — what happened to Tim?"

"Part of it. I couldn't find much to get excited about before that either."

"There must be something." She looked at the pad he had set on the bed. "What are you doing there? It seems to absorb a lot of time."

David glanced at the diagram of a *Dungeons and Dragons* adventure. "I've been running some games at Karen and Paul's runaway rehab farm. It helps them learn to solve problems." He frowned. "It doesn't help me solve mine. What I want most seems impossible."

"What is that?"

"Get away from Hugh."

"Why?"

"Christ, he thinks he's the reincarnated George Patton."

"That's an opinion, not a reason."

"He hates me."

"He says you hate him."

"Maybe we just hate each other."

"He says he doesn't hate you."

"Bullshit. I'm a constant reminder of Dad." David looked away from her while he dumped the cold ashes into a wastebasket. Instead of turning back, he stared at his hands. "I want to live with my father. You've kept me away from him for five years. I don't think it's fair." He was tense, as if he expected her to react with shock or anger. When she said nothing, he raised his eyes to hers.

"David, I don't know where he is." She met his stare openly, easily. "If I knew where he was, I'd be willing to let you visit him."

"Hugh wouldn't let me go."

"Why not?"

"He'd like me to drop dead, but he doesn't want me to go to Dad."

"I don't agree with that."

"He doesn't want to give you any chance to go back to Dad."

"I have no reason to go back to him."

"Why did Granfather put that restriction on my trust fund?"

"What restriction?" The change of subject caught her off-guard.

"That I couldn't touch any of the money, even the interest, until I'm twenty-five, without your signature."

Sharon looked down and scratched at a rough fingernail. When she raised her eyes, his clear, violet-blue stare penetrated her defenses. "So that if you did go back to your father, he couldn't use the money."

"But it's mine."

"It's your grandfather's money. He gave it to you in trust because he's trying to save you from heavy taxes when he dies. The taxes on the interest are paid by the interest, the excess added to the principal, which is not taxed as long as it remains untouched. It's for you, but since it is money he earned, he has the right to dictate the terms."

"What happens if I die before I'm twenty-five?"

"It goes to me because I'm his daughter."

"And if you die, it goes to Hugh?"

"No. It's divided equally amongst my surviving children. Becky's and Scott's trust funds are set up the same way."

"There's no restriction on theirs."

"There's no reason for it on theirs."

"But there is on mine because Granfather thinks I'd give the money to Dad?"

"That's one way to put it."

"I'm not stupid enough to give away my money."

"You wouldn't even realize you were doing it." She started to smile. "That man could get Scrooge to blow a fortune on him. He spends it as fast as he gets it, and he never buys anything with investment value. He never buys a house, only rents them. He travels, lives high, gambles, and buys fast cars."

"Cars have value."

"Not when he's through with them." She gave him a sympathetic look. "Right now, I think your father would be good for you — if he isn't in jail, or if one of his victims hasn't pounded his brain to jelly."

"Stop it, Mom. You're sounding like Hugh." His voice was angry, his eyes narrowed.

"I sound like your father. Those are the kind of excuses he used whenever I mentioned documented marriage. They were real possibilities. I find it ironic that I spent thirteen years expecting someone to shoot Marc, only to have it happen to Hugh for no reason I can think of."

"Accidents don't usually have reasons." David's answer was a flat reiteration of the official statement, but his jaw tightened.

"I have never believed it was an accident."

"I can't think of anyone who would want Hugh dead, except you."

"Me?" She stiffened. "David, that's a terrible thing to say. Why would I want that?"

"You're the one who would benefit the most from his death. You'd end up with everything and could go back to Dad. It's not a bad plan."

"Why would you think that? David, I don't want to go back to Marc. To you he may be the greatest person in the world. You weren't married to him."

"You love him." His strong eyes burned into her.

"I love Hugh," she answered as firmly as she could.

"Not as much."

"I don't know how to answer that."

The way he could sense her emotions agitated her. It was his father's uncanny ability to read through a person's shields, stir up deep feelings, and draw them out. People told Marc the truth. People told Marc things they would not tell their best friends, or their psychiatrists. People trusted Marc. That was what made him a successful con man.

"I love Hugh differently, maybe more realistically, more maturely."

"You still love Dad. If he was here, you'd know it."

She felt him study her expression while she thought about her answer. "Maybe that was true five years ago, I'm not sure now."

"Maybe he is here, and you already know it."

"That's absurd." His insinuation turned her cold.

"That's why Hugh doesn't want you to ever see Dad again. I heard him tell Granfather to keep Dad away from you."

"When?"

"Last fall when Granfather came back from Europe."

She sat back against the cluttered desk, feeling confused and uneasy. A swell of excitement filled her chest and quickened her heartbeat, just as it had a year ago when she saw Marc's name in a battered sports magazine. Before that, she had almost convinced herself Marc was dead, gone from her life forever. Now, his reality filled her, leaving her with a thrill she couldn't deny.

She took a breath and steadied her voice. "Why were they talking about Marc?"

"I don't know because, of course, they changed the subject as soon as they saw me. It was at the Changebrook Trials. They were talking with Colin Trombley, who said he saw Dad in Devon before he left England. When Colin left, Granfather said, `Breton tried to contact me in Zurich in July.' Hugh said, `Can you still keep him away from my wife?'"

"What did my father say to that?" Anger hardened her voice when she realized her father was still interfering in her life.

"That's when they noticed me, but Granfather nodded and said, `Nothing's changed.' Do you understand it?"

"No, but I don't like it. I wonder why Marc tried to contact my father?"

"Maybe he wants to see us." David jerked to his feet and snatched a pack of cigarettes off the night table. "That bastard Hugh has been keeping Dad away from me for five years. When I heard that, I wanted to kill Hugh right then."

"David." Sharon grasped his arm and jerked him around to face her. "David, what do you mean?"

"Don't you know why he hates me? It's my fault he's in that wheel chair. And he knows it."

She gasped when he spun her toward the bed and rushed for the door. She stumbled into the bed before she could turn and grab for him. His elbow hit her in the eye when he yanked his arm away and bolted out the door.

"David!"

The door slammed, and Sharon dropped onto the bed. While she stared at the closed barrier, an icy hollowness imploded inside her. She buried her face in her hands, grasping with tense fingers until the shock turned to pain.

The horror spun into an emotional void and left her with a splitting headache. The numbness lost its paralyzing grip, but hollow pain still gnawed at her. Her feelings refused to believe David had shot Hugh, but there was no way she could forget what David had said and she had to think about what it implied. If he had tried once, would he try again? She told herself no, especially after what he had just said. But what would he do about her suspicions? Surely, he would realize she would never tell Hugh or anyone else something so horrible. David said Hugh knew. But Hugh never put any blame on David. Her thoughts confused her even more and she wondered if, by saying what he had, David had been letting out a dreadful guilt. Had he run because he was afraid to face her reaction? The thought of him running off with so much anguish in him frightened her.

Glancing out the window, she saw one of the farm pickup trucks back out of the equipment shed and knew it was David. She ran down the hall, almost falling when she tried to take the stairs in long leaps. When she jerked open the front door, the truck turned out the front gate. It fishtailed on the gravel road before it disappeared over a rise, leaving a wake of red-brown dust.

"Damn you, David." She smacked a hand on a smooth, white column. When she turned, she saw Hugh and his wheel chair framed by the doorway.

"Did he take a truck?" Hugh asked in the roaring voice that could fill a riding arena.

"My talk didn't work out the way I wanted it to." The headache jabbed at her and she pressed her fingers against her forehead, just above the nose.

"Did he hit you?" Hugh stared at her left eye.

"No." She jerked her head up to look at his tight, angry face.

"Sharon, is that the truth?"

She shuddered at the hardness in his face, his eyes, his clenched fists. "He shoved me. His elbow hit me when I tried to keep him from leaving."

"If he ever hits you, I'll make sure he regrets it."

"He wouldn't hit me."

"Just as his father wouldn't?"

"It was reciprocal."

"I can't see any basis for you defending him."

She leaned against the pillar, staring toward the road. "I guess you had to be there."

"Do you want me to send the police after my truck? I could tell them I thought it was stolen."

She continued to look away from him while she controlled the racing tension inside her. "No. He'll come home when he cools down." There was no way she wanted the police chasing David, who might think they were after more than a stolen truck.

"Please talk to me, Tim." David stared at the back of Tim's bandaged head for a while before he dropped his own head to his hands and looked between his fingers at the tiled floor. "I've listened to other people, but it doesn't mean anything until I hear it from you."

"Hear what?" The voice was uneven, little more than a harsh whisper.

David snapped his head up, but the face was still turned away, as it had been whenever anyone visited, locked deep in the depressive side of Tim's personality. But Tim had spoken. He had reached him, maybe he could pull him out. "Do you hate me? Can you forgive me for doing this to you?"

"Can you guess what it's like, David? Alone, in pain, every breath an agony."

"I'm sorry. I couldn't let you do it."

"It's an indescribable hell. But it's something else, too. It's life. I've found out how much I want to keep it. When I came out of the void, I was glad to feel pain. It meant I had another chance. I just don't know what to do with it. I don't hate you. I think I'm grateful, but it's hard to feel anything like that now."

"That's the best thing I've ever heard." He wanted to squeeze Tim's hand, hold him to him, but it was impossible. Tim's hands were gauze boxing gloves, his body a loosely wrapped mummy. Instead, he grasped his own knees while tears spilled from his eyes, ran down his face. "I need you, Tim. It's lonely out there."

"It's lonely here, but it's all right. It takes all my efforts just to keep living and coping with the pain." Slowly, Tim turned his head. His eyes were dark with pain and stared out of a swaddled face. "It wasn't the way I thought it would be. It was all pain and fear. No sense of release or satisfaction. And it wouldn't have made any difference, would it?"

"I don't know what you mean. It certainly wouldn't have changed a tick of the world clock."

"It wouldn't have changed them. They say it was the acid. They don't even blame me, David. They never in my whole goddamn life blamed anything on me. My damn parents are still trying to blame everything on someone, or something else."

"You took it, Timothy, and plenty of people told you not to fuck with it. Why did you do it?"

"I won't answer that yet."

"Where did you get the acid?"

"What difference does it make?"

"I want to know."

"From Howie, but he's nothing. He's dogshit on the big shits' boots. You'll never dry it up. You couldn't keep me from finding it, even after you scared Saunders away from Haskill. You can't keep Liz away either. She doesn't want to see the truth any better than I did. I knew what it could do to other people, but I was different. I knew how to handle it."

"Are you still different?"

"I don't have answers anymore. But I know I'll never take chemicals again. When I get out of here, I'll do what you said and find someone who can help me."

David sighed. "I think they'll find someone for you. Suicides don't get sent home like appendectomies. They take it seriously, Tim. And please, when they send you to a shrink, give him half a chance, will you? Don't make up what you tell him or play parts. How could that other guy help you? He never met you."

"I never wanted him to. It was my mother's idea, not mine. This is different." He paused, then added. "This time I scared the shit out of myself because I forgot it was real."

"I'll get them. I don't care how long it takes. I'll work on them one at a time if I have to, but I'll find a way to put them in jail or keep them away from kids."

"Sure, David, you do that." Tim's eyes started to close as if he were giving in to the pain and the exhaustion of fighting it. "You always wanted to be in Marvel Comics, but you don't have a cape. And you have to have a power to be a Super Hero."

"Maybe not. I knew one who didn't have a power. He just wanted to get back at the bastards." He stood up, giving Tim a thumb's up sign. "We're going to make it just fine. We can still see each other's shit."

"Thanks, David. And I was wrong. You do have a cape. I'm sorry I singed it."

"No problem, Red Leader — just remember to believe in the force and stay on target." David gave him a thumb's up sign before he sauntered from the room, showing more nonchalance than he felt.

During dinner and all evening, Sharon's mind circled endlessly while she tried to put the David situation into focus. There was a lot against him. He resented Hugh and felt he could benefit from his elimination. She knew Marc had killed men in defense and suspected David also knew it. David did own a shotgun, which he occasionally used to hunt rabbits, squirrels, ground hogs, or barn rats. She remembered seeing him with it this fall before the shooting, but no matter how she strained her memory, she could not recall when. Nor could she remember where he had been on the day of the shooting. It had been November, a Saturday, one week after Hugh's elation from a Michigan victory over Ohio State.

David had been in the barn when the police arrived. He had come to the house, looking apprehensive when he saw the state police car, but he had been there to hold her and help her think straight. David had taken charge of things at the house after she left with one of the policemen driving her car.

She realized David must have been out riding, which only made things look worse. She had been painting on the sun porch. Becky and Scott were wrestling and tumbling in piles of late autumn leaves under the old oaks and maples in the side yard. She didn't remember how David reacted to the news. She only knew he had been there — calm, strong, and helpful, the way David always reacted in emergencies. David thought well in tense situations, just as Marc did. When others fell apart, David and Marc were sharp, agile, mentally alert, and rock solid.

Sharon found the only thing on the positive side was a deep-down feeling that David could not kill an unsuspecting person anymore than Marc could. As far as Sharon knew, the men Marc killed had tried to kill him or someone else. He never killed for money or hate. She was sure David was no different. He wanted to live with Marc, but not enough to kill for it. He said he hated Hugh, but she knew his hate was not strong enough to make him kill. In spite of what seemed to be true, she believed David was innocent. He was her child, and when she hashed it out, she could not accept him as a murderer. The tiny barb of suspicion buried itself inside her mind.

Sharon knew Hugh sensed her distress, but did not want to discuss David again, which relieved her. When they went to bed, he held her and let her cry. When the tears ran dry, he made gentle advances until she responded and made love to him with deep hunger and a desperate desire to reassure him, or maybe herself, of her love.

Hugh fell into a deep sleep, but Sharon was restless until she heard David come home at two. After his door thumped closed, her tension ebbed away and was replaced by uneasiness she could live with, maybe even sleep with.

Sharon slept badly with thoughts and images in her mind that were jumbled, out of time and context. When the dream clarified, it took her back to England and the most terrifying moment in her life.

At six weeks, David was a strong, healthy baby, and the doctor assured her he would easily survive what was only a minor respiratory infection brought on by a stretch of miserably wet English weather. Sharon had been awake several times already, listening to David's rasping cough. She had gotten up each time and hurried to the crib across the room, but there had been nothing to do. Her baby lay on his side, undisturbed by the cough that frightened his mother.

When Marc's arm slid around her and gave her a comforting squeeze, she sighed and decided to stay where she was instead of making another trip to the crib. Comforted by Marc's embrace, she lay awake, listening to rain water gurgle down a rain spout outside the bedroom window. When she felt Marc roll away from her, she thought about checking David again, but she was drifting on the edge of sleep and unable to drag herself out of the downward spiral toward slumber.

In what seemed the next instant, her mind was jolted awake by the frantic barking of her Skye terrier.

With her body still locked by deep sleep, she stared toward the open hall doorway at a silhouette with a raised arm, a bulky fist, a gun barrel with a lump of silencer. The bed shifted beneath her, and the gun barrel pointed past her toward Marc's side of the bed.

She screamed a silent, paralyzed scream, just as a gunshot shattered dark silence. The arm in the doorway jerked. Two more shots smacked into the crumbling body that thudded onto the hall floorboards. She jerked to a sitting position and turned to see Marc crouched on the far side of the bed with a revolver in his hand.

When Marc rose to his feet, she started to tremble and scream uncontrollably. He sat beside her and wrapped strong arms around her, but terror controlled her. She was cold and rigid and shaking so hard her muscles cramped with pain.

"It's over. He can't hurt us. He's dead." Marc's voice penetrated to her senses. She stopped screaming, but her body continued to tremble. She was cold with shock.

"Oh, God, Marc, he would have killed us all." When his arms relaxed and he started to stand, she clutched at him. "Don't let go of me."

"Go to the baby. He's crying."

Awareness of David forced her to function. She rushed across the room and, with steady, mothering hands, lifted her bawling son and cradled him in her arms. The small body relaxed and nuzzled for the security of her breast. The nurturing instinct overpowered her fear and she sat on the edge of the bed, offering a milk-swollen breast to her hungry son.

When she had the nerve to look toward the hallway, she stiffened, almost jerking her nipple from the suckling infant. Marc had thrown a blanket over the body, but the left arm was uncovered. The steel pincers of an artificial hand clutched the lower leg and clawed foot of a fighting rooster. Sharon shuddered and looked up at Marc.

"What does it mean?"

"It's a trademark. He leaves it with his victims. This time *l'artiglio* gets to keep his own cock's claw."

"Throw it away. It's sickening."

"It's important the authorities see everything as it is. I need to make some phone calls."

"Don't leave me with that thing." She looked away from the lump beneath the blanket.

"It can't hurt you."

"But the man who hired him can. Marc, he knows who you are. Someone else will come to kill you." Her voice bound up in her chest. She was frightened and pleading. "I want to get away. I want to go home."

"I can't go with you, Sharon."

"You could play soccer in America."

"Maybe in Siberia. Certainly not in the States." He stood beside her and pressed her head against his side while he looked down at the nursing baby. "I want you to stay with me. I want you and David with me."

"I won't stay where my child is in danger."

"He won't be in danger. The man will be dead in three days."

"No, Marc, don't kill him." She snapped her head up to look at his face. It was hard, unreadable, and determined. "It would be murder, no matter who he is."

"And what was this?" He gestured at the body.

"It was different. He was trying to kill you."

"It's time to destroy the Hydra instead of slicing off its heads."

"Just run away to America."

"I tried running to here. You're right, he knows who I am. There's no where to run that he can't find me. I may not be the one to kill him, but I promise you, he will be eliminated. Now let me make some calls to ensure that." He stepped away and hurried from the room.

Sharon was unaware of her tears until one of them dropped onto the baby's cheek. He was asleep again with his face pressed against her breast. A thin line of milk marked the corner of his mouth.

She brushed away the tear and slipped her forefinger into his curled hand. When the tiny fingers closed around her finger, she lowered her head and kissed his cheek where the tear had landed.

"I'll keep you safe, David. I won't let him endanger you again."

In her dream, Sharon was in the house in England on that oppressive, stormy night, but this time it was different. David held the gun. She was standing in front of Hugh's wheel chair, trying to shield him, shouting with no voice. Marc stood behind David, his eyes drawing her to him as he had that first night when she had wanted him so desperately nothing else mattered. There was only Marc's face, Marc's eyes, while he held out his hand to her.

"No, no, it's different now. Please, please, don't ask."

She woke with the sensation of weeping filling her chest. But her eyes were dry, her heart racing. She was sitting up in bed, staring at the small window panes across the bedroom. Hugh was beside her, still asleep.

The dream was not new, except for the ending. It had always been the same before, just as it had actually happened. She had only been frightened and always awakened when she saw Marc with the gun. The lingering pain of grief had never been there before. Sharon had no trouble understanding the dream, only the horrible, depressing grief that made her want to shout the truth at David until he understood that she had done it for him, not herself.

Sharon had no thought of leaving Marc when he told her he was going to Cairo with a widow, whose wealth was estimated in millions of pounds sterling. It hurt her, infuriated her, caused a terrible spat. When he said he was taking David, he roused her maternal instincts and changed all the rules.

"Is this why you're going to Cairo?" Sharon smacked the folded sports magazine on the kitchen table beside Marc.

He looked at the photograph of him signing an autograph, and his gaze took in the platinum-haired woman reaching for the autographed program. When he looked up, his expression was resigned. "She is very rich and very influential. She is also a criminal. I need to know how her operation works."

"It's that same woman."

His mouth twisted into a scowl. "I was hoping you wouldn't recognize that."

"What does she want?"

"Me."

"It's been thirteen years."

"Things weren't good after her husband's operation was broken up. After his death, she left Rome to restructure her life. It took her a long time, but she put the operation back together. It's stronger now, and she runs it with tight control."

"You said she was stupid."

"I was wrong about that. She was ignorant and had little education or reason to use her brains when he was alive. She has since gained an education and lost her ignorance. It seems she has a shrewd mind and a highly developed instinct for survival."

"You were responsible for her husband's death. You jilted her in Rome. You want to put her in jail. Why would she want you any way but dead?"

"Because she doesn't know I killed her husband—"

"You mean had him killed."

"It's the same thing. I told her I jilted her because you were having my baby. Being a woman, she accepted it." He shrugged and added. "She has remained a good soccer fan, so it was easy to reacquaint myself with her."

"Or for her to make herself available so she can get back at you."

"She doesn't want back at anyone. She hated *l'artiglio*, and is not only happier but better off than she was when her husband was alive. This woman is powerful and well insulated, but she still has the same weaknesses."

"Big men and expensive jewelry." Sharon snapped. "It's disgusting."

"Nothing else has worked." He cut back at her. "I tried to keep away from it, but they made me an offer I couldn't refuse."

"Who and what offer?"

"It doesn't matter who, and enough of a payoff to make the next few years very comfortable for us. Plus a no questions asked agreement about anything I can con out of the deal on my own."

"How many times do I have to tell you that I don't care about money? I only care about you. I want a live husband, and David needs a living father, not a dead memory."

"This one job will give me enough security to get away from it for a while."

"You've said that before, but you always go back. Someone always talks you into one more job, and it doesn't make a goddamn bit of difference. There are always more drugs, more killings, more criminals. It doesn't stop. You'll get killed trying to stop up a river that just goes underground and pops up somewhere else. I'm sick of the terror of waiting for you to come home, imagining the horror of having to identify your body or having to tell David he will never see his father again because some drug smuggler blew him apart." The fears that had been suppressed for years crested in her chest and broke loose in a tidal wave of pain, an incoherent cry of anguish that crumbled into sobs.

Marc's arms were around her; and although she was furious, she clung to him, begging him to listen to her and believe her.

"It's not dangerous. I'm going on a cruise with her. She calls it a Mediterranean holiday to Cairo. She doesn't know what I do or that I know she will be doing more than sightseeing in Egypt."

"You have a weakness, too. It's in your understanding of women. I've conditioned myself to accept that there will be other women because most of them are meaningless flings and you read them fairly well. But this time you are wrong. There is no way that woman has forgiven you. She may want you, but not the way you think. She either knows the truth and wants revenge, or she wants to own you and will not let you jilt her again."

"It isn't that way. She just wants a pleasant cruise."

"Bullshit. If she still wants you after thirteen years, she either wants your soul or your head."

"I hope you're wrong because I'm leaving tomorrow evening." He held her upper arms in strong hands. "David's going with me."

"What?" She gaped at him with disbelief.

"Her fourteen-year-old son will be with her. She thought it would be nice for him to have a companion, and it makes my role more believable."

"There's no way David will go with you."

"I talked to him this morning while you were out. David will do very well. I've been training him to think and observe for years. He's always known what to say and what not to say."

"What do you mean you've been training him?"

"The tricks of the trade is the best way I can word it. David will be helpful."

"He's not going. I will not allow David to face your dangers."

"Damn it, he's almost thirteen. That's old enough to leave his mother's teat." He pivoted and strode toward the back door, signaling that the argument was ended. He had spoken and expected her to accept his ultimatum.

"He's not going." She shouted at his retreating back.

When Marc spun around, his face was stone, his eyes blue arcs. "We'll ask him what he wants to do when he gets home from practice. If he wants to go, he'll go."

"Over my dead body."

"I hope not. I've never had any interest in necrophilia."

"I'm serious, Marc. I won't give in."

"It's David's choice, not yours. I'll be back for supper. I have to meet someone in an hour."

After his car drove toward the highway, Sharon went to the desk in the office and searched the drawers until she found her passport and David's. There was more than enough cash in the safe. She only needed to pack a change of clothes and night wear for herself. She found a leather suitcase in David's room. It was already packed, telling her what his decision would be if he were given the choice of going with his father or staying with her.

Reservations were easy. The tickets would be waiting at the airport. David was the biggest problem. She would have to lie to him. And there would be Marc's reaction. She had no idea what he would say or do, but it was unimportant. She would face it later when he came to Michigan to get them.

Sharon never doubted that Marc would come after them. David was as important to his father as he was to her. Marc would never let her take his son away from him, just as she would never let David experience the dangers his father faced with what she saw as reckless aplomb. She never felt she was leaving Marc. She was saving David because she had promised to protect him, even from his father.

At the soccer field, she parked near the gate where she could watch the boys leave the field. She stood beside the open door of the grey Renault until she caught sight of David. He was at least a head taller than the French boys on his team, and his dark, curling hair was, once again, too long. It seemed that David was always two weeks past needing a haircut and reluctant to get one.

Sharon shouted and waved at him, expressing urgency with her voice and gesture. He looked startled and, excusing himself from the boys with him, ran toward her.

"Is something wrong?"

"Yes." She took her cue from his concern and played on it. "We're going straight to the airport."

"I'm supposed to leave tomorrow, not today." He was resisting, but more from confusion than alarm.

"Something's gone wrong, and his plans have changed. We had

no time to discuss it. We have to leave right away. We'll learn more when your father catches up to us."

"He's not going with us? Why not?"

"We're going to Michigan."

"I want to be with Dad?"

"He'll come to Michigan. David, I don't know any more. I only know we have to leave right now."

"Are we going home first?"

"No. I have your suitcase." She nodded toward the back seat. "I threw some of your books and things in an extra suitcase. I hope I brought what you would have."

"How long will we be gone?"

"Stop asking me questions I can't answer."

"Will Dad be all right?"

"Isn't he always?" She saw him flash her a knowing smile. "He can take care of himself better if he doesn't have to worry about us."

"You're right on that, but I wish I knew what was happening."

Sharon saw excitement flush her son's face, flicker in his blue eyes. She heard it in his voice, and it convinced her she was right in taking him before he went to Cairo and let his father reinforce his excitement for intrigue and daring games.

Sharon took a stand, and the battle lines were drawn.

David would not join Marc in his war against the bastards, whoever they may be. He was a boy, and she was going to keep him a boy until he was ready to be a man. Marc's father had thrown him into the excitement and violence of an adult world before he was David's age. It had matured Marc. It had also left scars. She was not going to let it happen to her son.

Over the years Sharon had learned to live with Marc's unfaithfulness, but she could not live without David. Nor could she let her child face Marc's risks. She and David had taken off from Orly airport only minutes before Marc should have walked into their rented house outside of Paris and found the note telling him she had gone to her father.

Five years ago, Sharon had taken David and run home to Michigan, where she felt safe — until now. Why had someone tried to kill Hugh? Why had Marc tried to contact her father in

Zurich? She didn't believe what David said about Marc wanting to see them. Marc was direct. If that were what he wanted, he would contact her, not her father.

She knew her father, through his computer business, was involved with Interpol, which may have had something to do with Hugh's question about keeping Marc away from her. Things had gone against Marc after she left him, but she knew little about it and had no idea if Interpol had even been involved. Marc had always told her Interpol was little more than an information and liaison network, not an actual police force. But there had been something important between Marc and her father and she was sure it involved Interpol.

Unfortunately, just after Sharon left France, the job blew up in Marc's face. There was no one to help him, no one to tell Sharon the truth. Marc disappeared from her life as abruptly as he had entered it. She was left to pick up the pieces of truth and paste them together for herself, but she still did not know enough about what had happened to give David answers to his questions. And some of what she did know she did not want to tell him. There were still too many holes, too many unresolved feelings, which made it hard to forget the man who was still an enigma.

🐎 4

David rarely rose before ten on Saturdays, unless there was a horse show. The show season would start next weekend with an unsanctioned, two-day horse trial that was called a pipe opener, an early taste of competition. He was looking forward to it with the hope that his restlessness would settle down when he was back to competing.

He and Casey Jones, his quarter horse gelding, had qualified for intermediate division this year. His mother was in the same division with her pinto gelding, Limerick, but David felt no rivalry from her. Since she never approached competition with the intensity he did, she was never out to beat anyone, just to do her best against the courses. David went to events to do not only his best, but the best. He competed to win, not to place.

This morning it was almost eleven before he finished his shower and clumped downstairs for breakfast. He had been out later than he had wanted to be last night.

After his talk with Tim, he had gone to the farm where Karen and Paul ran a loosely knit commune for runaway teens, who were trying to redefine themselves and live without the crutches of drugs and alcohol. His conversation with Karen had been interrupted by a fight between two of the newest tenants at the farm. Both boys had been drunk and the actual cause, which had been forgotten in the fray, was racial in nature.

The black boy pulled a knife first. Unfortunately, the Italian boy had a bigger knife, more skill, and an avenging fury. It had been a messy fight that was almost more than David and Karen could subdue. If Paul had not come home when he had, Karen may have had to call the police and an ambulance, which they had not wanted to do. Paul had sewn up the two fighters' cuts as well as one on David's side. It was sore, but concealed and unrestrictive.

Dominic was a runaway who had never talked about anything they could trace. After the fight, Paul was uneasy about whether Dominic was running from home or the law. It had taken two hours of questioning, most it by David in Italian, a language Dominic was more expansive in. By one o'clock, they had enough answers.

Dominic had knifed a black pusher, who pressed him for a debt. There had been a fight. Dominic, a first generation American, had panicked and fled from Benton Harbor to Ann Arbor. He had tried to look up a girl he met last summer when he worked at a resort on Lake Michigan, but the girl had left the university after one semester. It left Dominic alone in Ann Arbor and someone had brought him to the farm. He was only sixteen. David was sure Paul would convince him it was best to go home, take his chances on lenient probation, and keep out of knife fights. Paul was a convincing person.

The situation with Dominic had pushed all thoughts about Sharon, Hugh, even Marc, from David's mind. None of it seemed important on a beautiful Saturday morning while he sat in the kitchen, smoking a cigarette and staring at the vaporous surface of his black coffee. But he supposed it would be to his mother.

Mary Williams came to work at eleven. David nodded in greeting when she passed through the kitchen. A few minutes later, his mother thumped down the back stairs in riding clothes. With Mary to watch the children, Sharon was free to ride. David could sense she was anxious to get outside on a day when spring shouted its presence in the smell and feel of sun-drenched air. However, she did not look anxious enough to duck out on him without letting him know he had not slipped anything past her.

"Good morning, David."

"It looks like a good one." He gave her a testing look to see if the sarcasm in her cheerful greeting was accompanied by a smile or a scowl. He saw a smile, but her eyes were clouded, as if she couldn't make up her mind between anger and concern.

"Am I going to get an explanation for yesterday's actions, or am I supposed to ignore it like a childish temper tantrum?"

"I apologize for shoving you. I just couldn't talk about it."

"Talk about what?" With an obvious effort to appear unrattled, she turned to the coffee maker, plucking a mug off the wooden rack David had made for a 4-H project three years ago.

"The way Hugh and Granfather kept Dad away from us."

"You don't know that they did, just that your grandfather thinks he can. Somehow, I think that if Marc wanted to see us, he'd find a way to do it."

"Maybe they told him we didn't want to see him."

"Frankly, I don't think either of them has said anything to him, or if Marc would take their word for how we felt." After pouring the coffee, she looked steadier, but she took a swallow of the hot liquid before she carried it to the table and sat opposite him.

"Mom, I can't accept that he would let us walk out of his life. Maybe I was only a kid, but I think I knew him well enough to feel that was impossible. He would have been furious when he learned we left. More than that, he would have been hurt. Dad didn't run away from trouble, and he didn't let it run away from him. When he was mad and hurt, he did something about it. I knew that, so I waited. When nothing happened, I invented a lot of things that could have kept him from coming to get us. They ranged from heroic secret missions in Russia to severe amnesia. I would like to know the truth because I can't believe he didn't try."

Sharon wrapped both hands around the solidness of her mug and a shiver of agitation crossed her face. David met her eyes but said nothing. His tight silence made her drop her eyes to her coffee.

"I wanted him to come for us, too. When he didn't, I thought I'd die of emptiness. I left him because I wanted to stop what he was doing, not lose him. I tried to call him, but no one knew what had happened. He was just gone. I assumed the other woman had won and he'd gone with her. There was nothing inside me but a

bitter, emotional vacuum. I let Hugh fill it. He was strong. He
was warm. And he'd been there before."

"Dad wouldn't do that." Hurt bored into his chest and his
feelings rejected her answer. "Dad wouldn't desert us. I won't
believe it. He never gave up, not when it was important to him.
He loved us, Mom. He told me he could never love another woman
as much as he loved you."

She met his burning eyes with a look of resigned hurt, almost
defeat. "I didn't learn anything for six months. Maybe I should
have told you the truth then, but he didn't want me to. He did try
to come after us." She reached across the table and closed her
hand on his tight fist. "He was arrested at the airport on a drug
trafficking charge and was sent to a French prison."

"Did he write to you?"

"He told me several times that if he were ever sent to prison,
I was to go home, start a life of my own, and forget him. He said
he had too many enemies in too many prisons and was sure one of
them would find a way to kill him. I didn't want to believe him,
but when I heard nothing for so long, I guess I did."

David was numb. It was not a scenario he had considered.
"How did you find out?"

"Six months after I left, I received a large amount of money
and a brief explanation of the arrest from his solicitor."

"Why didn't you tell me?" He felt cold and numb. She had lied
to him and it infuriated him.

"The solicitor said Marc requested that I not tell you. He
didn't want you to feel the shame he had as a boy when his father
was in prison. It was true, David. He never resolved his feelings
about his father being a criminal." The grip of fury relaxed when
he felt the truth of what she was saying. "David, I couldn't make
myself tell you I thought he was dead. And I did believe he was
dead until almost a year ago when I found his name in a British
sports magazine. It said he was playing for a team in Northern
Ireland. In June, he dropped out of the soccer world and
disappeared again, which is why it startled me when you
mentioned he was in Zurich last summer."

"Could Granfather have had anything to do with that arrest?"
David asked. He was willing to accuse Hugh of any underhanded

act, but he was not so willing to accuse his grandfather. He had never had an intimate relationship with his tall, silver-haired and dignified grandfather, but he liked him and saw him as an honorable person. "Could that be what he and Hugh were talking about?"

"I don't know. My father has a lot of international connections. I don't know how much he can do, but I doubt if he could or would do that. He honored my decisions as long as he felt I wanted to stay with Marc, but I know he kept his eye on him, or at least, he kept appraised of our status. By the time I learned Marc was alive and out of prison, Becky was two and Scott was a year old. I'd made my new life. I guess Marc had, too, because he hasn't tried to contact me. I made the decision to leave your father's world. Maybe there are some regrets, but there's nothing I can do about them. I don't like what you said yesterday about me wanting to get rid of Hugh because that's no answer at all."

"I didn't make the decision to leave him."

"No, you didn't. However, if I hadn't made it for you, the French government would have. You still might be able to go back to his world. I can't. I have Hugh's children, too. They're not much more than babies and need their father, just as you need yours."

"Let me go to Europe this summer. I'll find him."

"Europe is a big place with an awful lot of people. There isn't even a guarantee he's in Europe. Now that he's out of soccer, he hasn't any ties with anything."

"He was in Zurich last July."

"That was nine months ago. He could have been around the world in that time. One of the reasons Marc never bought property or used credit cards was because he didn't want anyone tracing him. He could pull up and walk out without leaving more than memories behind. He does keep an account and safe deposit box in a Swiss bank, but no one can get any useful information out of a Swiss bank. They keep no personal records. He's a number with no address."

"Do you know the bank or the number?"

"Your father is the only one who can use the account or get into the box, except an executor with a death certificate."

"Who's the executor?"

"Mr. Angus MacInnis in London. He can't help you much. Marc never tells him where he is."

"How would MacInnis know if he was dead?"

"Your father's passport is British. He was born in England, as you were, which makes you British subjects for life. The solicitor is to be notified if Marc is found dead. It's possible he won't be found. In that case, no one touches the account or deposit box. There may be a period of time on that, or some other check. I don't know what he arranged, but I'm sure Angus does."

"Would Granfather be able to find him?"

"He won't help you. Since he thinks we're better off without Marc, you would be foolish to even suggest it to him. I think Marc was foolish to try contacting him. It doesn't feel right. Marc was rarely foolish."

"All I want to do is see my father. Why won't any of you let me do that?"

"Because there's no way to do it — with or without Hugh." She looked into his eyes with no sign of contention. "I'll help you as much as I can. I'll give you names and addresses. Maybe you can learn something by writing. I won't keep you from looking for him, but I won't let you go off on your own looking for a man who can disappear whenever he wants."

"At least there's something I can do. Thanks, Mom. I had some wrong thoughts about you."

"I think we both did. Let's try to do less of that." She smiled when he slipped a strong hand over hers. "The horse trial at Babcock's is next weekend. Do you want to ride over and look at some of the fences? Harold said we could ride the trails as long as we didn't go on any of the course."

"That would be great." He broke into a wide smile. "I'd like to check out that new section in the ravine. I've heard there are some tough ones in there."

"Especially the drop." Sharon made a twisted face of horror.

"Mom, you always overreact."

"That way I either get used to the idea or approach it in complete terror."

He laughed at her. "Head Limerick straight into it and close your eyes. He'll take anything if you tell him you mean it."

"Keep this to yourself. Sometimes, that's exactly what I do. I can breathe with my eyes closed, and they never feel as big as they look. When I see the ground disappear ahead of me I tend to go into a state resembling rigor mortis."

"My problem will be keeping Casey down to a controllable speed so we don't fly past the turn to the next fence. I know he'll jump them all. The problem is getting him aimed right."

While David rode along the trail to look at three steps of reinforced banks where the intermediate course angled down the west side of the ravine, Sharon stopped her pinto at the edge of the ridge trail and looked at the dark structure of the dreaded second obstacle in the ravine series. After the stepped banks David was studying, the ravine was steep, almost a slide, to a bank that ended in a vertical obstacle of interlaced utility poles. What made it more difficult, more trappy, was what was, unofficially, called a coffin just in front of the obstacle.

The coffin was a shallow, rectangular hole that ran the entire breadth of the jump. In order to clear both coffin and jump, a horse had to be bold and moving with good pace. It had to take a long, strong leap, not a hesitant pop. A rider had to know how to prepare the horse and ask for the right moves or the animal could jump short and hit the top pole, or balk, spilling his rider into the sand-lined coffin. The main intent of the coffin was to put psychological pressure on both horse and rider. Technically, the coffin made no difference. If the fence was ridden properly, the horse would treat it as any other ascending oxer. However, the sight of a hole in the ground unnerved many horses and riders.

The psychological pressure was further complicated by the approach — a steep slide that leveled in the last dozen meters, giving only three or four strides to the optimum takeoff point. On the approach side, the jump was only three feet in height. The landing, five and a half feet below the highest rail, was sloping, gravelly dirt. Even in rain, the footing would be safe.

Sharon felt squeamish while she studied obstacle number eight, nicknamed the coffin drop, and could see why it was the most talked about jump on the course.

When she looked beyond the landing, she understood why David was concerned about steering Casey. Because he could get his haunches under him and use their power to control his momentum, David's big horse was agile downhill. Unfortunately, he liked to pull and give David a fight when he was rolling. At the bottom of the landing slope, the course took a quick turn to the right, Casey's stiff side. It would be a bad time to lose control.

After the drop, the course crossed the service road to fence number nine, a stack of logs on the stream bank. From nine, the horse landed in the shallow stream, which was running fast in early May, and splashed upstream for three strides to a jump made to look like a rustic boardwalk with heavy cedar side rails. This last fence in the series was a leap out of the stream to a gravel road.

As David had said when he studied the course map, the ravine was a series of fences where there was no room for mistakes in timing and no place for a change of mind. Once a rider left the smooth, ridge trail, it was concentrated, aggressive riding with no time to stop thinking or counting. First it was number 7 a,b,c, the three steps — one stride and a three and a half foot drop for each bank. Next was a short downhill run to eight, the coffin drop, which was a long leap into space, a slide, and a quick turn to the right. There was only a short run to number nine, the splash, and a strong leap out of water over the parallel rails of number ten, the boardwalk. The road at the end of the series offered a clear, level run, where a horse could make up time.

"Intermediate is set at 535 meters per minute," she said when David stopped Casey beside her.

"I've been pacing it right on the nose in workouts. He was always ahead at prelim, so it wasn't hard." He looked at the coffin drop just below them.

"I hope they keep the fence judges and spectators up here. It's a good view and keeps them safely out of the jump zone. I sure don't want anyone in that ravine when I go through."

"I can understand that." She lifted her eyes from the slide and felt her breath catch. "David, do you see the Jeep down there?" She pointed toward a heavy line of swamp maples across the service road. "Do you recognize it at all?"

"It's probably one of Harold's workers taking a lunch break." David answered with a casual shrug, but his face tightened and alarm brushed across his features.

The explanation sounded right, except Sharon had seen the same vehicle yesterday when she and Colin Trombley had been at the gravel pit giving their horses practice on slides. She was sure it was the same vehicle — sand colored with a heavy roll bar.

Yesterday she had the feeling she was being watched. Today she had the same feeling but, for a twisted moment, it was reversed, as if she had ducked his surveillance and come up behind him when he was not looking for her.

A man was sitting in the driver's seat — red ball cap, dark-blue T-shirt, faded blue jeans. His back was to them while he looked across the road over the stream. His feet were on the dash, ankles crossed. He was drinking something from a blue cup, while an aluminum Thermos beside his feet glinted in the sunlight knifing from behind a snow bank of clouds.

While Sharon watched, the man finished drinking, shook the cup free of droplets, and lowered his feet from the dash. He grabbed the Thermos and spun the cup-cap back onto it before he set it on the passenger seat. When his hand came up, there was something in it. Sharon saw a flash of reflected sunlight when the man turned toward them in a slow, sweeping search until she was staring directly into a long camera lens. Embarrassed anger tensed her. She jerked up on the reins and thumped the sides of her boots against Limerick's barrel. The horse threw up his head, white mane tossing, and backed him away from the ravine drop-off.

She looked at David and realized he was not indignant. He was furious. He pivoted Casey and surged onto the trail, heading for the dirt road so he could come in behind the Jeep and trap it in the ravine above the bridge. Before Sharon turned to follow her son, the man lowered the camera and started the Jeep, which backed onto the road, then spurted toward the bridge. She could hear the vehicle change gears while it accelerated and knew David would be too late.

Sharon had a better look at the driver today, but it did her no good. He had been too far away to see any details or expression. He was a heavy-set man in sunglasses with a thick, squarely trimmed, black beard. He was wearing a red baseball cap over dark hair. At this distance, he looked like most of the local four-wheelers. It was not unusual to see a Jeep in either place, but it was unusual to see the same one, especially that way — poised, like a spider waiting for prey.

When Sharon reached the service road, David was waiting by the stream, scowling at a cloud of dust on the road beyond the bridge. "Missed him, didn't you?"

"By a country mile. As a driver, he's crazy. Good, but crazy. He may need that roll bar. What does he want?"

"Damned if I know." She shrugged. "Why did you take off like that?"

"I don't like being spied on."

"All you did was scare him off. Your father would say, 'That was a damn fool thing to do'"

"Why?" David screwed his face into a scowl. His heavy brows drew together in an attempt to look cross, but he couldn't keep from smiling at her imitation of Marc. She knew he, too, had heard that expression more times than he could possibly recall.

"Because you let him know he's affecting us. Unless you know all there is to know, the best thing to do is play dumb while observing all you can. Your father taught you that. Patience, David, never make a big move until you're ready."

He sneered with exaggerated disapproval. "It's probably someone from Schmidt's trying to catch cheaters schooling on the course. They raise chicken-shit protests so much they're a T.D.'s nightmare."

"I don't think Schmidts, or anyone else, would go to that much trouble for one of Harold's pipe openers. He's very casual about them. They certainly wouldn't have been watching me at the gravel pit yesterday."

"Any idea why?"

"No." Sharon shook her head to flip away the hair that had slipped out from under her scarf onto her forehead. "That's why I asked if you recognized him."

"You asked if I recognized the Jeep. I didn't give you a

straight answer. I've never seen the Jeep, but I have seen the man. I wasn't sure until I saw the beard and sunglasses. I think he has bad eyes. The lenses are very thick and dark brown."

"Where have you seen him?"

"He was hanging around school talking to people around Thanksgiving time. He didn't talk to me. I thought he was a narc."

"A narc?"

"A narcotics cop." He gave her a funny look. "You should know what a narc is. Dad was a self-appointed one."

"Oh, I know what a narc is. I was curious about why a narc would be interested in us."

"There are a slew of them at the high school and on campus. Sometimes they check Haskill out, too. My name came up, but no one said he showed any special interest in me."

"That's unsettling, especially that your name came up. Maybe I lived with your father too long. When things seem out of the ordinary, I get apprehensive and think that maybe someone hasn't been straight with me about a lot of things." When she picked up the reins and started to walk toward the bridge, David's hand caught her wrist, making her stop the horse and look at him. His hand was hard, firmly restraining, with a strength that told her he would not let her shake it off.

"What has been out of the ordinary?"

"I can't put my finger on specifics, but I feel I'm left out of too much that's happened around here." She looked away from his eyes because she didn't know how to say what was upsetting her. David said nothing, but he continued to hold her wrist. She had opened a Pandora's box, and he was not going to let her close it or brush him off. When she looked back, his penetrating gaze seemed to see right into her. "You upset me, David. You and Hugh."

"There are things between Hugh and me that you don't know about."

"What things, David? Ever since Hugh was shot, you've been different."

"Different? Different than what?"

"You haven't been open. You've been unpleasant."

"Oh, come now, Mom." He huffed. "I was never a model child."

"No, you certainly weren't. There were times I couldn't keep up with your mischief. You could make me more furious than anyone, except your father. But you always believed in yourself, even if you weren't a model child." She was surprised when he laughed and let go of her wrist. "What's so funny?"

"I don't suppose the psych books would call you and Dad model parents, either, but we fit together. We were three people who had fun and liked each other." He looked puzzled when he settled into the saddle and started the horse walking toward the bridge beside hers. "I never had the feeling we were trying to play out roles and do things the way other people did them. I was a real part of your lives. I knew I had to obey you and that when it came down to brass tacks, Dad had the final word, but I didn't feel I was a separate species the way I do now. Sometimes I wonder how Becky and Scott will see it all. You and Hugh, especially Hugh, are so ideal and structured with them it's almost impersonal. You listen and give them such nice pat answers. I'm not sure you see them as real people."

"They're only two and three years old."

"That's just what I feel. I never felt my child's world was different from your world, that I wasn't a people the same as you were. If I got obnoxious, Dad blistered my ass, but he never tried to make me feel like an inferior being the way Hugh does. Maybe you don't see what I believe in because it's unorthodox. I still believe in myself, Mom, and I believe in people enough to feel it's important to give strength to those who can't find it in themselves."

"Then why do you drink and smoke pot? It's not the reaction of someone who's satisfied with himself."

"By your definition, most of the social strata you associate with aren't satisfied with themselves. Why should teens be denied the crutches of adults? Are we that much stronger? Do we have fewer identity problems? Most teenage drinkers come from homes where the parents are problem drinkers."

"You're a whiz with generalities. Most of the people we know use alcohol as a social aid, not an emotional crutch. But you have a valid point. I'd say a large percentage of people aren't satisfied with themselves. I don't care about them. I care about you. What's your excuse?"

"That's where I find them, Mom. The ones who need help. I hit bottom last winter. I don't regret it because I can share it with them. I don't drink much now. I rarely smoke pot. Once in a while I find it relaxing. It lets me drift with my imagination or let out hurts."

"It lets you escape facing those hurts or inadequacies. I used it until I learned from your father that I didn't need an excuse to express what was inside me. What you said before about us not playing roles is interesting. Your father played roles superbly, but always intentionally, as a cover or disguise. With us he was totally himself, uninhibited and unconcerned about an image. He was the most self-satisfied person I've ever known. He only used alcohol or marijuana when he needed it to fit in. You're using crutches."

"I'm fitting in. The kids don't want to talk to straights. While we're on the subject, what about your husband? He drinks and turns into a hard-ass."

"He certainly isn't satisfied with himself. I understand what Hugh's trying to smother. I don't understand you."

"Maybe Hugh's accident has something to do with it." David jerked his eyes from hers and glared toward the bridge. "How in hell am I supposed to get back at a helpless cripple?"

"Don't see him as helpless. It would be a mistake."

"That accident changed all the rules."

"Was it an accident?"

His jaw clenched. His face turned to stone. "It has to be seen as an accident because I have no defense."

"David, please tell me the truth." One of her hands twisted in the horse's white mane while she clutched the buckle of the braided rein with the other. His face was tense when he stopped on the bridge and stared down at the stream, where crystal sheets of water rushed over irregular stones and sent up sparkling sprays of droplets. "Why did you say it was your fault? Why do you need a defense?"

David twisted to look at her. "You don't know why he went up there? Doesn't he tell you anything?"

"I guess not. He said he went to look for poachers."

"That's what he told the police. I thought he told you the truth. Hugh didn't go after poachers." He looked back at the stream. "He went after me."

"Why?" She moved Limerick's haunches over so she could face him.

"He wanted to pound hell out of me."

"Hugh?" She made a wrinkled-nose face. "He's not a violent person."

"You mean he isn't a hotheaded scrapper. Did you ever watch him when a horse balks?"

"He's firmly patient."

"Yeah. He firmly and patiently lays on the whip until the horse either does what he wants or is a quivering wreck. I'm not a horse, and I don't like it when he starts on me because I'm too damn stubborn to give in easily."

"He wouldn't do that to a person."

"He may not be as quick to be physical, but he is unrelenting and degrading. I guess he rationalizes it as, `When all else fails . . .'"

"Why was he after you?"

"It's a long story."

"We have a lot of time."

"I told you I hit rock bottom. I needed money because I'd borrowed too much. Hugh's tight and you aren't exactly overgenerous without a lot of questions I didn't want to answer. I got involved in a marijuana racket. I was buying from a student in Ann Arbor and selling it at school."

"Haskill?"

"The easy thing about Haskill is the kids have plenty of money. The profit can be high and there isn't much haggling. Somehow, probably through his brother, who was also buying from me, Rob Williams got wise to it and told me to drop it. When I didn't listen, he told his father. Leon, of course, told Hugh, who made a big noise over it. I played innocent. He didn't believe me, but he didn't have any proof so he couldn't do anything. He did tell me that if he ever found the proof, he'd pound the shit out of me and feel justified because I was a goddamn liar. Hugh doesn't make false threats. He punched out a drunk groom once."

"When?"

"While we were still in Europe. The groom was passed out drunk when he was supposed to be watching a colicky filly. She died of a twisted intestine. There are several stories about Hugh's wrath if you look for them — a G.I. in Nam with shattered ribs from the butt of Hugh's rifle. The only thing that saved Hugh from court martial was that the G.I. had tried, in front of witnesses to grab him by the balls. Hugh doesn't have a wide view of deviates."

His answers startled Sharon but failed to shock her. She chose to show little reaction. "Maybe I wouldn't have blamed him too much."

"It's not his concern." He raised his chin and hardened his face. "It may be yours, but it isn't his."

"Where does the cabin fit in?"

"I was grounded. Since I couldn't go to Ann Arbor, I was using the cabin as a meeting place as well as somewhere to stash what I didn't want to carry around. I could get there by horse and the student by trail bike. Leon found out about Bruce and made him tell all. Leon and Rob are straight as saints and merciless toward sinners." His growl was caustic.

"So Hugh was going to catch you with the proof?"

"That's what he told Leon. Bruce tried to save me by getting through to Tim, who intercepted my student, who met me on the trail and told me Hugh was on his way to the cabin. I got there first, picked up any evidence, and took off for home through the recreation area. I figured Hugh would be burned when he didn't find anything and would come after me like a storm trooper, but he still wouldn't have his damned proof."

"But who shot him?" Her demand was exasperated.

"I don't know." He shouted back. "That's the truth. I feel responsible because I was the reason he was there. I'm trying to find out who shot him because the police would try to pin it on me if they heard that story."

"Why haven't they?"

"I don't know that either, except Hugh doesn't want them to

hear it. I also know the student didn't shoot him."

"Are you sure?"

"It would be impossible."

"What about Tim? Or someone the student bought from? What about this bearded man? You said you started seeing him around then. Could he feel you know too much?"

"It's remotely possible, but I didn't see him for more than a week later. I'm inclined to think he's a cop, or a detective of some kind. He's nosy enough to be one. It's even possible Hugh hired him because he doesn't want to take the risk of believing it was an accident. My student did see a man in the woods with a gun, but assumed it was a hunter and, since the trail was rough and needed to be watched, hardly looked at him. Tim only had a car. I don't think he could have gotten there in time on foot. Nobody higher up in the drug chain would have been interested."

"Why not?" She remembered three men with guns chasing Marc for some stolen marijuana.

"It was only a student with some grass. Marijuana is common stuff in Ann Arbor. No one is going to shoot a man with Hugh's connections for a little grass deal. I wouldn't have made it so complex if Hugh hadn't been breathing down my neck. I was worried about him, not the law."

"Has Hugh said anything to you about it?"

"Plenty. He caught me alone a few days after New Year's. He wasn't very nice, and Leon was there looking as if he wanted to rearrange me."

"Did it have any effect?"

David shrugged. "It shook me up, but it was pointless. I wasn't selling it any more."

"Did you tell him that?"

"Of course not." He gave her a patronizing scowl that was a carbon copy of the one his father always used in response to what he saw as a dumb question. "It's a little stupid to tell him I'm no longer doing something I already told him I wasn't doing. It rates with, 'Have you stopped beating your wife?' and other unanswerables."

"You told me."

"I don't lie to you." His answer was a simple statement of

fact.

"Why do you lie to him?"

"Because he expects it. Hugh thinks I'm an incorrigible criminal with larceny in my genes."

"Lying to him doesn't make him think any better of you."

"Mom, it pisses me to be told I eat, sleep, and breathe in comfort because of his generosity. He told me he'd be damn sure I didn't become a crook like my father as long as I was living under his roof. It made me damn eager to get out from under his roof. I'm still here because it's also your roof and Dad made me promise to always stick with you. He said someone had to take care of you when he wasn't around. I've never seen Hugh as a great replacement and want to keep you aware of it."

"What do you mean?"

"Without me to keep Dad alive in your mind, Hugh would overwhelm you with his opinions. It seems to me Dad spent most of his efforts getting back at crooks who took it from honest people. He wasn't a crook to me."

"It's a matter of viewpoint. He conned the rich because you can't con much from a poor man, and a lot of rich people made money in dishonest ways. He did like to go after the bigger crooks, but he didn't always do it legally. His philosophy said that committing crimes against criminals was fair practice. David, I'm grateful for your concern, but no one is going to overwhelm me with opinions that aren't mine. I lived with the man for a long time. Hugh never met him. Why should I believe him?"

"I guess I know that now." He flushed with his half-smile. "It was a self-assigned mission that kept me going when I felt like an outsider."

"Then it served its purpose, didn't it?" He looked startled, then he obviously understood what she had said and laughed. "David, why didn't Hugh tell me about any of this?"

"I guess he decided he could handle it himself and didn't want you involved. The trouble is he makes a big deal out of a little thing. It wouldn't be the first time."

"Why haven't you said anything?"

"I didn't want you to know."

"I'd hardly go into shock if I heard you sold a little marijuana."

She added facetiously. "When I met your father, he was stealing it."

"You never approved when he drifted over the line. You pointedly stressed you did not believe in the ends justifying the means."

"I still don't, but I won't go into shock over it. Hugh is straight and legal and has trouble with narrow vision."

"That isn't what I didn't want you to know. That isn't what I can't cope with all the time."

"What is?"

"When I heard about it, I didn't care. Mom, I wasn't sorry. I was glad." His eyes bored into hers. "I'm only sorry he's crippled. I wanted him dead. The whole time he was in surgery, I wanted him to die and get out of our lives. I know it's wrong to feel that way, but I did, and I didn't like myself."

"Well, thank God for that. Do you still feel that way?" Her direct question startled him, and he looked pensive.

"No, I don't care anymore. I just want to get away from him." He picked up the reins, tightened his legs, and with a quick thrust of his pelvis, lifted the horse into a long-framed gallop.

When her horse tried to follow David's, Sharon shortened her reins and held him to a restless jog then eased him back to a walk. She wanted to let David go on without her so he could straighten things out in his mind and emotions.

While she rode alone, the tight knot inside her relaxed. She knew David had told her the truth when he said he hadn't tried to kill Hugh in more than thought. In spite of the burden on his conscience, wanting someone to die was much different from actually trying to kill him and couldn't be classified as a crime.

She was more upset by David's recounting of scenes with Hugh and wondered how far back and how deep his resentment went. She had often sensed tension, had a feeling they were only putting up with each other on account of her. She had never liked it but had learned to accept living between David and Hugh, who were on opposite sides too often and were both guilty of a reluctance to compromise or negotiate. They both threw out no choice challenges that turned into fights Hugh usually won. He had all the ammunition on his side — money, food, car keys, housing, strength, age, and horses.

But then, there had been times when David and Hugh had come together in a way that encouraged her. It had usually been about horses, occasionally about hunting, or guns, or physical skills, when David had seen a reason to admire Hugh and learn from him. Before last summer, Sharon actually thought they were going to make it as friends.

Last summer had been the crisis with Cavendish, a horse Hugh had declared an outlaw and sold to the killers against hers and David's protests. That had been just before the Changebrook trials. She could understand why David had reacted so bitterly to Hugh's comments about Marc.

Sharon was uneasy about what David said about Hugh's wrath; but when she thought about it, she realized she shouldn't have been surprised. Hugh was used to getting his own way, as his father had been before him. The old general had been a harsh, exacting, often humiliating, disciplinarian. Some of it had rubbed off. Hugh was not exactly brutal to disobedient horses, but he was harsh and argued that some of them needed to be broken to his will in order to respect him. It made sense that he could be the same with people who defied him. On the few occasions Hugh had disciplined David around her, he had been harsh and cutting in his manner, as if he were dealing with an outlaw horse sent to him for retraining.

Sharon decided she would try to talk to Hugh if she could get him in a receptive mood. When it came to David, that was difficult. She knew it would not be today. Her father would be arriving soon. Tonight was the spring dinner-dance at the hunt club. She hoped Hugh was ready to face the pressure of a large social event without depression and too much alcohol.

While he galloped away from his mother, David felt oddly calm. The anxiety that had agitated him when he admitted his guilt was gone. The whole horrible guilt was gone, as if it had been a festering thorn she pulled out. Once it was gone, the vindictive hate that had blinded him drained out of the wound. He felt tremendous relief and started to realize it wasn't Hugh who was keeping his father away from him. It was Marc himself. Hugh and his grandfather may have had some way to keep Marc out of the States. They had no way of keeping him from communicating with his son. Marc knew, or could easily discover, David's address, even his phone number. No one screened his mail or his phone calls.

He slowed the horse to a relaxed canter, feeling he had made an ass of himself by childishly blaming other people for something that was clearly his and Marc's doing. The reason was simple. Karen had hit it dead-center. He was afraid of the answers, and there was buried resentment toward his father. The truth made him feel naked. For the first time in five years, David wondered if Marc really cared about him. Was it possible he felt David would not want a father who had let him down by getting arrested and sent to prison? Could Marc feel his son's silence meant he wanted to forget him? Or had prison changed him?"

David had no answers, but he wanted to find them. It made him more determined than ever to find Marc. He wanted to talk to his father about things he couldn't ask anyone else. More important, he felt Marc needed to know how his son felt. It was hard to believe the father he had known could feel wrong or guilty. If it was true, something had to be done about it.

With his change of view toward Marc, David saw Hugh differently. He no longer felt overpowered by Hugh. It no longer mattered that Hugh was alive or that his mother wanted to stay with Hugh for the sake of their children. If Hugh was her choice, he didn't have to be David's. He still disliked Hugh, but he viewed the conflict from a different angle. Hugh wanted him to obey his authority without question, while David refused to recognize that authority. Without guilt turning Hugh into a tormentor, it was a clear-cut battle of wills to David. That was something he could deal with, had been dealing with for most of the five years since he left Europe.

🐎 5

When Sharon returned home and saw a dark-grey, 1932 Rolls Royce parked in the front drive, she realized she was actually looking forward to seeing her father, who always seemed to be tied up in Europe or Washington. She was also eager to see Grace, the woman he had married nine years ago, ending fifteen years as a widower.

Sharon hurried in the back door and cleaned up in the small bathroom off the television den. Her father would be having a drink with Hugh. They would probably be discussing business, which she was sure would bore Grace.

While Sharon crossed the carpeted front hall, Hugh's voice was loud, his words clear. She stopped before she pushed open the heavy office door that was only partly closed.

"Charles, I don't think the boy has the slightest respect for the law. It's generally accepted that students smoke marijuana in Ann Arbor, often so openly teachers and police chose to ignore it. But he doesn't just use it. He sells it. He may sell more than marijuana for all I know. I had some control over him when he was afraid of me, but I couldn't make him see that he was wrong. Now that I've been cut down, he gives me the finger and does whatever he wants."

"How does Sharon feel about it?"

"She doesn't know about it. I'm not sure she'd take it seriously if she did. Thanks to Breton she tends to shrug off what she sees as victimless, petty misdemeanors. David not only wants to be like his father, he thinks his mother would go back to Breton if she had the chance."

"So do you." Charles Collingwood's oboe-toned voice was low, gentle in delivery, cruel in revelation. "He took her from you once. You're afraid he'll do it again."

"I just don't trust him."

"Hugh, ever since he was released from prison, you've been telling me you were afraid he'd hurt her again, or try to get money out of her. The truth is you've always been unreasonably jealous of Marc Breton."

"Do you blame me?" His question was a sharp demand.

"No, I don't. In fact, I've often empathized with your fears. The man is a scoundrel, but he has a charisma that makes him damn pleasant to be with. Like David, he was controllable when he was afraid of me. But I've lost my ace in the hole."

"What do you mean?" Hugh sounded startled and vulnerable.

"He won complete acquittal, which threw me for a tailspin. It was mostly handled in chambers and there was a lot of pressure and evidence from powerful, although publicly unidentified, sources. I get the feeling he is not the total scoundrel we think he is, but I can't tell you why. My ace was strictly clerical. I can't change or influence what the courts decide. If the decision had gone against him, I could have made sure it was enforced, but that was my limit. I have also lost him."

"You've what?"

"Lost him. I don't know where he is. He disappeared last October, but at that time he was still unable to get a U.S. visa. He surfaced in December and spent the winter ski-bumming from Scandinavia to Spain. I can't get a single item on him after February, except a rumor that he went to Brazil with, believe it or not, an Austrian countess. He said he wanted to improve his Portuguese."

"I can believe it. You suspected he was financially strapped after he quit playing soccer. He'll probably stay with her as long as she can support his gambling habit."

"We can hope that's the case, but I can't get any positive identification in Brazil. He's more identifiable now. He came out of prison missing most of his left ear with several deep scars on the left side of his face."

"How did it happen?"

"There are a lot of stories: a knife, a guard's chain, a sick torture by other inmates, an attempt on his life that failed. Prison authorities are, of course, blind to it."

Nausea twisted Sharon's stomach. Her eyes stung with tears. She pulled in a breath and held it while she rushed into the living room to be alone.

In the office, Charles Collingwood dropped a match into a heavy glass ash tray. After drawing on a slender cigar and letting the smoke out in a slow stream that curled toward the ceiling, he raised cold, marble-grey eyes to Hugh. "I found out why Breton tried to contact me in July." He held Hugh's attention for a moment while he thought out how to say it. "When I was in Zurich last month I told Duval about your accident. His secretary was horrified. It seemed that in October Breton had sent a message that said it was important he talk to me about my daughter's past or she could end up a widow."

Hugh grayed and swallowed while he composed himself. "Is that exactly what he said?"

"She swears to it. She thought I'd received the message and acted on it. I only knew he wanted to talk to me. I assumed it was about his acquittal. I took some risks for him when he lived with Sharon, but I had no intention of doing it again. I ignored the message. Now, I'm not sure if it was a warning or a threat."

"Why would Breton want to warn me?"

"Because, if Sharon is right, he's a decent man."

"That's ridiculous. How would he know there was anything to warn me about?" Hugh scoffed. "From Breton, I can only see it as a threat. But was it Breton himself, or someone acting for him?"

"It's not his usual style."

"Prison could have changed his style. I wonder what he wants?"

"Your money or your wife." Charles saw that his quip was not appreciated by Hugh, but it did relieve some of the tension that tightened his face.

"Or both." Hugh lifted his drink and stared into it. He raised his eyes to Charles. "Don't say anything to Sharon. The less she knows of all this the better."

Sharon stood in the living room, gripping the back of an upholstered sofa. She heard someone on the sun porch and looked up to see Grace watching her from the doorway.

"I hope you don't mind," Grace said. "I was looking at some of your paintings. I really like the Italian olive grove. Did you paint it from memory?"

"No, I have a picture." She pulled herself together and forced a smile, hoping it would push away the pain the conversation in the office had given her. "But I suppose there's a lot of memory in it. It was one of our favorite picnic spots."

Sharon walked onto the sun porch with Grace. "I started it one dreary winter day when everything was grey. It made me miss the scenery around Naples so much I had to recreate a piece of it."

"Do you miss Europe?" The woman paused until Sharon met her eyes. "Do you miss Marc?"

"I don't regret him if that's what you mean." She looked at kind eyes edged with soft, crow's-foot wrinkles. "But it is the past. There are things and people I'd miss here, too."

"The first time I went back to Europe with Charles, I tried to recapture some of the feelings I'd felt with my first husband. I couldn't do it. I'd changed, and Charles wasn't Allen. You're wise to understand that no matter how much you enjoyed the past, it can never be the present."

"I'm not sure Hugh realizes I understand that. He resents my memories until I feel I shouldn't have them." She gave Grace a smug, teasing smile. "I keep them alive in nostalgic daydreams. The smell of my paints, passages in novels, shapes and colors of trees, a certain sky, traits or word inflections in David can stimulate a rush of memories that seem to belong to a world experienced by someone else. I don't long for the reality. I cherish the nostalgia."

"An excellent adjustment." Grace's arm hugged around Sharon's shoulders. "An artist's refuge from the pragmatism of men of business and net worth."

"Hugh has the horse affliction as badly as I do, so we don't bore each other or have nothing to do together. Horses are addictive. They can fill your life and leave little time for anything else. Marc left a hollow place, but I've padded it over with Hugh, horses, and competition in a very comfortable lifestyle."

"Charles has the antique cars, which brought us together. Shows and rallies filled the loss I felt when Allen died." She smiled wryly. "Thank God for rich men's obsessions."

Sharon felt comfortable with this willowy woman she had grown more fond of as a mother than the woman who had died from alcohol-induced complications when her only daughter had been fourteen. She remembered conflicting things about her mother and could best describe her as having three personalities: a paranoid insecurity when sober, an uncaring, unreachable depression when drunk, and a shrewish, nagging cruelty when she was somewhere between drunk and sober. Sharon had become adept at sampling her mother's moods, then acting accordingly by making herself compliant, silent, or scarce. She learned self-preservation early and knew how to show the proper face while keeping her feelings and fantasies inside. They were expressed in paintings, drawings, and with Marc, the only person who had been able to tap into and share the intense inferno of her passions.

Grace understood about Marc. Her stepmother even admitted she had fallen for him the first time she and Charles visited them in Europe. Grace had chuckled over Charles's wariness of Marc and told Sharon that if Charles Collingwood's father had been a genuine thief without family honor, instead of a legal thief with a family name to uphold, Charles would have been a worse rogue than Marc Breton.

"Hugh doesn't like this painting," Sharon said. "Do you suppose he can sense how much feeling is in it?"

While she stared at the canvas of a sunny, hillside olive grove, Sharon felt herself drawn into the somnolent warmth of green and gold. She sensed the heaviness of olive scent, which stimulated memories of the man and boy, who had laughed and rolled on the hillside. She laughed at David, who wrapped his seven-year-old body around the checkered soccer ball and refused to give it up in spite of frantic tickling.

Finally, Marc sat on the ground, pulling the rolled up boy onto his lap. "That is strictly against the rules."

"I don't want rules."

"You can't do that. It takes the challenge out of life when you don't have rules."

"You don't always follow the rules."

"The challenge lies in outwitting some of the rules. Remember, David, people need rules to make civilizations work. Don't scream unfair if you get caught breaking the rules. Admit it, take the foul, and play more carefully next time."

"Some rules are dumb."

"Because some people only look at the rules and forget they were made for people. Look at people and decide if a rule is good for them. See if breaking a rule will cause real harm before you defy it. Now give me the ball. There's no game if you kill the ball."

Marc's face was clear in Sharon's memory. She winced when she thought of him scarred, mutilated by cruelty. Marc had been caught breaking the rules. She wondered if he had willingly taken the foul. Did he play more carefully now? She doubted it.

"Hugh may not sense the feelings in the painting but in the way you look at it," Grace said.

Her stepmother's gentle comment pulled Sharon out of the past and turned her from the painting. "You may be right. I get lost in it. I painted it with intense concentration."

She saw Grace smiling at a small painting of a fantasy scene she had created for the children. "That's my version of Elrond's elfin world from *The Hobbit*."

When Grace looked back at her, away from the paintings, Sharon said, "I've been letting what you said last time you were here bounce around in my mind. You're right about Father and Marc. They're two of a kind. Father eats up foolish businessmen and manipulates the law. Marc drains the foolish manipulators and outmaneuvers the laws."

"It's simple, Sharon. Charles doesn't trust Marc because he

knows he's the sort of target Marc zeros in on and sucks dry."

"Father isn't mercenary enough to interest Marc. He hasn't hurt enough people. Father always misunderstood Marc's real motives. He only sees the monetary incentive behind Marc's cons. Do you believe Marc conned me? Hugh and Father won't see it any other way."

"Marc was in love with you. Unfortunately, he was so continental in his beliefs he couldn't understand your American morality and sense of equality."

"That's for sure. Shall we join Father and Hugh for a drink before we dress?"

"It is expected."

By ten o'clock, Hugh was on the verge of drunk, and Sharon wanted to go home. So far, everything had gone well, but his apprehension had made him drink too much. Hugh was not a pleasant drunk. Alcohol sharpened his tongue and made him brutally blunt. Some of the conversation tonight touched on club politics, a subject Hugh could be devastatingly outspoken about.

There was a lot of friction between older, staid members, who wanted to keep the hunt club solely for hunting, and a growing knot of members, who supported eventing. In spite of the purists, more and more hunter people were crossing over to combined training, at least in curiosity if not full participation. Tonight, there was a lot of talk about the pipe opener at Harold Babcock's Pheasant Run Farm and the issue was stirred up.

Sharon's interest in eventing had started in Europe, and she had come back to Michigan a devout convert. It brought her back to Hugh, an avid follower of Harold Babcock, who had once been an international three day competitor. Eventing caught her with its challenge. Hugh won her with his security.

David had gone in his first American horse trial at thirteen on a fearless Irish Connemara pony named The Irish Rover and had been a strong competitor ever since. Hugh had trained David's horse, Casey, and ridden him in a few training level trials before he gave him to David. In three seasons, David had taken the horse through training and preliminary to intermediate.

Sharon spotted David across the room surrounded by a flock of girls. She tried to guess which one he would take home, then gave it up as a hopeless problem. David never seemed to have much of a local social life, but Sharon was not fooled into thinking he had none. He was too attracted to girls. The opposite was even more obvious, and from what Sharon observed, he could take several of them home. David collected girls, as friends, never seeming to fall for one at a time. As his mother, she was unsure what that said about him, but he was too much like his father for her to believe he was at all innocent.

David had the big car tonight — the Buick that had been equipped to haul the horse trailer. Since Hugh couldn't drive it any more, he grudgingly allowed David to use it for special occasions. Tonight, Sharon had given David the keys. Hugh had given her a sour look when she told him.

"May I ask you to dance?"

Sharon turned at the deep voice and felt Colin Trombley catch her hand with a firm, warm grip. "Of course. I was beginning to think you were giving me the snub."

She moved into his arms and looked into deep-set hazel eyes. Colin had a strong brow, high cheekbones, and a bowed mouth with a long, golden moustache. He was aesthetically attractive with what the Victorian British would have called features of good breeding, an aristocratic bearing. He was a man born to horses and hounds, who knew how to flatter and set people at ease.

Sharon had met Colin fox hunting in England and enjoyed a brief affair with him while Marc had been on a soccer tour. There had been fun trips in Colin's old Bentley to archery contests and medieval festivals with nights in tiny country inns and slow walks by the sea. She had no regrets. Colin, always a gentleman, had been discreet and had not tried to continue the affair after Marc returned.

Marc had disliked Colin, but Sharon didn't suspect she had anything to do with it, unless it was an uneasy awareness. Marc had told her one scoundrel could recognize another, but she had never seen Colin as a scoundrel, just a bored young man with an alcoholic wife and no need to work for a living. He had inherited sizable incomes and properties from his father, his aunt, and a beautiful bride, who had been kicked in the head by a horse after only fourteen months of marriage. He told her the second marriage had been a reaction of grief and a dreadful mistake.

Colin had ridden with Captain Mark Phillips and had a nodding acquaintance with Princess Anne that he tended to exaggerate when someone seemed impressed. He never bothered to put on an act for Sharon, which pleased her and made her feel he was on the level with her.

Colin had come to Michigan to train and compete for Dr. and Mrs. Harrington, a childless couple with a substantial fortune and a strong desire to see their stable in high competition. Colin Trombley was good, but Sharon doubted he was that good. He must have given them quite a sales pitch to get the job. Since arriving in the states, he had mostly been the old Colin, a little jolted by an automobile accident that had killed his second wife and her lover a year and a half earlier. Actually, Sharon felt it was for the best. Sybil had been a shrewish lush with a title she had always been quick to point out was far above Colin's standing.

"What do you think of the intermediate course? Harold told me you and David popped by to have a look at it."

"It terrifies me, but David's champing at the bit."

"Nothing frightens that boy. Danger tempts him as it did his father. Caution him, my dear. The horse is too bold, and David is thrilled by it. He'll break his fool neck if he doesn't take back on him."

"David takes care of himself. I have faith in him."

"Does Hugh?"

"He has faith in David's ability to survive."

"There is a good bit of the Breton instinct in him." He looked past her shoulder and asked, "Do you know the girl with David?"

"Which girl? He was with a bevy of them a few minutes ago."

"She showed up late with Karen. They weren't at dinner." Colin's expression was more alarmed than curious and she turned to follow his gaze.

"I don't know her." Sharon no longer doubted what girl would be leaving with David. She remembered Arlene Metzger's gossip about David dating a college girl much older than he was and could understand the alarm on Colin's face. The blonde hanging on David's arm was beautiful — stunningly beautiful. She was almost as tall as David — supple, graceful, golden tan, golden hair, sea-green eyes. After starting at Colin's bold stare, the girl's expression became confused and her pretty green eyes looked strange, as if she were not aware of just where things were happening around her.

Out of the corner of her eye, Sharon caught a flash of movement and saw Hugh spin his wheel chair and zip across the dance floor. It confused her until she saw him cut David off, momentarily trapping him between a wall and a wooden railing, where a short stairway led to the lower level lounge and foyer.

"I think I better break this up." Sharon moved away from Colin. "I doubt if there will be anything pleasant in that encounter."

"Where are you going, David?" Hugh pivoted the chair to face his stepson.

"I don't see it as your problem."

"Where my car goes is my problem. Give me the keys." Hugh thrust out his hand.

David stood immobile, meeting Hugh's eyes with a contemptuous stare. "No. I have the car tonight. I haven't done anything wrong, so I won't give it up just to please your drunken whim."

"Nothing wrong? Cutting school is right? I still make the rules and can insist that you obey me."

Hugh's voice had been low. David's was not. "I don't listen to you when you're a drunk hard-ass. Now get out of my way." Setting his foot on the front of the wheel chair, David shoved it backwards, right at his mother, who caught it and stumbled back a few steps before she stopped it.

When Sharon strode around Hugh, David jogged down the steps with the girl. Sharon was right behind him and each tense step made her more furious. David had a way of doing that to her, just as Marc had. The voice and tone brought back that night in Rome when Marc had told her to keep out of the way, as if nothing was important but him and his deal, his job, his con. She had backed away from Marc, but she was not going to let David treat her that way.

Outside, Sharon followed David down wide stone steps and into the parking lot until he reached the car and stopped to unlock the passenger door. Even though she tried to keep a hold on her anger, she found herself shouting. "That was an outrageous display of behavior."

After he twisted the key in the lock, David jerked open the door and thrust the girl into the car. When he closed the door and turned, he took two strong strides toward his mother, making her draw back just enough to give him the edge. He stared at her stunned face, then said, in a relaxed, arrogant voice, "Yes, he was both outrageous and drunk. Let's face it, Mom, you didn't want that scene to go any farther."

"He only did it to exert his authority. You kicked hell out of his ego. He won't let that go by."

"Tough shit. It's not my job to boost his ego. I only obey what makes sense to me. Hugh trying to boss my life doesn't make sense."

"Why do you hate him so much? Hugh didn't take me away from Marc. I left him."

"That has nothing to do with it. That only makes me see you as a fool. Why don't you ask Hugh about it? Ask him about his methods of breaking rebellion. Ask him why he sold Cavendish to the killers. Or why he can't turn his back on Thistle."

"What are you talking about?"

"Ask your husband. It's his problem. I have to leave."

When he turned to walk around behind the car, Sharon started after him. She froze when she looked across the parking lot and saw it — a sand colored Jeep with a heavy roll bar.

"David! Where are you going?" The alarm in her voice made him pause with the driver's door open. "For God's sake, don't do anything wrong."

"What are you babbling about?"

"That Jeep is here."

His gaze followed hers to the vehicle. "There's no one in it."

"If he's what you think he is, he's waiting for you to do something."

"Hey, Mom, there's nothing to get worked up over." He raised his hands and gave her a wide-eyed look of innocence. "Relax. I'm not going to do anything he could care about."

"Who's the girl? Isn't it polite to introduce your mother to your date?"

"She isn't my date. And she wouldn't make sense out of an introduction right now. She did something stupid. I'm trying to get her away from here before she goes whacko on me."

"When you act like this, I feel like going whacko."

"Don't do that, Mom. I really am on your side." He slid into the car and chunked the door locks closed before he started the engine. When he backed past her, he winked and laughed. His tires chirped when he shot ahead then squealed around in a tight arc onto the driveway.

"Oh David. I never knew whether I wanted to spank you or hug you. You haven't changed a bit." She glared after him with her feelings churning in confusion.

When the sound of a starting engine alerted her, she pivoted in time to see the Jeep careen around the end of a row of parked cars and out the back entrance of the lot. It turned left in time for the driver to see which way David had turned at the intersection down the road.

While Sharon watched the Jeep's tail lights move away from her, something nagged at her mind. Something wrong. Then she recalled what it was. The left backup light on David's car was on when he left. The man in the Jeep would have no trouble following him.

When she turned back toward the Tudor style clubhouse, she almost bumped into Colin, who wrapped his arms around her and held her pressed against him. He was strong, sheltering, and she broke into tears. "Oh, Colin, I don't know what to do. I'm scared, but I don't know what I'm afraid of or which way to turn."

"The first thing to do is get a grip on yourself and try to explain what happened."

While he held her, she cried and let it tumble out in a jumble of run-on thoughts. "David left with that gorgeous girl who was spaced out with the backup light on and the cop in the Jeep was following him and she looked as if she wanted to seduce my son right in front of me."

"Hold up a minute. What cop in what Jeep?"

"The bearded man in the tan Jeep. David thinks he's a policeman or detective, but I think he's after David because David knows too much."

"Sharon, you're not making sense." Colin remained calm, but his voice was frustrated. "What does David know too much about?"

"About Hugh and who shot him."

Colin's face sobered. "What does David know?"

"I don't know. He said a student who met him in the woods on a trail bike saw a man with a gun that day. I think it's that man and he wants David to lead him to the student so he can kill them both."

"Good Lord, Sharon, you can't really believe that." He held her by the arms and gaped at her.

"Can't I? Tim was in on it. Look what happened to him."

"He tried to commit suicide. No one tried to kill him."

"I don't know what else to believe. He's been watching us, taking pictures of us like some crazy man. He was watching me the day you and I rode at the gravel pit." Her statement startled Colin, who, apparently, had not seen the Jeep. She looked at his shocked face and said, "A cop wouldn't care about me, but a killer who thought David knew too much and had told me would be interested in both of us."

"Has David told you anything?"

"No, but the killer doesn't know that."

"No one killed Hugh."

"Someone tried. That makes him a killer to me."

"Have you said anything to the police?"

"What is there to tell?" His question confused her. "Colin, I don't know anything. I only feel it. I don't know who to talk to and I don't have any evidence to support my feelings."

"You can talk to me. I'll listen to your feelings and give them credence. I want to help, but you'll have to tell me something more solid." He handed her a handkerchief and led her to a bench in a copse of trees beside a gurgling brook. "I'll try to understand."

"There isn't anything more solid."

"Then that's that."

He squeezed his arm around her shoulders. It was a warm,

caring gesture that made Sharon feel less alone with her apprehensions. Colin was a steady friend, and she needed one right now. David and Hugh were too close to the problem. She had known Colin for a long time and could rely on him.

"Sometimes I think I'm going crazy. I don't want to believe someone would want to kill Hugh, or that David and Hugh could be such enemies."

"I suspect maybe Hugh blames David in an indirect way for his condition."

"Why?" She twisted to look at him. "That's what David said, but I didn't think anyone else knew about it."

"I overheard Leon telling Hugh how he could find the proof he wanted if he was at the old cabin about three. Hugh was furious and said, 'This time I'll catch that damn kid red-handed and take him down to size'" Colin mimicked Hugh with an accuracy that made Sharon frown. The rough voice made her see Hugh's hard, angry features.

With a shrug, Colin said, "I had the feeling he'd taken David down to size before, which I dare say wouldn't endear him to David, who's too much like Marc to accept it. Personally, I thought Hugh was overreacting; but since it wasn't something I belonged in, I wasn't about to say so. I slipped out and went home before they were embarrassed by my presence." He gave her a nonplused look. "I didn't know Hugh could get so angry."

"Hugh can get very angry, sort of like a persecuting zealot out to destroy sin."

"That describes it. If I were David, I certainly wouldn't have crossed Hugh. But then, I always give violence a wide berth. A Breton invites it. I mean even getting knocked around on a soccer field was too violent for me." After an expansive chuckle, he turned serious. "It was a natural conclusion to think it could have been David; but frankly, I can't believe it of the lad."

"Sometimes I think Hugh believes it and is pushing to see if David will break over it. I don't know what to do about them. I don't know what to do about the man in the Jeep. I have this terrible feeling about him, a deep inside feeling that's strong and frightens me. I'm afraid for David. Colin, I need help. Where should I go?"

"The police would suspect David," he answered quickly.

"I know that. If that man isn't the killer, he's a policeman out to prove my son tried to murder my husband. David says he has no defense and there's too much evidence against him."

Colin thought for a moment, then asked, "Sharon, do you want me to see what I can dig up? Maybe I can learn something about the girl. If I could keep an eye on David and/or the man in the Jeep, it might tell us something."

"Would you, Colin? It's an awful thing to ask you to do. What if he is the killer? It could be dangerous."

"I'll keep a wary eye on him. It's not too much to ask. You were and still are special to me." He lifted his hand and held it against her cheek for an instant before he leaned forward to give her a light kiss. "The rub is you always have a handsome husband."

"Thank you, Colin. Just having someone to share it makes me feel better. Maybe it's all in my mind, but I want to know more. I can't talk to Hugh, and David is frustrating. He's so glib and cool, only I don't know what he's doing most of the time. He has his father's bearing and cleverness, but not his experience. David is young and vulnerable and not as invincible as he thinks he is. I'm sure he feels he can solve it all by himself, the way Marc would. The thought terrifies me."

"I'll do what I can to help. It's important to me."

"Sharon!"

She jumped at Hugh's shout and turned to see him on the walk with her father and Grace. "Thank you, Colin. Call me if you learn anything at all." She stood with him, took his arm, and walked to where Leon was pulling to the curb with the van Hugh could drive the wheel chair into. They had ordered one he could also drive, but it would be another month before it was ready.

"When you said you were going to talk to her, Trombley, I didn't expect an abduction." Hugh jabbed at Colin with too much bite in his voice. Sharon knew Hugh disliked Colin and saw him as an idle wastrel, who talked horses a lot better than he rode them.

Sharon slipped into the van while Leon pulled out a short ramp for Hugh, who seemed calmer than she expected. But the hardness was there.   When his eyes drilled into hers, she confessed. "I couldn't stop David. I don't know where he went."

"I hope for his sake he enjoys his night out. He isn't going to like what I'm going to tell him tomorrow." Hugh gave her an angry glare. "You will not give him my car keys again."

6

David pushed the car over the speed limit on both the twisting, undulating gravel roads of Wellington Township, and the expressways into Ann Arbor. When he exited at Main Street, he was distracted by the girl, who draped her left arm around his shoulders and tried to chew through his neck. Her right hand fumbled at his fly, searching for the zipper tab.

"Cut it out, Liz." When he shrugged his shoulder to shake her off his neck, she tightened her arm and bit into him, sucking hard, until he jabbed an elbow into her ribs and pushed her away from him. "I'm trying to drive a goddamn car."

Liz flopped back against the seat and stared out the windshield. "Oh man, it's great. All the lights are dripping. They're making big, hot puddles."

"What the hell did you take?"

"It was dust. I smoked some dust." She giggled. "And I took a little, tiny, red thing Howie gave me. He gives me lots of them." She slid onto the seat and pressed her face into his groin while she growled deep in her throat.

"I said cut it out." He smacked his hand down on her squirming rump. The blow was hard, releasing the anger that surged through him at the mention of Howie. She jerked her head back, banging it on the steering wheel.

"We're almost to your apartment. Sit up, cross your legs, and behave yourself." He grabbed her by the hair at the back of her head and yanked her upright. "Try to act like a human, not a bitch in heat."

Liz rubbed at her rump before she sat back. She rocked on the seat with her thighs pressed together and bit at her lower lip. Much as it irritated David, even disgusted him, it drove him crazy. Liz emanated a sexual energy that aroused him in spite of his disapproval.

"I got the itch bad, Davy. You gotta stop it. You do it best."

"I hate it when you take that shit. Why did you do it? You promised me you wouldn't take anything."

"I forgot." She twisted her face and squirmed on the seat until she slithered to the floor boards. "I didn't mean to forget." The childish voice upset him and he ignored her while he fought a battle between anger and lust.

Liz had been an intelligent girl when he met her last fall. She was into drugs then, but not like this. Now, even when she wasn't on something, she didn't appear to be all there. She was getting more childish, more unstable, with uncontrollable urges for sex and, occasionally, punishment, which annoyed him. He had no interest in a whining, pouting sex partner.

It seemed that in the last month or so Liz had stopped caring about anything but sex. The way David saw it, her body craved more and stronger sensations while something in her mind demanded punishment for her failure to resist. It was a layman's diagnosis from a thin veneer of psychological knowledge, but he was willing to bet he was close to right.

When Liz was like this, he was tempted to walk out on her. He didn't for three reasons. First, there was a lingering hope that he could turn her around and find the girl he had fallen in love with. The second reason was more practical. Liz was the student who had agreed to meet him at the cabin. She had seen a man with a gun but not well enough to give a good description. Last fall, David wanted Liz as an alibi. He no longer trusted her to give good answers. She only remembered bits and pieces of what happened and when she was spaced, she had a way of screwing up what she said. It could well come out of a jumbled association pattern like — cabin, David, gun, or — cabin, David, gun, shot man. His third reason was one he did not like to admit. She made him crazy for sex.

He drove in the driveway at Liz's apartment complex and stopped at the lowered gate, where he pulled a card out of his shirt pocket. He thrust it into the slot on the red-eyed machine, which digested the code and popped the card back at him while the gate tipped up to let him drive through. He parked in a long carport beside her car in the apartment's second space. Liz was still piled on the floor, arched back with her shoulders and head flat on the seat. She was staring at the dome light fixture with an absorbed, but pouting look on her face.

After opening the passenger door, David grabbed Liz by the arms, hauled her out of the car, and hoisted her across his shoulders. By the time he climbed four short flights of stairs and dug in his pocket for the key, she was giggling and rubbing her hands on his buttocks in a stimulating way that was getting more results than he wanted.

Inside, David locked the door and carried her to a bedroom, where he dumped her on the big, unmade bed. When he turned to leave, she caught the back of one of his pant legs in a firm hold and tugged him toward her.

"Stuff it, Liz. You're blasted. I told you I don't like it that way."

"You have to, Davy." Her voice cajoled with breathy urgency. "You can't leave when I need it."

"I'm sick of being your stud dog." He grabbed her wrist and shook it until she let him go.

Before he made it to the door, her arms wrapped around him from behind. Her face pressed against the back of his jacket. Her hands locked on the front of his belt. David knew he should pry her off him and leave, but he was reluctant. Liz wanted sex. If she couldn't get it from him, it was likely she would find it somewhere else. She was in no condition to drive or even leave the apartment. He also knew that if he didn't leave right now, she would get what she wanted.

"All right, but it's the last goddamn time I'll fuck you when you're stoned." He turned when her arms released him. "That's all it is to you, isn't it?"

A victorious smile split her face and she backed toward the

bed, tugging him by the end of his belt. "You want it, too. You always want it."

He stepped up to where she knelt on the bed and took her head in his hands, forcing her to look up at him. "I love you, Liz. Does that mean anything to you?"

"I'll do good things to you, Davy." Tears filled her eyes and her hands opened his belt. When he dropped his hands to her shoulders, she stripped his pants down to his knees. Her head dropped for a long moment of warm, engulfing ecstasy before she reared back, laughing, and flopped across the bed.

While David jerked off his suit jacket — the tie was already in a pocket — vest, and shirt, she rolled onto her belly and tried to reach the zipper in the back of her dress. He kicked off his shoes and pants, laughing at the way Liz flopped and rolled on the undulating water bed. The dress worked its way up her thighs in twisted disarray, showing that she was wearing nothing else.

"You look like a fish out of water." He grabbed the zipper tab and slid it down the length of her golden back. When she arched up on her elbows, he slid the dress off her shoulders and stripped it down her body.

Liz's long, dancer's back swelled into rounded buttocks. When his hands caressed their softness, he noticed the flushed mark where he had smacked her in the car. He touched it, felt its warmth.

"Why do you make me do things like that?" He dropped his head, kissing the lingering flush. She moaned and squirmed at the touch of his lips, the trailing movements of his tongue, the teasing nips of his teeth. He tasted the salty skin at the small of her back and moved up her spine to the soft hollow of her neck.

"Lizbit, you are the squirmingest thing I know. You can get me harder than a stone phallus just by the way you wiggle."

When his excitement grew to a core of molten urgency compressed in his groin, he slid his legs between hers. She moved her thighs apart and rose up on her knees. Breathing in the musky scent of aroused woman, David grasped her hips and teased her with slow, shallow penetrations. He entered her with a sudden thrust and her passion broke loose, turning her into a wildly thrashing body. She moaned and then yelled with deep, throaty sounds until her wildness peaked, and he let her slip away from him.

David ran caressing hands down her sides before he rocked back on his knees and looked at her while she lay, spread-eagle, face down on the rumpled bed sheet. Her rib cage rose and fell rhythmically. Her eyes were closed, her mouth partly open. Lying beside her with his head propped by his arm, he felt the relaxation of after-sex, but he felt alone.

Silently, he studied the woman beside him, marveling at the blending of flesh and muscle in a body shaped and conditioned by years and thousands of dollars of dancing lessons, exercises, and recitals. When he first met Liz, she loved to dance. In the last year, dance lost meaning and she stopped caring.

Although Liz still danced, still exercised, she did it without purpose. Now, even the habit of dancing was giving way to the pills, the dust, the weed. They were destroying her. They had already destroyed Tim.

David saw chemical drugs as a plague spread by two-legged rats. One rat, named Howie, loomed in his mind.

He ran his free hand down Liz's body from her shoulder, past the sideways bulge of a compressed breast, along the slim hollow of waist, across the soft curves of hip and buttock. He slid it back up until he reached her armpit. Moving his hand under her shoulder, he rolled her over. Her face, neck, and breasts were still flushed, but when she opened her eyes they were glassy and out of focus. The lids slid down over them, and her mouth was a slack smile close to idiocy.

There had been a time Liz had been cuddly and giggly after sex, a time she had been able to laugh and talk with him, a time she knew who the hell he was. Now, she just let it blow the top off her mind and crashed into oblivion.

David looked at her expressionless face, wondering if she had really known who he was tonight. She had called him Davy, her pet name for him. One of his friends had told him she called any man Davy when she was spaced.

When he tossed the sheet over her, David glanced at the underside of her breasts. Small, round, festering sores marked them. He snapped on a brighter light. There were more of them

on her belly and thighs. Alarmed, he tried to shake her awake.
"Liz, wake up. Talk to me."

When he could get no more than a few muttered words of
nonsense out of her, he rolled off the bed, finished covering her,
and dressed. He shoved his vest into a jacket sleeve, turned off
the light, and carried the jacket out of the bedroom.

A light was on in the kitchen. Liz's apartment mate, Pam, sat
at the table with a cup of coffee.

"Hello, David, I was hoping it was you. The kettle's hot if you
want some."

"Thanks." He dropped the jacket across the back of a chair
and fixed some strong, black coffee. "Why are you up?"

"She woke me up. She usually does when she has sex with you
because she yells so much," Pam answered with an unconcerned
voice and laughed at his embarrassment. "Don't blush. It makes
me think my fantasies about you are true."

"I'm not that good." He smiled slowly and winked at her. "But
of course, if you want proof, you can try me sometime."

"Ask me sometime." She shot the comment back at him with
an answering wink. "But seriously, David, I need to talk to you."

"And I need to talk to you." He sat across from the short,
chunky redhead, whose crystalline eyes fascinated him, as did her
habit of wiggling her freckled nose like a rabbit's. "Do you know
how she got the burn marks."

Pam watched him light a cigarette before she answered,
"Yeah. From a cigarette. A few days ago she brought home that
big slob Howie, who hangs around the arcade and sells her stuff.
He's a sicko. She woke me up yelling that night, too. But it was
different." David tensed and read sympathy in her expression.
The thought of Liz with Howie made him sick. "She was
screaming in pain — bad pain. I broke in on them. The bastard
was burning her with a cigarette. It was gross and infuriated me.
But it made sense, considering the way she's been and what he's
like. I started yelling and threatened to hit him with her tennis
racket. It was a crazy thing to do, but it worked. He threw down
the cigarette and ran. I ignored him because I was afraid the bed
would catch fire. Afterwards, I was too scared to call the police or
tell anyone. David, I'm still afraid for her, afraid for me because

I don't know what he'll do about it."

"Nothing. He's a coward. I can't believe she wanted anything but pills from him."

"There were enough of those. There were so many spilled on the bed, it looked as if they'd been popping them like M & Ms. When she came out of it, she couldn't remember anything."

"Shit, she never remembers anything." He scowled. "Pam, I don't need applause, but I'd like to have my performance remembered. Sometimes, I don't even feel I'm a needed part of the act."

"She always says she wants you."

"There may be a burned out memory of the times we really made love without her goddamn junk. I could have gotten as much out of an electronic sex doll tonight."

"You're more than that to her. You're different."

"Not any more." He looked away from her and drew on the cigarette.

"There was something about you that could get through to Liz. She listened to you. Sometimes she'd cry and talk like she was pleading with you to forgive her, but you weren't there."

"I'm not sure there's much to get through to."

"The most horrible thing about that night with Howie was that she didn't even know what was happening. She was shrieking from pain, but she wasn't trying to get away." Pam tightened her hands on the edge of the table. "It made me furious."

"Call her parents. Tell them they have to stop pretending it will go away. Tell them the Coleman-Breton therapy system couldn't help her. A hospital would be best." He spoke calmly, coldly. Inside, he was a rigid block of fury.

"I was afraid you'd be mad if I did that."

He stabbed out the cigarette in a heavy ash tray from a nearby bar. "I don't trust her. There's no sense putting you in danger." He looked at her for a moment, reading the uneasiness in her eyes. "I think Howie was trying to O.D. her."

"Oh God." Her eyes rounded. "Then somebody knows what she saw."

"It looks that way." He slid his hand over hers, holding it with a tight grip of reassurance. "What are you going to do?"

"I can't afford this apartment without her. Her folks are paying for most of it."

"Why don't you move out with Karen and Paul? You've been helpful with Liz, and they could use another level head. There isn't much luxury and you'd have to contribute time to the garden and farm chores, but I think you'd like it. We kept trying to get Liz to stay out there, but it wasn't for her."

"I feel I'm giving up on her."

David reached out and lifted her chin. "You've done all you can. We've done all we can. Liz is killing herself and doesn't care. Maybe she wants to. Maybe that's why she let him give her all those pills."

"Did she tell you about the man who came here last week asking questions about you?"

"Don't tell me he was a bearded man with dark glasses."

"Then she did tell you."

"No. I've become very aware of him. What did she tell him?"

"Not much that day. She may have talked to him again."

"That dude is a pain in the ass." Some of his rage snapped out through his self control before he clamped down on it. "How close a look did you get?"

"As close as I am to you. He had coffee with us."

"Notice anything special about him?"

"He had a thick beard trimmed very square, medium length dark hair. Some grey in it, mostly by the temples and salted through the top. He kept the glasses on. I think they were prescription. They were thick and sunlight made him squint, even with the tinted glasses. He was your height, maybe a little shorter. He was wearing a blue, mountain parka, which he opened but didn't take off." She shrugged helplessly. "He was just a normal man, a little round shouldered, blue collar speech."

"Obviously, someone isn't satisfied with the word accidental in regard to the shooting of my mother's husband. It also means Liz is no longer a secret. Shit, I thought he gave up months ago. Now he's making himself too conspicuous. If he's trying to make me nervous, it's working. There's no way to prove anything, and I know I didn't shoot Hugh. But circumstantial evidence points right at me, and it scares the shit out of me. There's no way I can hide the fact that I can't stand the son of a bitch."

"Liz said you wouldn't have had time to shoot him."

"Did she tell him that?"

"He never asked about that day. She told me that right after it happened. She never talks about it now. Why do you want her to forget it?"

"She has trouble remembering what day it is. Who would believe she had a sense of time then? I'm going to have to sort it out myself. The bearded man is a key, but I can't get to him. Howie I can get to."

"Liz did see a man in the woods — the hunter with the gun."

"But she had no idea what he looked like. She only knew he had an army colored coat and a black knit hat. That isn't exactly what your safety conscious hunter wears in the woods. But then, it isn't so damned unusual either. Now, she hardly remembers how to get there."

"I thought you wanted her as a witness."

"I wanted her as an alibi, but not now. Call her parents. Encourage them to hospitalize her fast. I don't want her talking to people. She babbles and confuses things."

David finished his coffee and stood. He grabbed his jacket and when she stood, reached out and hugged an arm around her. "We can't help her. Maybe a hospital can. Maybe no one can. If we leave her to Howie, she's likely to end up dead."

"First thing tomorrow morning."

"Sounds good." He started for the door, stopped, and turned back to face her. "One more question. Do you know anyone named Ivan?"

"There's an Ivan who danced with Liz." She looked puzzled. "He teaches at the studio on Washtenaw."

"Did Tim know him?"

"He took jazz dancing from him. Why?"

"Tim mentioned the name. I couldn't place it."

David wasn't sure what made him drive past the old railroad station that had become the Gandy Dancer restaurant. Whatever attracted his attention was forgotten when he saw the Jeep backed up to the embankment across the lot from the restaurant. He hit the brakes and slowed to a crawl while he drove through the lot, wondering if he should check to see if there was a bearded man in the bar. He decided it would be the wrong thing to do.

He accelerated up the hill toward the Division Street bridge, then angled across the deserted street, heading away from the Gandy Dancer toward Main Street. At the corner of Main, he felt uneasy. He had somewhere to go, but he didn't want anyone following him, especially not a detective in a tan Jeep. He turned right, away from town, instead of left.

While he drove toward the M-14 interchange, he checked his mirror. There was no car behind him. There was no car anywhere, only a motorcycle pulling out of a side street. David took the expressway east, away from I-94 and home. He was still alone with only the single light of the motorcycle falling away behind him. He switched to 23 south, exited at Plymouth Road, and drove back into town from the northeast.

After David cut through the University's North Campus, he was almost back where he had started by the Huron River below the complex of University Hospital buildings that clustered together like crowded mammoths on top of the hill to his left.

The hospital was a maze of hooked together buildings, displaying over a hundred years of architectural vogues. It was cramped and confusing, but it was the fifth largest hospital complex in the country and a leading medical center for the Midwest. It was where Tim was receiving the best possible care in one of the world's most modern burn centers. When he glanced up at the buildings that climbed and crested the hill, David felt a twist of angry pain.

"Damn it, Tim, what made you do it?" he asked the question Tim had refused to answer. "Something had to have made you do it beside acid."

While he renewed his hate of drugs and whatever is was that made them so available to kids, he decided mass extermination wasn't a bad answer.

"Pushers don't deserve humane treatment." He snarled to himself, then sobered. Less than a year ago such a rash solution could have eliminated him, too. Well, maybe there was no simple solution.

The more involved with life David became, the more complex it became. Nothing was all right and all wrong any more. Except Howie. He was all wrong. David had no compassion for Howie.

After passing the hospital hill, he drove into town and turned west on Huron, back to Main Street three blocks south of where he had turned north earlier. There had been no sign of the Jeep. He paid little attention to the motorcycle that swung in behind him after Liberty Street.

David zig-zagged across town beyond the official campus area and found a parking place in a small, dark lot beside a narrow building. Bright, round bulbs flashed in random order around a doorway and curtained window with "Arnie's Arcade" painted on it in gold letters. Outside the building, David unbuttoned his shirt cuffs and rolled them back, almost to his elbows. He shrugged and pushed through the heavy door.

He found Howie leaning against a support column in the back, where he always seemed to be. He was watching a group of rowdy teens play an electronic game where the primary objective was to drive a death car over as many pedestrians as possible in a ninety second turn.

"I need to talk to you, Howie." David offered him a cigarette and gestured for him to follow.

"What do you need? Who sent you to me?" Howie asked in a voice that was too high, too staccato. He took the cigarette and crossed the room with David, who was younger, shorter, and much lighter.

"No one sent me to you. I need some information about someone." David pushed open the side door and let Howie step out ahead of him. In the lot, he kept walking, lighting his cigarette, then Howie's. He stopped in the back of the lot where his car was parked.

"Who do you want to talk about?"

"Liz. You do remember Liz, don't you?" He looked at the glowing end of the cigarette he held straight up in front of Howie.

"She wanted me to hurt her. It's true, David."

"So what? You don't have to be animal enough to do it."

David swung with a crossed, backhanded blow that started

from his knees and slammed the back of his doubled right fist against the corner of Howie's mouth. He felt the jaw shift and teeth cut into his hand.

His next hit was a straight-armed punch right into the softness of fat and weak muscles about eight inches above the downward pointing belt buckle. When Howie dropped to his knees and fell forward, retching, David lifted a knee, smashing it into the pasty face, crunching the nose cartilage and laying him out flat on his back.

While Howie gagged on the blood pouring from his nose and filling his mouth, David planted a knee on his convulsing chest. He ripped open Howie's shirt before he took the cigarette from between his clamped teeth. He held the burning end against white belly skin until the body under him leapt like a gaffed tuna. Howie tried to scream, but only choked on his own blood.

"Fun, isn't it?" David rolled him over to keep him from drowning in blood and vomit. He tore off the back of Howie's shirt and grabbed a handful of greasy, tangled hair while he sat astride the ample rump.

"How long were you supplying her? How long did it take to get her spaced enough to let you take her home and try to kill her? I want to know why, Howie."

David pressed the cigarette against the small of Howie's back. When the heavier man reared up, bellowing like a wounded moose, David tightened his grip on the hair and clamped powerful rider's thighs around a thick waist. With a snap of his hips and trained use of body weight, he flattened Howie to the ground again.

"And what about Tim? You're a son of a bitch, Howie. Why the fuck do you think you have a right to live?"

"I didn't do nothing to Tim. I only give him the envelope. Some asshole paid me to give it to him with the acid."

"What was in it?"

"Nude pictures of him with some fruitcake dancer."

"Who gave it to you?"

"The same guy who paid me to make a zombie outta Liz."

"Who was it? What did he look like?" He drew the cigarette across the exposed loins. The body trapped between his knees thrashed and lurched, but David's legs tightened as if he was clamping onto a runaway colt.

"I never saw him." Howie gasped. "It's the truth. He called me on the phone. I picked up the envelope at a P.O. box. That's how he paid me."

"What box?"

"It was always different, even in a different P.O.."

"What did he sound like?"

"Foreign. I think he was foreign."

"What kind of foreign?"

"I don't know. Foreign is all I can say. I didn't know it would push Tim off the edge. Liz is fucked-up anyway."

"You're slime, Howie, parasitic, blood-sucking slime. Get the fuck out of this area before I find you again."

He relaxed his clamped legs and ground out the cigarette in the middle of the bared back. When Howie started to struggle to his knees, David released his hair and stood up. The blue-jean covered rump rose like a swaying hippo, and David kicked up between heavy thighs. Howie's scream was a strangled squawk and he pitched, face first, onto the gravel of the parking lot. David left him that way, writhing on his belly, retching and blubbering.

When David's car turned out of the lot and chirped away from the arcade, a man hunkered beside Howie. His black-gloved hand clamped on the hair at the crown of Howie's head and yanked back until it hurt. A left knee dug into the middle of Howie's back, right between the shoulder blades.

"If you so much as think about mentioning the name David Breton or pressing charges, I'll make sure you go where they'll ream your ass out big enough for a bull elephant. I don't want some punk asshole fucking up my case. Do you understand?" He jerked back on the hair until he received a croaking response.

Releasing Howie's head, the man struck with a fast, hard rap at the base of the neck. The fat pusher went limp and the man checked for a pulse. He found a weak one and then made a quick, thorough search of Howie's pockets. They were loaded with pills, powders, grass, in bottles, phials, and small packets.

The man jogged to a phone box near the front of the arcade

and made a call to the police. It was short, direct, and one-sided. "There's a man behind Arnie's Arcade. He's in shock. Send an ambulance."

Across the street, the man put on a helmet and kicked his leg over the seat of a black motorcycle. He fastened the chin strap over a thick beard before he started the machine.

While he drove away from the arcade, David felt detached. He knew what he had just done, but couldn't understand it. In his rage, he had seen the ugly, festering burns on Liz's smooth, golden skin — burns that would leave scars, permanent blemishes on an almost perfect body. And he heard a scream of agony from a pillar of flames. He had done it for Tim, who had tried to help a friend and been dragged into something he had nothing to do with. He had done it for Liz, a helpless torture victim without a mind rational enough to know what was happening to her.

Liz had turned her brain to jelly by not caring, not finding anything worthwhile in life. She had been a beautiful young woman with wealth, intelligence, and talent, her body movements poetry when she danced and sensual when she made love. She had become involved with David and saw more than she should have. Now she was a burnout.

When the street blurred in front of him, David realized he was crying. He tried to wipe the tears from his eyes, then gave up and let them stream down his face. He turned down a side street and hopscotched with the one way streets until he found the one he wanted. After parking where it was quiet, away from lights and traffic, he locked the doors, took a packet of tissues out of the glove compartment, and lay down on the seat.

David let himself cry for Liz, the girl he had felt reaching for him until she slipped away and there was no one real to love. He cried because he had failed to see what was happening and felt overwhelmed by the impenetrable mystery he was trying to unravel. He no longer felt like a hero. He felt like a boy who had made a mistake and been punished for it.

"I didn't see it, Dad." He spoke to a memory of the man he most wanted to emulate and please. "I thought I was doing it right when I kept Liz out of it. I tried to tell myself it really was an accident because I couldn't think of anyone who'd want to kill Hugh, except me and you. The horrible thing is, I still can't."

He dozed off but was awakened by the wailing sirens of police cars speeding away from the center of town toward the river and the apartment complex he had left two hours ago. He disliked the sound of sirens late at night. It meant tragedy, grief, or hopelessness.

He sat with his forehead pressed against the steering wheel until the throbbing pain in his head subsided. When he felt able to cope with people again, he left the car and walked across the street, around to the back entrance of a once grand, turreted Victorian house awkwardly appended by crude, iron fire escapes that would give the original architect a migraine.

On the lattice-enclosed, back porch, he pushed the button for apartment four, upstairs, in the front. She came to the door sleepy, rubbing her eyes and yawning while she tied the sash of a maize and blue, terry cloth robe that wrapped almost twice around her and dragged on the floor. When her small brown face peered through the narrow door window, her smile came alive and she unbolted the door.

"David, it's after three."

"Is that all?" He stumbled over the doorsill and slumped against the wall. "I've had a shitty night, Gwen. Can you offer peaceful asylum for someone who can't face driving to Wellington until he's had some sleep and a hot shower?"

"I for sure can." She slid an arm around his waist and let him hug her.

David looked down at a rich brown complexion that was soft, smooth, and beautiful. "It feels good to hold someone who's warm and good, happy and gentle." He smiled when she wrinkled her nose at him. "Don't you think you're that wonderful."

"It sounds good."

"Gwen, you and Karen are the best girls in the world." He made a wry face. "And you're both taken by great men."

"What happened, David? You look bad." She lifted his right hand and looked at the ragged cuts and swelling knuckles.

"I hit somebody's teeth. It's Liz. I stopped fooling myself

tonight. No one's ever going to help Liz."

"We tried to tell you that. Liz was too far gone when you met her."

He wanted to say she hadn't been until this spring when someone made damn sure she was beyond help. He didn't because he didn't want to involve anyone else.

"I'll be all right." He hugged her small body while they walked up the stairs together. "How are you going to explain to Rob that you took me in like a lost puppy?"

"You can explain it to me yourself."

David raised his eyes to the top of the stairs, where Leon's oldest son stood like a Nubian warrior in sweat pants. His dark face was set in a scowl, but a laugh tugged at his mouth. It rumbled out when he stepped aside to let them into the apartment.

"Rob, I wouldn't even think of upsetting one of the Wolverines' line backers."

Rob laughed louder. "For a white kid, you're damn smart."

When the phone rang, Sharon jumped as if she had touched an electric fence. For an instant, she was stiff with the tension of being awakened from a restless sleep. The second ring jolted through to her mind. She turned on a bedside lamp while she picked up the receiver.

"Hello."

"Sharon, it's Colin. There's been a real botch-up. It doesn't look good for David."

"Who is it?" Hugh winced away from the light.

Sharon spoke into the phone. "Could you call back in three minutes. I'll get it in the office. I don't want to disturb Hugh." She hung up and looked at her husband. "It's Arlene. She's had a few too many after a fight with Eric. I'll go downstairs."

"Please do." Hugh muttered. "That woman is a pain in the ass."

"It doesn't hurt to listen to her." Sharon slid out of bed, pulled on her robe, and yanked out the plug on the phone. "I unplugged it so the ring won't bother you."

"Thank you. Tell her to have her crises in the daylight."

"She does, Hugh. Believe me, she does."

The phone was ringing when Sharon reached the office. She snatched it up before she switched on the desk lamp and rolled the chair over from where it was shoved away so Hugh could sit at the desk in his wheel chair. "Hello, Colin?"

"Yes. Is David home?"

"Not yet." She looked at the digital desk clock. "My God, it's three-fifty. I must have slept more than I feel I did. What's wrong, Colin?"

"She's dead, Sharon. Dead as a drowned cat."

"Who? Colin, who's dead?" She clamped one hand on the hard receiver while her other one tried to squeeze information out of the coils of the phone cord.

"The girl with David. Liz Palmer. A night watchman found her floating in the swimming pool at her Ann Arbor apartment complex. He called the police."

"And David?"

"There was no sign of David."

"How old was this girl?"

"Twenty-one. She was a junior at the university. Her family lives in Grosse Pointe. She came to the dance as a guest of Karen Coleman."

"David was dating her?"

"Off and on. He'd been at parties at her flat. I assumed he ran with Karen and her crowd in Ann Arbor." He paused and cleared his throat. "Rumor is David's been sleeping with Liz."

"That shouldn't surprise me, but it does upset me. I think I'd rather not have heard it from you."

"Whatever does that mean?"

"It makes it too public. How do you know all this?"

"I hear things from the kids when I ride with them. When I talked to Karen before I left the dance, she said Liz wasn't feeling well so David took her home. When I reached the apartments in Ann Arbor, there were police cars and a large crowd for three A.M. I listened to a few stories, looked around for David's car but didn't see it. The Jeep was parked by the Gandy Dancer, which was closed. I guess she was dead for a while before the night watchman found her."

"The girl looked as if she was on some kind of drug. Could it have been an accident? I mean, if she tried to take a swim, couldn't she have drowned?"

"That's possible. It certainly looked like an accident — that is if you discount that it's an outdoor pool that hasn't been cleaned out yet. There was only one small thing that came to my attention as fitting in with what you told me. While I was mingling with the crowd, I noticed a Honda trail bike in the parking garage. It was in front of the car in one of the stalls for her flat number."

"You mean Liz was the student David met in the woods?" A cold lump clamped in her chest.

"It looks that way."

"Colin, do you know what that means? He's killed the only person who could possibly identify him. But what about David? Do you know where David is?"

"Not a bit of an idea."

Sharon pulled her fear in, telling herself David was all right and would come home soon. It had been this way with Marc too often. She remembered hours, even days, of dreadful waiting, when every phone call, every car made her tighten inside until she wanted to know something but was afraid to hear it. When Marc had come home, he was always relaxed, sure of himself. He never showed fear or apprehension. He never even seemed concerned. Sharon suspected David would be the same, with all his tensions wrapped inside him. He could cover his feelings and put on a convincing front, just as Marc could.

"I suppose the police will want to question David," she said.

"I'm sure they will. He's possibly the last person, beside her flatmate, to see her alive."

"Colin, I hope not." She pressed her lips together. "I hope six people saw her walk to that pool alone and stoned."

"That would definitely help." There was sarcasm in his voice. "I'll see if I can find out if there was a convenient party with enough people looking out the window at a fenced in, unlighted pool, just when she wandered out to take a swim — dressed in jeans and a sweater and carrying a purse."

"Please, Colin, leave some straws to clutch at."

"Sorry, Sharon, but there don't seem to be too many."

"David's not a murderer."

"I didn't say he is. He just seems to be too close to too much bad business."

"He inherited the talent."

"He's rooting around where he doesn't belong."

"I know, but he won't listen to me. He thinks he's as good as Marc, but even Marc made mistakes. I'll try to talk to him. Good night, and thank you."

After she hung up, Sharon sat for a few minutes staring at the small, black squares of the window panes. With a sudden movement, she jerked open a drawer of the desk and took out a bottle of Hugh's tranquilizers. He rarely took them. He preferred to get drunk.

In the large, new lavatory designed for Hugh's wheelchair, she filled a paper cup with water, took one of the capsules, and left the bottle on the counter beside the sink. She felt it was probably the wrong thing to do, but she was reluctant to face David with her nerves on edge. She also knew she couldn't go back to bed with Hugh.

Sharon curled up in a comforter on the couch in the television den. The pill was marvelous. All the tension unraveled and sleep crept in from the edges of her awareness until she tumbled into its softness.

7

"Mom? Mom?" David's voice floated on the edge of Sharon's mind, midway between dream and reality. When she felt him shake her shoulder, she accepted the reality and dragged open heavy eyelids. "Mom, wake up. Why are you here?"

"I was waiting for you." She shook away the grogginess of interrupted sleep and was confused by the bright sunlight streaming in the windows. "What time is it?"

"Almost eight." David sat on the coffee table. "Did I cause another quarrel with Hugh? You shouldn't get between us. Hugh and I can carry on our war just fine without you."

"I didn't say anything to Hugh, but he has things to say to you."

"That doesn't surprise me a bit."

"David, where were you?" Sitting up, she set a hand on his knee. She tried to sound alarmed; but instead, she yawned, still feeling calm, without the gnaw of apprehension.

"Don't worry about it."

"I have to worry about it. You have to worry about it. Liz Palmer is dead."

"Dead?" David stiffened, his face a mask of shock Sharon was sure could not be an act. "How is she dead?"

"A night watchman found her in the swimming pool at her apartment building."

"That's a bummer." He pulled in a breath and controlled

himself, leaving an expression of brittle pain.

"I guess she drown. I only know what Colin told me."

"Colin? What does that phoney have to do with it?"

"I asked him to try to find you."

"Oh Christ." He snarled, then laughed with a cynical cut. "That's like hiring the Three Stooges, all in one body."

"David, when you left, that Jeep was following you. One of your backup lights was on. I think he did it so he could follow you. Marc said it was common to knock out a light or mark a car in some way to make it easier to follow."

"That makes sense. I didn't know he was following me, but after I left Liz, I saw the Jeep parked near the embankment by the Gandy Dancer."

"When did you leave Liz. Was she alive?"

"She was breathing. I think it was about one."

"What was she wearing?"

David gave her a penetrating look and, with a lift of an eyebrow, said, "She wasn't wearing anything. She was in bed."

She made her face stern and looked at her son. He was wearing suit pants, no tie. The ice-blue shirt was open, showing a muscular chest with thickening dark hair. The sleeves were rolled up on hard forearms. His suit jacket was on the table beside him and the shadowy mustache was darkening. Somehow in the last two days, she had not only become aware of David as a young man, not a boy, but was beginning to accept it. "And you?"

When he chuckled with a short tone of irony, she flushed. "Mom, a girl is dead, and you're worried about whether your little boy went to bed with her first."

David stood and walked to the fireplace with his fists thrust into his pockets. He stared into the empty grate, trying to understand why, after the first shock of hearing the news, he hardly seemed to care. Maybe it was because he had already categorized Liz as dead last night. The news had hit him hard, then faded. He had already grieved for Liz and had no grief left, only a dull emptiness that made him feel defeated and detached.

He looked out a window at a clear, beautiful May morning and the brilliance of new flowers in the gardens. It was a day so removed from death he could not grasp it.

In a steady, factual voice, he said, "I suppose the police are going to want to know about it, too. They'll do an autopsy and find semen in her, unless the pool water eliminated it. I don't know much about the chemistry of it. They'll probably determine she was on the pill and spaced out on Angel dust and who knows what else. She could have decided she was a damn fish and could breathe underwater. Dust does strange things to the brain, especially one as burned out as Liz's."

"Most drugs do." When he turned to face her, his stare of assurance clearly surprised her.

While David studied the familiar planes of his mother's face, he saw details he had never noticed before: tiny lines beside her eyes, the roughness of scar tissue on her chin, the scattering of grey hairs that blended with the golden hues.

She had always been just his mother, unchanging, loved, but not always understood or even considered. He no longer felt like a boy, but he was not sure he could stop seeing her as a mother. David still wanted to protect her, hide a lot of what he really was from her. He knew she wanted him gentle, fair, honorable, and sure of himself — a sort of Superman, who acted with only good intentions from noble motives.

Perhaps that was what was wrong. She was his mother and he loved her, but that was not all he wanted. She said he had not been straight with her, but he wasn't sure how he could be straight with her and still feel she was his mother.

David neither wanted, nor needed a mother. He needed and wanted her as a person, a colleague, who could accept him as he was, not as an ideal son. He knew he had to be straight with her and stop trying to be what he thought she wanted — an image of his father, without the faults, without the dangers.

"Yes, Mom, I was in bed with her. But I sure didn't use any of that fucking shit she did." He ignored her disapproving mother's scowl. He knew she had listened to the same language from his father, from Hugh, and a lot of other people without disapproval. "Liz was a chemical freak. She was also the student I was buying the marijuana from."

"With the trail bike?"

"Yes."

"Did you sell that kind of stuff?"

"Only marijuana. I have ethics, Mom." He twisted to the kitchen doorway, where a towheaded girl in a long nightgown was rubbing sleep out of her eyes with tight fists. He walked to her and picked her up. "Good morning, Becky. Mom isn't feeling too peppy this morning, but I think I can make you some breakfast. I'm starved."

"I want French toast."

"One of my specialties. Go see if Scott's awake while I get started." He set the child down and gave her a gentle swat on the seat to propel her toward the kitchen. The girl giggled and ran for the stairs.

"Mom, take a shower, dress your kids, and join us for breakfast. I give the police about an hour. Pam will have told them I was with Liz and given them this address."

"How can you take it so calmly? You made love to a girl and two hours later she was found dead."

"I mourned her last night."

"You knew?"

"Not that she was clinically dead. The part of her that was Liz died a while ago. I just accepted it last night. I don't know what to call what was left. She went to bed with anyone. I don't think she remembered it afterwards. I don't think she cared. She took pills, powders, crystals, liquor, sex — all for a hell of a wild time. It was all sensation with Liz — bigger, better, higher sensations — orgasm or pain. I think she was trying to kill herself." He held out his hand to help her stand. "She cared about me when we first made love, but that seems like a long time ago."

"Aren't you afraid the police will think you had something to do with her death?"

"They undoubtedly will, but what can they prove? Making love to her didn't kill her. Her apartment mate was there and knows when I left. I had coffee with Pam. We talked about Liz. I wasn't even with her when she buzzed herself. I just took her home before she did something crazy. I guess she did something crazy any way."

"But she was a witness."

"The police don't know that. They don't know anything about that." He gave her a hard look. "I don't want them to know about that."

"Do you think it was suicide?"

"No. Suicide is intentional. Tim tried to commit suicide. He planned it. That stuff Liz took cross circuits the brain. As I said before, maybe she thought she was a fish."

"She was wearing jeans and a sweater and carrying a purse."

"She could have decided to do anything. When she saw the pool, she may have had a vision of mermaids and believed she was one of them. Logic and illogic, real and unreal are all mixed up."

"Don't ever take any."

"I did once." He thought back to an experience that still made him shudder. "The buildings started to melt. Then I watched a cloud of fluorescent bugs devouring my hands and legs. I was terrified and felt like an ass afterwards. I never want to feel like that again."

"I did some wild things, but by the time chemicals were in vogue, I was old enough to be afraid of them."

"I aged in one night. Mom, I will say it again — I don't take drugs. I'm involved with trying to get kids away from them, so I'm close to a lot of it. I smoke grass once in a while. I sold grass to get out of a mess and then to help Karen and Paul fix up the farm they live on."

"It's a commune of weirdos according to the rumors I hear."

"Please, that's the attitude we don't like. It scares us because it could cause Paul to lose the lease."

David glared at her skeptical face. "We're trying to give them something better to live for than drugs and a few kicks. Most of them are kids who have lost meaning in the way their parents live, but can't find viable alternatives. They won't go to neat clinics and establishment-backed centers. The land, growing things, caring for animals seems to turn some of them around. It didn't do anything for Liz."

He gave her a slow smile. "Don't worry about me, Mom. I like staying in control and healthy."

"I think I've been misjudging you." She was clearly relaxed by the new ease in his manner, but she scowled when he slid a cigarette from the pack in his shirt pocket. "That's not what I call a healthy habit."

"One has to play a few risks. Hurry up if you want *Petit déjeuner à la Breton.*"

After Sharon left, David opened the refrigerator, pulled out a carton of eggs and started cracking them into a bowl with the clowning flourish of a flamboyant chef. He whistled a French melody he remembered from his childhood. His mother said it was titled *Milord,* and credited its popularity to Edith Piaff, one-time Parisian singing sensation.

David's father had often whistled the same tune and had taught it to David, which was why it was so clear in his mind. It was jaunty. It fit Marc. It was Marc. It was also an infectious melody that David used to pick up his spirits.

The bang of the swinging door to the dining room cut off both the whistle and David's spirits. He stared across the peninsula of counter while Hugh's wheel chair purred across the carpeted floor and stopped, blocking the open end of the narrow, u-shaped work area where David stood.

"Where's your mother?"

"She went upstairs to take a shower and dress the kids. She was asleep on the den couch when I came home."

"When did you come home?"

David glanced at the clock. "About half an hour ago."

Hugh's face hardened. "David, I pulled back on restrictions and slacked off on your discipline because I had enough of my own problems and little energy to handle yours."

"Oh really? I thought you just realized it was ineffective."

"You had your independence. You were nct only a nasty winner about it, you've shown no responsibility. In my view, a boy of seventeen does not take a girl home from a dance and come home at eight o'clock the next morning. Your mother chooses to ignore your behavior, but I won't. I was raised by a strict military man, who expected obedience to an acceptable standard of rules."

"So why should I suffer for your misfortunes?" He watched Hugh's face redden and realized his tone was much too cutting, but he was angry, too, and not very good at controlling it. He saw no reason why he had to do things according to someone else's standards, someone else's morals. He had his own and believed in the logic of them.

"It grates on me to hear of your infamy and learn about some of the degenerates you run around with and then to be treated with arrogance."

"Well, it grates me to be humiliated, ordered around in public, and treated like a subordinate with no choices, no rights, no dignity."

"I won't tolerate such a brazen lack of prudence by anyone under my authority."

"I'm not under your authority, thank you."

"If I'm financially supporting you, I have the authority. If your father wants the responsibility, he's welcome to it. Unfortunately for you, he hasn't made any effort to take it."

"You won't let him near me, you son of a bitch." David shouted and slammed his fist down on the counter while he glared into Hugh's glowing, catlike green eyes.

"If he'd asked, I'd have shipped you anywhere he wanted — first class. You were an arrogant little brat when you came here. Now you're an arrogant big brat. Last night was one giant step too far. I won't ignore disobedience and disrespect like that. I'm clipping your wings. I want my car keys and your driver's license. Now!"

David pulled the keys out of his front pocket and threw them in Hugh's lap. "It's your car. But it's my license. There's no way I'll give it to you."

"Yes, you will, David." Hugh moved the chair forward, his eyes locked with David's. "You may not like me, but you will obey me."

"I told you to stay out of my way."

When David lifted his foot, Hugh jerked the chair forward with his left hand while he jackknifed at the waist. His powerful right hand closed on David's ankle and jerked up. The low, rounded furniture bumper on the front of the chair whacked into David's other shin, and he crashed to the floor. Before the boy could stand up, Hugh swung the chair and caught David's left wrist. He bent his arm up behind him, and, holding him on his knees, slammed him against the front of the cabinets. With the wheel chair braced in the corner, Hugh held David pressed against the hard wood.

"I don't take that, David."

Hugh's left hand and arm held David's arm so that any increase in pressure sent sharp pain coursing through his shoulder, reminding him that Hugh was still much stronger than he was with no qualms about inflicting pain.

"You can reach your wallet. Take it out of your pocket and give me the license."

"I need it, Hugh." He clenched his teeth but answered in a steady voice that showed no defeat. "It's identification."

"You have a school ID, and you aren't going anywhere. I'm grounding you so hard you'll taste the dirt. And you'll stay grounded until I tell you otherwise, which means until you start proving you can be trusted to behave the way I expect. Now give me the license."

When David tried to twist free, Hugh lifted up on the arm just enough for pain to tighten his stepson's face. He held it a second, then eased up. "Why does your temper always fight the inevitable?"

David was silent, still trying to break away or force himself to his feet. He refused to answer because he didn't know why. He did know he had lost. Something in him even said Hugh was not all wrong, but he refused to listen to it. It was the way he was, the way he had always been. He fought until there was no hope because maybe, just maybe, he could win and save his pride. It hardly mattered what the issue was. David did not want to give up, even though he knew it was useless. And he knew that even if Hugh regretted getting into such a battle of wills, he wouldn't give up either.

Hugh lifted up on the arm, slowly, steadily. "David, do you really need to relearn which of us is the more stubborn?"

"No." David's answer was a concession. The pain eased. "Take it."

"Give it to me."

When Hugh relaxed his strength, David pulled his wallet out of his hip pocket, flipped it open on the floor, and slid the license with his color picture on it from behind the plastic window. He held it out to Hugh.

Hugh took the license before he dropped David's arm, rolling him so he fell on his seat. His shoulders thumped painfully against the sink cabinet at the end of the work area.

"I'm going to Lansing with Harold Babcock to look at some horses. Tell your mother I won't be home for dinner. And you be here tonight when I get home. It that understood?"

"I'll be here." When he heard the door swing closed, David thudded his right fist on the floor. "Damn him!"

David was straightforward and confident when the police arrived. The two men were black and white, Detectives Reed and Stanwyck. They carefully explained that he did not have to answer any of their questions right now, but it would be easier on everyone and much more discreet if he did not make it necessary to get an arrest warrant and treat him as a suspect.

David told them the bare facts of his time with Liz. They were relieved by his direct manner and willingness to cooperate. They were relaxed, unhurried, and they were very good. They heard and taped his skeleton story with few interruptions. Then, their casual postures changed, just perceptively, and they took the initiative.

Stanwyck, the stout, bristle-haired man with the friendly, florid face sat a little taller on the couch. He shifted his eyes from David to Sharon, who was sitting on an upholstered chair off the corner of the long, low table made from one varnished slab of gnarled, black cherry wood milled on the farm by Hugh's grandfather, a tough old fighting cock of a cavalry officer.

After looking at Sharon, Detective Stanwyck moved his eyes back to David. "We have some personal questions. Do you want your mother to leave?"

"I don't have anything to hide from her."

Reed, the tall, wiry officer, shifted forward on the couch and looked directly at David, who openly returned his stare while he sat facing him on an ottoman. "What did you do when you first reached Miss Palmer's apartment."

"I thought it was obvious when I said I put her to bed," David answered. "I fucked her. Do you want it stroke by stroke? My memory isn't that good or that graphic."

"The girl was abused."

"Not by me and not last night. Pam said it was a few days ago. It was no more than three because I know the burns weren't there Tuesday."

"Do you know who did it and how?"

"His name is Howie. I don't know a last name. He hangs out around Arnie's Arcade. He peddles almost any drug in small quantities. He did it with a cigarette."

"Could he have returned last night?"

"I doubt it."

"How did you hurt your hand?" The man dropped his black eyes to the bandage on David's hand.

"I hit it on a sharp object in a parking lot."

"When did you arrive home?"

"About seven-forty-five this morning."

"Where did you spend the night?"

"With friends."

"What friends?"

"Gwen Laurette and her fiance Robert Williams, the oldest son of my mother's husband's attendant. 316 Richmond, apartment four."

"When did you get there?"

"Three A.M."

"What did you do between one and three A.M.?"

"I drove around for a while. I was upset."

"About what?"

"Liz." He looked straight into the onyx eyes in the sable face with boldly sculptured features. "I went to Arnie's Arcade, beat the shit out of Howie, and left him a few reminders of his abuse." David saw a look of painful regret cross his mother's face. He had seen it before when his father had been hurt or in a fight.

"How long did that take?" The police officer asked without showing a flicker of feeling.

"Half an hour, an hour?" David shrugged. "I didn't check the time."

"Did you call the Ann Arbor Police at one-forty-six to report that Howard Jenkins was injured in the arcade parking lot?"

"No." David was startled by the question.

"Someone did. Jenkins was taken to University Hospital at two A.M. He said he didn't know who did it."

"He knew who did it." David scoffed.

"He was very insistent about not knowing who beat him. Did you threaten him?"

"No. At the time, I didn't give a shit."

"Your times check out, but you didn't get to the Laurette girl's apartment until three?"

"Gwen said it was three."

"What did you do between the arcade and Richmond Street?"

"I parked across the street from Gwen's apartment."

"For how long?"

"I don't know. I cried and fell asleep."

"Why did you cry?"

"Because I didn't like what I'd done. And for Liz because it was all over."

"Why was it all over?"

"Pam and I had made the decision to tell her parents she needed to be in a hospital. The drugs had destroyed her ability to think rationally."

"There was a bruise on the back of her head that did happen last night about two hours before she died."

David looked confused, then he smiled. "She should have one on her fanny the same age. I smacked her on the ass and she cracked her head on the steering wheel."

"Why?"

"She was interfering with my driving. Does that classify as abuse, too?"

"I'm not sure." Detective Reed failed to stop the smile that tugged at the corners of his mouth and spread into a laugh.

When Reed lifted his coffee cup and sat back, Stanwyck cleared his throat and studied a small, lined notebook before he met David's eyes. "Did you telephone Liz Palmer at two-o-five?"

"No. When I left, Liz was asleep. I expected her to stay asleep."

"Someone called her. Her roommate thought it was your voice." He looked down at the notebook again. "After the call, Liz dressed and went out. When her roommate tried to stop her, she said, 'David says it's in the stars.' Does that make sense?"

"Liz was into astrology. Sometimes we talked about it. She was a water sign."

"The pool gate was opened with a key."

"That's reasonable. She has one."

"Death was by drowning, but marks on her neck indicate she may have been held underwater." He looked at the obvious red mark on David's neck. "Aside from a matching passion mark, can you explain why she would have bruises on her neck?"

"No."

"Was the sharp object you cut your hand on the top of a chain link fence around a swimming pool?"

"No, it was Howie the slob's teeth."

"Will you let a doctor examine it?"

"Certainly."

"What's your blood type?"

"O positive."

"Was your stepfather injured in a hunting accident last November?"

"No." David saw the man's composure crack and Sharon's hand tighten on the arm of her chair. "He's not my stepfather. He's my mother's husband. I have a father. I won't accept a replacement."

"Was your mother's husband injured in a hunting accident last November?"

"I refuse to answer any questions about that incident. I've said it all. If you want to know my answers, look them up."

"Do you have any thoughts on who might have wanted to kill Liz Palmer?"

"No. She was destroying herself with drugs, but she wasn't harming anyone else."

"Is there anyone whose recent behavior seems unnatural?"

"No."

"What about the man in the Jeep?" Sharon's question snapped out with an impulsive urgency. The hardness, the condemnation in David's sudden glare was meant to stun her and cut her off. It was a flash of instant fury so like his father's that he could see her throat tighten and her right hand flew to her chest.

"What man?" Both policemen twisted to Sharon.

"I don't know who he is. He's been around a lot. He has a beard and drives a sand colored Jeep." Her voice was uneasy while David projected his growing anger. "It might not be important."

"Did you see him last night?" The black man asked David.

"No. The Jeep was parked in the Hunt Club lot when I left. I think he's more interested in my horse's performance next weekend than mine last night."

"What do you mean?"

"If a horse is good, he merits watching. The man has been observing some of my workouts."

"Why are you concerned about him, Mrs. Jamison?"

"He just popped into my head when you mentioned unusual behavior." Sharon tried to act unconcerned. "He's been something of a nuisance when we ride. David's right. He is mostly interested in our horses." Sharon was trying to sound casual, but David knew she wasn't fooling anyone. The policemen had heard something new and would not dismiss it.

The two officers stood up almost simultaneously. "I think we've covered the ground well enough for now."

Detective Reed asked, "What will you be doing with your horse this weekend, David?"

"I'm in a horse trial at Pheasant Run Farm, so is my mother. There's a Dressage phase Saturday morning, followed by a short roads and tracks phase, then a cross-country phase. Sunday morning is stadium jumping. The same horse and rider must do all phases." David lifted an eyebrow. "During the official season, we do it for three days."

"Sounds interesting. Please stay in the area, Mr. Breton."

"I don't have much choice on that matter right now." When Detective Stanwyck looked puzzled, David said, "I can't go far if I have to work a horse every day. I like to win. One doesn't win without work."

David watched the car drive away then turned to his mother.

"And you told me chasing him was a damn fool thing to do."

"I'm afraid of him. I'm sure he's the killer and wants to kill you. He got Liz and he wants you."

"And you think siccing the police on him will make it any better?"

"If they arrest him, you're safe."

"They can't hold him without evidence. Just because you think he's a killer isn't any good. Beside, I don't think you're right. Something as obvious as a black beard should have stuck in Liz's mind as clearly as an Army colored coat and black knit hat." He lit a cigarette and walked into Hugh's office, letting her follow him.

"David, this is frightening. We can't hide things from the police."

"We have to. Everything stacks up against me enough they could arrest me, including the fact that I lied to them last fall when I said I was riding a long way from that cabin. Even Hugh lied about why he was going to the cabin."

"I don't understand that." She looked puzzled. "Hugh never lies about anything."

"I suppose he did it to keep my petty crimes out of the newspapers. He would rather write it off as an accident than have it hit the papers as a family scandal. I don't like him, but I have to admit he has guts."

"How can he live with the knowledge that someone who tried to kill him is still loose and may try it again? Or does he think it was you in a moment of desperation and knows you won't do it again?"

"If he thinks that, he could be in trouble. But I think he knows I didn't do it."

"Why?"

"Hugh knows how I feel about him. He also knows me well enough to know I don't fight that way. I give a warning." He laughed with a sudden burst. "I gave Howie a good ten seconds to realize I was going to knock him silly."

He found an ash tray on a bookshelf just before the ash fell off his cigarette and carried it to the desk. When he sat back against the front of the desk, Sharon sat on the leather couch under the big, square-paned window with her legs folded tailor-fashion in front of her.

"Mom, let's look at this as objectively as we can. Hugh is a rich man. He owns 60% of Jamison Aircraft, which is in a little trouble right now, but it is by no means on the rocks. His president owns 20% and your father owns the remaining 20%. Besides the company, Hugh has a substantial estate and stock portfolio. This farm is paid for and worth a bundle — 350 acres, valuable horses, good barns, a new, full size indoor arena, an older, smaller one, outdoor dressage rings, jumping rings, training rings, and cross-country courses. There are two tenant houses and this restored, 120 year old brick house, which has historic value since it was once an inn and post office as well as a temporary courthouse when a judge lived here. He also made good investments and is loaded with insurance."

"You have it pretty straight, young man."

"I like to think I'm intelligent. If Hugh dies, who benefits?"

"In what way? I don't feel I would benefit, even if it did all go to me." Her answer was hard, verging on anger. "I don't want to hear any more of your ideas about getting rid of Hugh."

"I'm not saying that." His rebuttal brought her up short. "I believe you, but maybe someone else doesn't."

He softened his voice when she looked uncomfortably confused. "Killing Hugh does little good without you in the picture, unless money is not a factor."

"David, you aren't making sense."

"Just listen a minute. First suspect is me. If Hugh is gone, my mother is unbelievably rich and can be persuaded to spend some of it on me — pure greed as motive. Or she can be persuaded to go back to my father — added emotional motive."

"But it isn't true."

"So we'll have to try someone else. Leon? Not much motive, except I'm sure Hugh has left him plenty. But Leon almost worships Hugh."

"I wouldn't call it worship, and it hasn't always been that way. Their relationship went bad just after I left for Europe. There was a woman."

"A white woman?" David asked with a quizzical lift of an

eyebrow.

"Does it matter?"

"It could. Leon can be touchy about racial hurts."

"David, you will never be able to brand Hugh as a racist. I don't think he considers skin color any more than eye color. It was a black woman. I see Hugh and Leon as I would brothers. They have their ups and downs."

"Aside from all else, Leon is a sharp shooter, an expert with a rifle, shotgun, or bow. In fact, damn near anything that shoots. He wouldn't have hit low, nor would he have misjudged the gun's range. If Leon wanted to kill Hugh, Hugh would be dead."

"If you want to consider everyone, what about Bruce? He knew Hugh was going after you. Maybe he only wanted to hit him in the legs, just to stop him, not kill him or cripple him."

"Now you're thinking." David ground out the cigarette. "But you're wrong on that one. Bruce was home nursing his hide because Leon about wore a belt out on him when he learned he was still involved. Bruce called to warn Liz, but he was home with his mother. Mention grass to Bruce now and he bolts like a skittish yearling. Then there's Colin Trombley, but he didn't know about my grass dealing. He's also an ass, who lacks backbone."

"Colin isn't an ass." She straightened with her indignant retort. "He isn't macho, but that doesn't make him an ass."

"Has he been playing up to you with his suave self-importance?"

"Colin is more genuine with me. He likes to impress, that's all."

"Mom, he's conceited and obsessed with himself. He thinks he's really in with the girls. They mostly ignore him. Colin is irritating and a parasite, but not dangerous. He's sort of an agreeable clinger. Besides, the only way for him to benefit is if he married you. I can't see you willing to marry him."

"You certainly have your opinions on my taste in men." Irritation was making her testy, and her hands gripped her knees.

"You like tough men. Hugh's three times the man Colin is and Dad seven times." He chided her gently. "With men like that in your life, how could you be interested in Colin Trombley?"

"Well, he's polite, gentle, kind, flattering." She relaxed her hands and shrugged with her answer.

"And he's stuck on himself and a dreadful bore."

"David, he can be a lot of fun, and politeness does not make a man less than a man. It's something you would profit from learning." She leaned back and folded her arms across her chest. Her face had a scolding mother look. "Colin grew up with manners."

"Do you want to marry him?" He shot the question in a voice that precluded all argument.

"No, but—"

"That's all you need to say. There's also your father."

"My father?" Her face twisted in an expression of exaggerated disagreement.

"Sure. If his daughter owns 60% of Jamison Aircraft and he owns 20%, he has the whole mess in his hands because you'll turn the responsibility over to him. Hugh and Granfather spend a lot of time condemning Dad for using you because of your money. Do you realize that Jamison Aircraft was in serious trouble when you returned from Europe? After Hugh married you, he talked his mother into selling her 20% to your father. He received large loans from Collingwood Electronic Data Systems, Inc. with generous terms for repayment. That money enabled Hugh to develop a jet prototype and keep in stride with Leer."

"That probably would have happened any way."

"Would it? Do you really think Charles Collingwood would have been so generous if his daughter hadn't been involved?"

"Why not? It gave him a tax break and turned out profitable." Her tone was a touch cynical. "He was never so stimulated with paternal generosity when I lived with Marc."

"Dad wasn't a 60% owner of tangible assets. You stand to inherit control of that corporation, which is almost the same as him inheriting it, except it isn't added to his taxable income. He can't lose."

"How do you know all this?"

"I'm nosy." David lifted himself to the desk and looked down at his swinging feet. He sensed a loosening of her disapproval, a curiosity that was becoming conspiring. "I've learned a lot by listening and snooping in this office. Hugh started it when he laid down the law and made me spend three hours a night in here doing homework that took me less than an hour. My inquisitive mind was really sated when I learned the combination to the safe."

"How did you do that?"

"Do you remember Philipe Roudin? He was a friend of Dad's. He was also a safe cracker. He taught me how to hear tumblers and told me I had the sensitivity. I had enough time to keep at it until I figured it out. Sort of like sticking to Rubic's cube."

"Why did you do that?" She gave him a cross look.

"I was tired of hearing Hugh tell me what a scoundrel Dad was and decided to find out how much of a scoundrel Hugh was. I've done a lot of research on him in the last three years."

"And what did you learn?" she asked with a smug look.

"That he's a pillar of ethical perfection and a straight-laced zealot. He's honest and his business is on the level. Jamison Aircraft produces quality planes and is very safety conscious."

"I could have told you that. I think his propriety was what turned me off at first. Hugh's father was hard as ice, and he was tough on Hugh. It rubbed off."

David nodded with reluctant agreement. "The only disgraceful thing about Hugh is his unrelenting temper. He's no saint when he's challenged. Personally, Hugh gets what he wants, even if he has to exert force — physical, financial, or emotional. In a battle of wills, he has no compassion. But we don't need to talk about Hugh. He didn't shoot himself." David veered away from a subject he could not be objective about.

"My father wasn't even here."

"But he was in Detroit a week before. A man like your father rarely does his own dirty work. If he could have a man picked up in Paris and sent to prison on a false drug charge—"

"You don't know that."

"But I believe it."

"My father would not have a man murdered."

"I said to look at it objectively."

"I am. Your grandfather likes Hugh, has no desire to control Jamison Aircraft, and no need for money. He doesn't know what to do with all he has now."

"That doesn't seem to matter with men like Granfather. He

wants to acquire more control, more worth, as if it's a measure of his success. Jamison is a way of spreading out, maybe for a tax write-off if it keeps slumping. The computer business is going out of sight. Granfather must be rolling in thousand dollar clover blossoms."

"You're being ridiculous." Her defenses rose against his line of thinking. "You've had your brain immersed in too much *Dungeons and Dragons,* war games, spy novels, and fantasy."

"Murder can be a fantasy." He lifted one foot to the desk and hugged his arms around his bent knee. He let his voice go soft and stared beyond her. "It's a daydream that becomes more and more prevalent until it starts to take rational form. Suddenly, when it happens, or almost happens, it becomes stark reality and the fantasy image shatters like an image in a crystal ball. Real murder, real death, real tragedy hits like a huge mallet and all the rationale is gone." He paused when he felt her staring into him as if she was awed by what he was saying.

"That's the way it was with Tim about suicide. The way it was with me about Hugh. I used to daydream about him being gone and it being just us — and Dad. When it almost happened and I had to face the reality of it, it was much uglier. Hugh's shooting twisted something inside me because part of me was horrified by my own wishes."

"What do you mean?" She looked a little dumb-founded and out of touch.

"I went through hell over that. Karen and Paul, Pam, even Liz and Tim were a lot of help, but what helped the most was telling you yesterday." He met her eyes and pulled her awareness to him. "Something let loose, and I stopped turning away from you. This winter I wanted to hide everything from you. I was bitter around Hugh and ashamed around you."

Still holding her gaze, he crossed the room, kicked off his shoes, and sat on the couch. He faced her with his knees drawn up in front of him and rested his chin on his knees, staring into her eyes, capturing her attention with his intensity. "You were right when you said I wasn't satisfied with myself. I tried liquor. I tried drugs. I tried sex. The drugs scared me. The liquor made me sick."

"And the sex?" Her smile grew until her eyes crinkled and she looked like a peevish imp.

"It didn't scare me, or make me sick; but sometimes, it made me lonely."

"People have often told me you were very intelligent, intuitive, and mature. Lately, I've had trouble believing it. Today I can feel it." She turned to face him over her bent knees. They sat like two book ends, staring at each other across an empty shelf, two blue-jeaned figurines on a doll house couch.

"Okay, Mom, let's say that's what happened with Hugh. Someone planned a fanciful murder, where the victim would just disappear and make everything right without causing tidal waves. But it didn't happen that way. Hugh didn't die. He didn't go away, and the guilt is hovering like a noose ready to snare him, or her. There's a person somewhere who's guilty and frightened. Liz was a witness of sorts. She wasn't of any value because her mind was such a mess, but the murderer doesn't know that. He's scared. It keeps building in his mind. He finds out some cop seems interested in Liz, or that she babbles a bit at times, so he kills her."

"Then it's someone who's been watching Liz."

"Probably been watching everyone close to it. Guilt's a funny thing. If you put pressure on it, it cracks in unexpected places. Hugh said I was a nasty winner because I rubbed it in when he gave in and eased up on me." He gave her a perplexed look. "He was wrong. I felt like a loser. Fate had cheated me out of winning. Every time he glared at me, I was sure he was saying, 'You wanted to destroy me and now it's done.' I couldn't stand it."

"What about now?"

"It's out in the open again. He infuriates me, but I can take that. If this guy with the shotgun is guilty enough, he may not stop at Liz. She saw him, but he doesn't know how well or how many people she told. Eliminating her may ease the anxiety for a while, but there's a chance something will stir it up again and it will grow until he has to do something else."

Sharon shuddered. "I hope you have too active an imagination. That was my reassurance when you were a precocious child and told me you knew things about people."

"Dad and I always played games about the whys behind people's actions. He drew on my intuitive insights and taught me how to analyze behavior. He was a master psychologist and taught me to think that way, too. I've never stopped playing the games with myself. Now I play them with Karen and Paul. They listen to me and encourage me. I like to know what makes people tick." David broke from her eyes when his thoughts refused to form into words.

"So who ticks right, David?"

The question was right to the point. His throat tightened on the answer he knew he had to give. It came out flattened and toneless. "Besides me, the only person with a super motive is Dad."

"You've thought about this, haven't you?"

He nodded at her throaty answer. "For quite a while. Hugh took you away because of a move that put Dad in prison. I can remember the way he talked about prison." He looked into her eyes without the demanding intensity. He wanted her to feel his hurt. At the same time, he wanted her to understand that he had to find answers to his doubts. "Mom, he was afraid of it — deep down afraid."

"He couldn't get a visa last fall." Her answer was too fast, too defensive. She was avoiding the bared emotional pain that vibrated between them.

"How do you know that?" He tightened his stare, reached deeper into her, begging her to drop the last barrier to her inner feelings.

"I heard Father tell Hugh yesterday. Marc couldn't enter the country."

"Not legally anyway." Her answer offered a thread of hope that tempted him, but it wasn't enough to change the reasoning that made too much sense. "He rarely let simple legality thwart him."

"Marc's like you. He couldn't shoot a man that way, not in the back, not like a sniper."

"Unless the time in prison did something to him, changed him, twisted him inside."

"Not Marc, he—" She wrapped her arms around her knees and

pressed her forehead to them. "Please, David, you're upsetting me."

"Why?"

"Because you may be right." The realization left her face pale and drawn.

"How?"

"Father said Marc came out of prison missing part of an ear with scars on his face."

The revelation turned his churning feelings into a frozen wad of fear. "Maybe they made him hate, too."

"No." She shook her head and gripped his forearm. "He had deep, intense passions, like you, David. But he never hated — never." She lifted her face to look into his eyes. "David, why do you say you hate Hugh? Tell me, David."

"He broke me." His hand tightened on his wrist while he hugged his legs. His face felt drawn. "He didn't just punish me. He broke my pride until I had nothing left and surrendered completely."

"Did he beat you? I know Leon gave his boys terrible hidings, but Hugh always disapproved. He said there were times when Leon was barbaric."

"I could have taken that." David saw her face sour. "Leon gets mad and has it out with them in a burst of violent anger, which doesn't last very long. They yell at each other and let it all out. Hugh wouldn't lose control that way. He uses pain, but differently. He hurts, calmly and slowly. He won't stop until I crawl to him a little. Now, he just reminds me, and I give in."

"Reminds you of what?"

"That he wins." David stood up, then sat back on the wide arm of the couch and looked into her eyes. "It started when I was running around with a gang of rowdies in eighth grade trying to prove I was the biggest rowdy of all. We kept getting into trouble in school and in town. Nothing you said or did made any impression, so Hugh got in on it."

"I lost patience and asked Hugh to do something about it."

"Hugh did something. I don't blame him for most of it. Remember when I was picked up by the police after I threw a homemade pipe bomb into a paint display?" She gave him a scowling nod. "It was the most Godawful mess of surrealism I ever saw."

"It was that all right. Anyway, three of us were caught trying to cut through the park. I knew it was wrong and expected to be punished, so it didn't surprise me when Hugh cut off my allowance and made me work to pay damages. I could even understand why he grounded me and chewed hell out of me. I even remember feeling a little respect for him because he'd finally stopped scowling at me from behind you. It didn't even upset me that much when he slapped me for fresh-mouthing him. When he demanded I tell him who else was involved, things changed."

"How did they change?"

"Hugh and I have some basic differences in philosophy. I feel that personal integrity, honor, and human dignity are to be respected, even in someone who has violated established laws. Hugh feels that once a person becomes a rebel and has broken the law, he has no honor left. I wasn't willing to break my word to others and turn them in. We had agreed, even pledged, that if any of us were caught, we wouldn't tell on the others. I swore to keep my vow and meant it."

"I take it Hugh didn't agree with you."

"Not one bit. I felt a tremendous loyalty to my vow and refused to tell Hugh what he demanded. But Hugh had told the police he would find out what they wanted to know. He didn't try to convince me it would be better to tell him. He didn't give me time to think about the issue. He just demanded I tell him."

David walked across the room to the wall with the pictures and trophy cases. He took a dressage whip off the rack of assorted tack items and tossed it to her. "It wasn't a violent beating. It was one or two solid whacks at a time, then a demand. I kept saying no. Maybe I was a fool, but I held out for a long time. When I broke, I told him everything he wanted to know. I turned in six boys and two girls. I was dirt to more than that. Most of them beat the shit out of me. I didn't blame them. I broke my pledge and was the only one who pointed at anyone else. I've never forgiven him for that."

"I don't think I could forgive a beating like that either."

"It wasn't the beating. It was the destruction of my will, the demeaning of my belief. I'd never been treated like an honorless piece of shit before. I betrayed my friends and my dignity. He cowered me and felt right. To Hugh, I was wrong, so my ethics were not to be respected. He was upholding the law, which made him right. Might is right. The law is right. A lawbreaker has no right to dignity or personal honor. That's what Hugh believes."

"Your father would applaud that speech. He had strong ethics, but they were his own — as I think yours are. Are you afraid of Hugh?"

"No. If I don't defy Hugh, he won't hurt me. What I resent is that he forces me to live by his standards and won't give me a chance to have my own. I hated Hugh when he reduced me to an honorless coward and shamed me to myself. I also know he could do it again. I might have been able to respect him if he hadn't destroyed my pride."

"You don't knuckle under to him."

"I did once, and I've always been afraid to admit it. I still get my pride up and make a brave stand, but it doesn't take much of a reminder to get me to back down and let him win. I haven't had to choose between giving in and something that important to me again. Maybe it would be different now. He calls me stubborn when I won't bow to him. I argue, or put up a fight, or yell at him and tell him what I think. He doesn't feel wrong. His view is simple, `I have the money and power, so I'm right and I'm boss. If you dare challenge me, I'll break you to obedience.'"

"That's a horrible story." Her soft statement stopped his diatribe. "I have never sensed that part of Hugh. I don't like it and cannot condone it, but I'm not sure I can excuse you either. Why do you keep antagonizing him? Are you daring him into a showdown?"

"Mom, I am stubborn, not stupid." He watched her slump in relief and laughed gently. "I snap around when he says the right words or gets a good hold on me. He's strong and I know I can't outlast him. We both fight to win. But I'm passionate. Hugh is ruthless. The hate was in me, waiting until I had the power to defeat him. This winter, while I was so messed up, it was overpowering. Now, it's just a strong desire to tell him to go to hell. I don't want to smash him, but just once, I want to hear him apologize to me and allow that I can be right even when we see things differently."

Sharon grimaced and handed the whip back to him. "Your father could become passionately proud, too. You're so alike. He was beaten to his knees a few times, David, but spirits like yours and Marc's don't stay broken. They keep springing back. You're like that horse Cavendish. You think Hugh turned him into an outlaw, don't you?"

"I know he did. Cavendish had more spirit than any horse we ever had. He could have been a world class eventer until Hugh pitted himself against him."

"Hugh doesn't treat Vulcan like that." She sounded confused. "He's very gentle with him."

"He has no reason to. Vulcan's not a rebel. He wants to please and has no fight in him. Vulcan broke to Hugh early, easily, and respects him. Hugh doesn't enjoy being cruel. I think he dislikes it but feels it's some kind of duty. He's only ruthless in that he has to rule and will use all the force he needs to win. Cavendish and I didn't break right. He could send the horse to the killers and not have to live with his failure. I'm a little different."

"I think you've made more of it than he has."

"Of course. I lost."

"I'm sorry, David. I didn't know about it."

"As I told you this morning, Hugh and I can wage our war without you. You don't belong in it."

"What did he do to you this morning?"

David flopped onto the couch, tipped his head back, and stared at the wood paneling on the ceiling. "He grounded me and took my driver's license."

"For how long?"

"Until he decides to relent." Rolling his head, he gave her a wry, appraising look. "I don't suppose you could get him to change his mind?"

"No, David. In the first place, I'm not wholly in disagreement with him. Secondly, Hugh doesn't give in to my remonstrations either. When I cry and yell at Hugh, he slams a door in my face or turns to stone. I got so mad at him one night, I put both feet in his back and shoved him out of bed. Marc would have turned it into a scorcher of a spat, and ten to one we would have ended up laughing. Hugh stood up calmly, like a stiff-necked officer, told me to learn to control myself and walked out on me. I threw all the pillows at the door then pounded on the mattress. Hugh says Marc was barbaric because he hit back once in a while."

"Like a striking snake." David added in a tone of admiring awe. "He had the fastest backhand I've ever seen. One flash and it would be over, like a cobra strike."

"I keep telling myself to grow up because Hugh is more civilized."

David snorted. "He's a hard-ass." He reached over and, catching her big toe, jerked her foot to him and tickled it. He kept laughing when she thrashed and kicked at him.

"Stop it, David." Laughing, she grabbed a throw pillow and started pounding him with it.

When he ducked away from the thudding blows, David let go of her foot and grabbed her wrist. She banged her heels down on his thigh until he leapt at her. Wrapping his arms around her shoulders, he hooked a leg behind her knees and pulled her off the couch. They rolled across the floor in a tangle and lay in each other's arms shaking with laughter they couldn't stop.

Finally, weakened from laughter, they lay on their backs looking up at the ceiling. He took a deep breath, sat up, and winked at his mother. "God, we're uncivilized."

"Hugh would never understand such childish abandon." She smiled at him and grabbed a handful of his dark curls. "David, it's great to have my fun-loving, feisty son back. But please, get a haircut before the event."

"Yes, Mother, anything you say."

"That means you're going to ignore me."

He twisted his face and ran his hand through his thick hair. "No. I think you're right. You are allowed to be right once in a while."

🐎 8

By Thursday, David was getting impatient about the event and wanted another look at the section in the ravine. A few things hung up in his mind, and he needed to set them straight. The stepped banks were no problem. As long as he came into the first one well in hand with enough impulsion, Casey would take them in even strides because that was the way they were built. Harold Babcock's courses were excellently designed, carefully constructed. He used big, solid fences that rode safely at good pace.

The coffin drop concerned David. After the three short banks, he knew he had to lengthen stride and take the big drop with a leap long enough to clear both coffin and fence. He was sure he had planned three long strides on the level run to the drop, which would force Casey to jump in a long arc. His memory kept telling him there was only room for three short strides but too much for two long ones, unless he took the last step big. That was not only difficult, it was wrong for a Babcock course. Harold's combinations were evenly strided. The steps should ride with metronome precision — blip, blip, blip, down the hill.

David could have waited until the official course walk on Friday, but it was nearby. If he stayed on the roadway above the ravine, he wouldn't violate the rules by riding on the course. Besides, it was a nice afternoon. Casey needed some galloping and a few wind sprints to keep the edge on his conditioning. 535 meters per minute was fast. He wanted Casey fit enough to come in right on optimum time or just under it. He wanted a clean cross-country ride with no time penalties to mar it.

It was four miles to the ravine overlook on a good, sandy clay road over smooth, rolling hills. David planned to walk the first mile, trot the next three as a warmup. After he studied the jump, he would return to the lower road at a gallop via five miles of state owned riding and snowmobile trails.

The trails twisted through rugged hills and ravines that taxed Casey's agility and made use of the powerful haunches, gymnastic muscling, and quick mind of his quarterhorse ancestors. When the trail straightened out in open fields and mature pine stands, David could push into a full run and feel the elastic lengthening of the horse's muscular body, hear the even cadence of long, ground-covering strides inherited from the thoroughbred side of his breeding — bloodlines that traced back to Eclipse, the English forefather of American thoroughbred racing.

David's best laid schemes went *a-gley* after the first two miles when he saw Colin Trombley's white Triumph parked where the road split. The west fork climbed above the ravine, the east angled down to cross the stream just below the course turn after the drop. The ravine was steep below the plank bridge, and the stream cascaded through a narrow, rock-choked crevice toward the paved county highway. The water vanished under the highway, where it was tamed by a cement culvert that turned it to follow the curve of the elevated roadbed. Beyond the curve, it surged out of the pipe in a foaming rush and plunged down a rocky stream bed in the woods below the scenic sweep of the highway.

David stopped Casey beside the car and looked around for Colin. He saw nothing but the racing stream and the steep hillside thickly carpeted in delicate pink and white spring beauties, patterned with clumps of purple and yellow violets. Here and there, trillium stood out, snow-white, above the low cover of fragile flowers. Tree buds were bursting with tiny leaves, and afternoon sun gold-washed the straight trunks of beach and etched the roughness of bark on towering hardwoods. The warm light brightened smooth, slender shafts of saplings growing at the feet of giant trees, and fragmented into an arching rainbow above a cascade that sprayed off a jutting rock.

David turned when he saw Colin running down the hill from the top side of the ravine. He chuckled at the frantic look on the man's face while he ran faster and faster, trying to keep up with his own forward motion.

"What the hell are you doing, Trombley?"

"Trying to get down this hill without a nasty spill." Colin reached out and wrapped an arm around a small ironwood tree at the top of the roadside bank. His other hand clutched a camera slung around his neck. "I wanted some photos of the jumps from straight on below them."

"Why didn't you drive up the road?"

"It's on the wrong side of the stream. The water's running too high to cross on the stones."

"You climbed all the way up that hill just to take pictures?" David watched the man pull in deep breaths. "Colin, I didn't know you had it in you."

"Harold likes good slides of his fences. That's the only way to get a straight-line shot of the drop with the steps behind it. The angle is right to get a good perspective on the whole run."

"I guess it would be. I like looking down at them from the edge of the ravine."

"Already got that shot." The Englishman jumped down to the road, where he set his camera onto the passenger seat of his car. He sat back against a front fender to pack his pipe.

"You had your mother quite upset, Davie-lad." Colin tipped his head and raised a sandy eyebrow. He looked up at David from under an uneven fall of red-gold forelock and sucked the lighter's flame into the tobacco stuffed pipe bowl.

"I've been doing that most of my life."

"She thinks you're trying to play detective in a matter that should be left to professionals. I can't agree with her more."

"It seems to be popular to stay uninvolved. I've never been a trend follower." David gave him a sour look.

"When it starts to hint of murder, that's not only a popular move, it's a wise one."

"Look, Colin, I appreciate that you want to help Mom out, but I also feel I know what I'm doing."

"I don't think you do, David. I don't think you know the half of it."

"But you do?" He hardened his voice and played with Casey's mouth when the horse, sensing his rider's tension, shifted his feet and pawed impatiently.

"I know I've seen more than I want."

"And I know someone is trying very hard to put the blame on me. I want to know who."

"Be careful, David. Curiosity has killed more than cats."

"But only a fool believes ignorance is a solution." He lifted his reins to back the horse away, then hesitated when he saw a disgusted look on the man's face.

"You're a bloody ass." Colin muttered and dug the lighter out of his jacket to relight the pipe. "You're going to get yourself killed. And how will she take that?" He started to strike the lighter, then stopped and dropped it back into his pocket. Holding the cool pipe in the palm of his hand, he gave David a cutting look. "It will devastate her, but you haven't thought of that, have you? You'll just keep prying until you know too much."

"You listen to my mother too much." David pivoted the big chestnut horse and trotted up the hill while Colin puffed on his dying pipe.

When David reached the overlook, he dismissed Colin and his advice along with his mother's fears. He had an event to win and no time to let his imagination build on unrealistic paranoia. But he was uneasy. He could no more pass off Liz's death as an accident than he could Hugh's shooting, or Tim's attempt at suicide. He knew they were all tied together, but he had no solid feeling about anybody. All evidence pointed at him and only him. He was anxious, but he didn't feel he was in danger. He couldn't even sense where he should expect danger.

When he looked down at the coffin drop, he was only concerned with how he was going to jump it on Saturday.

David's smile spread when he reevaluated the distance from the spot of landing after the last bank to the takeoff spot for the drop. It was easily three strides — three powerful strides. He knew he would pace it off carefully tomorrow, but at least he had set his mind at ease. Harold had designed it right.

While he backed the horse away from the edge of the ravine,

David followed the course with his eyes, wanting it to be Saturday when he and Casey would meet the challenge of Harold Babcock's new course.

In his mind, he was leaping the logs on the stream bank when he saw a glint of sunshine on polished chrome. He jerked his thoughts away from jumping and studied the bushes beside the stream. The glint turned to a flash. An instant later, a man rolled a black motorcycle onto the road below David. The man was wearing blue jeans, a dark, heavy sweater, and a deep-blue helmet with a smoky visor that concealed his face.

Although David saw no face, he never doubted that if the visor was lifted, he would see a dark beard. It was a moment of *déjà vu*, but this time, he was sure the man had not seen him. He felt that if he could backtrack on the trail without alerting the man, he could confront him and find out who the hell he was.

David heard the motorcycle start while he cut around the bottom of the hill. With relief, he noticed Colin's car was no longer parked beside the road and fresh tire tracks showed it had been driven toward the county road. David didn't slow Casey's gallop when he noted these facts. He digested them while he passed, then pushed the horse into longer strides over the wide, plank bridge.

When David spotted the man on the cycle, he was looking up at the coffin drop while he swung around in a circle with his right foot dragging on the ground. He stopped halfway around, swept his gaze from the jump to the dense thicket of swamp maples and alders beside the stream, then to the hill where Colin must have taken the picture.

When he started to look back at the jump, the man became aware of David. Snapping his head toward the bridge, he pushed the cycle forward, made a sliding, dust-showering turn and roared away from David on a dirt road that dead ended at the end of the ravine.

With a smirk on his face, David pounded after the cycle. He was sure he could box it in and hold the man long enough to get a good look at him, possibly talk to him. He realized he may be chasing a murderer, but he was not deterred. He was sure this murderer wasn't bold enough to kill him in a face to face confrontation that couldn't be passed off as an accident. But fear mingled with his excitement — a tightening in his scalp, a warm wash of sweat turned clammy, a twist of nausea in his gut. His hands tightened on the reins, his legs pressed against Casey's sides. He dropped his weight down into his heels, ready for any sudden move from the horse, who was apt to shy away from a charging motorcycle.

The cycle reached the cul-de-sac at the end of the road, swung left. David collected the horse and braced himself for a herding game to keep the man from speeding past him, but there was no confrontation. Without hesitation, the cycle bounced off the road and roared up the hill, zigzagging through the woods in angled switchbacks.

Sweeping his eyes along the hill, David picked a trail that would take him on a wider route without the switchbacks. The cycle was unable to use it. He would have to leap a runoff stream that cut a gash in the side of the hill and clear two decaying log jumps from a past cross-country course before he joined the side trail leading into a network of rugged trails.

With his upper body bent forward, David grasped a handful of mane right at the crest of Casey's neck and held himself firm and balanced over the horse's center of gravity. He gave Casey his head and closed his calves against sleek flanks. The animal leapt ahead with his hind legs reaching under his barrel. Shod hind hooves dug into gravelly dirt and the powerful haunches thrust the horse upwards in long, surging leaps that climbed straight up the hill.

David heard the motorcycle to his left and asked for more effort. He bonded himself to Casey, balancing with him, pushing with him as if the animal's body were his own. Casey accepted the bond, letting David control his movements and efforts until he was a powerful extension of David's own muscles, nerves, and brain. David didn't need to think about controlling Casey. The gelding responded as if he were his rider's legs.

David and Casey topped the hill just as the motorcycle's front wheel reared up over the crest. The cycle's rider thrust his weight forward and down, grounding the wheel and throttling ahead on the smooth trail. Cursing, David lengthened stride. Casey soared over the stream cut in a long leap and cleared the two jumps in even strides.

With the jumps behind them, Casey sensed David's urgency and stretched to cover more ground with each stride. His nostrils widened, drawing in more air, his heart pounded, forcing more oxygen rich blood to his muscles. The horse was working in a smooth, steady rhythm at full capacity, but the cycle was winning. Here, on a smooth trail, the machine was in its element, capable of a sustained, all out speed that flesh, blood, bone, and muscle could never match. Casey could possibly match the speed, but it would push him beyond aerobic effort into emergency flight. A horse could sustain that kind of speed for minutes, instead of the hours the machine could. But the machine was also limited, and David saw his chance.

This motorcycle was a modified road bike, but it was unable to handle the same terrain Casey could. It could not jump, it could not swim, and it could not handle the dune-like sides of the old gravel pit ahead. On this trail, there was only one gate out of the fenced gravel pit below the hill. If David could reach it first and drop the iron pipe barrier across the road, he could stop the cycle and confront the driver.

The motorcycle was circling the lip of sandy gravel on the only road it could use. David knew he could never catch the machine on the road, but he had a good chance of beating it to the gate if he went down into the pit and crossed the shallow spring-fed lake that filled the bottom. He made up his mind when he saw the cycle lose speed on a rocky, washed-out stretch of road. He could do it. He just had to find the right spot.

The bank to his left was badly undercut, unable to support Casey's weight all the way to the edge. David was reluctant to ask him to leap a full stride early. It could upset Casey's timing, undermine his trust in his rider, and break the mental rapport so important to the physical bond. Then he saw the windfall oak tree lying with its trunk along the edge of the bank, its full top hanging over the rim of the gravel pit.

It would mean a drop of almost eight feet, but the landing was good sand, the seventy-five feet of remaining slide about sixty degrees. It made the coffin drop look like a piece of cake, but

David never hesitated. He turned Casey and headed for the center of the branchless trunk.

While the horse pounded toward the rim of the pit, David looked beyond the fallen tree at the emptiness of blue sky above greening treetops on the far edge of the gravel pit that had been gnawed out of the side of the hill. He let his instincts judge the distance to the jump, sighted his takeoff, set his strides, and went for it. Casey trusted his judgments and jumped in a leap that took him over the fallen tree, out over nothing.

As soon as Casey's hind legs cleared the bank, David sat back hard, driving his seat into the saddle. He thrust his pelvis forward, forcing the hindquarters under the horse so they could break the fall and control his momentum while he slid toward the floor of the gravel pit on his haunches. He had six running strides before he hit the water, splashing it around him in a fountain of spray that hit him in the face, soaked his shirt, and chilled him with its icy touch. The lake bottom was firm sand over clay. The water was over Casey's chest.

The horse's pace slowed when he surged through the cold water like a breaching whale. David twisted his hands in the drenched mane and pulled his chest close to the thick crest while Casey rose and fell with strong bounds that reminded David of the gait on a painted carousel horse — a tremendous push up, a slow float down until the hind hooves found the bottom and thrust him forward with head lifted, nose reaching ahead of him, nostrils flared. Then they were out, scrambling up the bank and galloping toward the framework of an old, fallen conveyer. Casey snorted in a quickening tempo, blowing a spray of water out of his nostrils with every stride.

When they arced over the weathered wood and iron hulk of the gravel conveyer, David looked to his right, bending the horse in midair and changing his lead. He was turning when he landed and, after bounce striding up a steep bank, they charged across the level floor on a sand road that had been packed hard by vehicles.

David saw sun glinting off the cycle when it rounded the far edge of the pit, almost onto the graded road to the gate. He urged another notch of speed from the horse just as the cycle popped out of the last dip of the rough road, giving the man his first view of the horse and rider he thought he had outrun. The bike hit a rock, stuttered, went into a sideways drift, then righted itself on the level road and roared ahead.

Now it was an all out race David felt he was winning. The cycle's engine sounded as if it were running flat out while David was closing with the road a good fifty yards ahead of the laboring machine. Casey still had a reserve of sprint speed, a last burst of effort needed for a run to the finish flags. When he reached the main road, David would give it all they had.

All David had to do was reach the left hand gate post and yank out the rusted pin to release the long, metal arm with the octagonal stop sign bolted to it. The cycle would have to stop or crash into the gate. David was sure that if he closed the gate at the right time, the rider would be forced to turn so suddenly he would lose control of the machine and fall off it.

The race turned when a foaming emergency flare landed on the road ahead of David. When the spitting, fuchsia brilliance skittered toward him on the sand, Casey slid to a stop and reared in fright. David grabbed mane and clung to the thick neck like a sailor on a yardarm. He tried to use his weight to force Casey down and forward, but fright had replaced trust. The cycle sped toward the gate. Casey wheeled and bolted — away from the flare toward the road the cycle had been on.

By the time David regained control of the horse, he was livid with fury. He spun around in time to see the cycle zip out the gate.

"You son of a bitch." David bellowed at the disappearing cycle. "Turn around and face me, you gutless coward."

When the shout died away, somewhere in the back of his mind, David heard a gentle, teasing voice ask, "Didn't it ever occur to you that you might be outclassed?"

He vividly remembered the incident. He had been ten and attacked a particularly nasty bully of fifteen. The question had been his father's, asked while he held an ice pack to a cut and swollen eye and pressed gentle but firmly probing fingers along a bruised rib.

The memory made him chuckle, and he gave his answer to the

horse, whose ears flicked back at the sound of his voice. "It must not have occurred to me because I wiped him out a month later. Everyone has weak spots, even this bastard, and I don't give up. Who do you think he is, Casey? If he's the killer, why would he keep snooping on me and risk identification? If he's a cop or detective, what would he be looking for in the ravine? If he's trying to irritate me, he's doing it. But why?"

He laughed when Casey snorted and tossed his head. "You're not much help, but at least you listen."

David leaned forward to pat the gelding's neck and then vigorously rubbed along the top line of muscle. The horse stretched his head out and down in relaxation. "I'll bet you loved that whole hair-brained, foolhardy chase as much as I did, but let's keep it between the two of us. Mom would have a coronary."

🐎 9

David finished his dressage test with a center line so balanced and straight he could hardly believe it. Casey halted at G, square and immobile. With a snappy flourish, David removed his hat and held it beside his right leg in salute to the judge, who returned it with a formal nod of her head and a strong smile.

Returning the smile, David reset his hat and lengthened his reins. He pushed Casey forward and felt the supple back muscles stretch into a relaxed free walk. The ride had been good, better than he had expected. Casey was with him, responding to his body language and confidence. Thursday had been a breakthrough with the horse-rider bond stronger than it had ever been. It was as strong today.

David rubbed his hand on the smooth neck and straightened one of the small, tight braids while he left the arena on the big chestnut, whose coat gleamed like burnished copper and showed dark, half dollar size dapples in the sunlight. David, as Casey, was a fit, well-tuned athlete. He had buckled down and worked out all week, running, exercising, lifting again, even working with an enthusiasm that had stunned Matt Stone and made Hugh wonder what he was up to.

It was a beautiful day, cool enough to be invigorating, yet spring-soft, bright with greens and blues, all washed and gilded with sun-gold. The air was scented with the May freshness of new life and a profusion of wild flowers. David refused to think about problems today — not Liz, not Hugh's tyranny, not bearded strangers, not even Annie Babcock, who was home from a term at boarding school in Ireland that her letters called a concentration camp run by sharp-eyed nuns.

With almost two hours before his next starting time, David took care of Casey and left him tied to the trailer with a fresh bag of hay and bucket of water. His mind was full of tempting visions of lunch when he hurried into the trailer's dressing and tack room to hang up his black coat and change into jeans.

Inside the small, crowded tack room in the front of the trailer, he started to change out of his formal dressage attire, which included the white breeches he hated. He could never keep the damn things clean and always wore overalls until just before he mounted the horse. As further defense against the magnetism of dirt, he changed out of them as soon as he could after his dressage test.

He was standing on one foot, pulling the tight-fitting breeches off the other foot when the room brightened with a flood of sunlight.

When the door swung closed again and the lock clicked, he turned and stumbled sideways against the steel wall at the front of the trailer. He was still on one foot, the other knee bent, the breeches gripped around his foot and bunched in his opposite hand. The light was dim from the high, screened windows with jalousy panes, and he could see that she had closed her eyes for a moment to adjust from the brightness outside.

He managed to free his foot from the clutch of the stretch fabric so he could stand on both feet before she opened big, brown eyes that melted into him. She smiled with full, soft lips on an almost pouting mouth. He was in his jockey shorts, a white dress shirt, and a tie. He had one sock on. The other sock was still inside the balled up breeches he dropped into an open tack trunk. He felt like a fool.

David had not seen Annie since Christmas. The encounter had been brief. He was partying in Ann Arbor, which was not for Annie. Her parents would never have allowed her to stay out late and any hint of alcohol or tang of strong smoke would have sent her big-voiced, fire-breathing father after David like a raging gladiator.

Harold Babcock was proud of what he saw as his daughter's wholesome, clean character. He did his best to preserve it, while Annie did her best to preserve his myth. Actually, most of his image was true. Annie had no taste for alcohol, disliked smoke of all kinds. She thrived on health foods, vigorous exercise, and what she called good, wholesome lust. Annie said she was a good girl — damn good. David fully agreed.

The fallacy was that Annie's father was still ardently protecting a virtue Annie and David had ended a year ago in a deep bed of golden wheat straw. Secluded by a fortress of stacked bales, they had leisurely experimented in the arts of sex, while their horses greedily cropped grass and devoured fallen apples in an old orchard behind the big storage barn where Babcocks kept their straw and idle farm equipment.

Lately, David had been too involved with Liz and his own upsets to think about Annie. He thought about her now when she walked toward him with her shirt unbuttoned enough to show plump bulges of uplifted breasts and a deep cleavage that drew his eyes to the strained button.

Annie certainly was wholesome. David's word was ripe — like a softly fresh, juice-laden peach, tempting him to bite into its flesh.

"You're very impolite, David." She stepped up to him, catching his tie in her hand, and winding it around her fingers until she was pressed against him, warm and shifting. When she looked up, her spicy warmth breathed from between parted lips, just below his chin, only inches from his own mouth that was suddenly moist. His jaw slackened and his tongue moved against his teeth.

"I've been home three days, David. You haven't been over to see me, except for yesterday when you came to walk the course with your mother. I could have been a turtle for all the attention you paid me."

David raised his hands and slid them up her neck, grasping two handfuls of tumbled auburn curls. "I'm stuck at home. Hugh grounded me and literally keeps me under guard — his, Leon's, Mom's, or Matt's. The only time I'm not in someone's sight is when I'm in bed or the bathroom."

"I saw Liz's picture in the paper." Annie's eyes narrowed. She tipped her head and slid her lower lip forward in a pouting way that was half little girl, half seductive nymph. "Rumors say you were going with her. She was a beautiful girl."

"She was beautiful, but I wasn't going with her. I guess she was a friend, someone who needed something from me. It wasn't anything like it was with you."

"It can be that way again, David."

"Maybe I can get Mom to look the other way for a while tonight, but you'll have to drive. I lost my license."

"Points?"

"Hugh. He must keep it in his wallet because it sure isn't in the house, not even in the safe."

"I think I can get a car. Your test was good. You rode him so powerfully, so forward." Her hands undid his tie while she rubbed her leg on his. "You don't ride for two hours."

"I want some lunch."

"I'll get you lunch later. Mom made some great fried chicken." Annie unbuttoned his shirt and pressed her face against his chest, nibbling at him until he tightened an arm around her and lifted her chin to kiss her.

When her body molded to his, David sighed and gave her a crooked smile. "Oh, what the hell."

David pulled off his shirt. When Annie unbuttoned hers, he reached out and unsnapped the front of her bra, watching it fall away from what he called an unsurpassed set of bare mountain peaks. Annie's breasts were big, firm, and ripe. He had a sudden change of appetite and stopped thinking about lunch. The ripe peach brushed his lips, and he opened his mouth, biting into its softness, drawing the pleasure into him until he felt his arousal surge out of control. Hot blood flushed through him and hardened him while the cool deftness of her hands stimulated him.

He broke from the kiss and reached behind her to grab Casey's shipping blanket. She helped him throw it over two unopened hay bales by the door.

He muttered. "It isn't much, but it beats a steel floor."

Annie giggled. "Or a classic M.G. in the winter."

"Don't remind me. I thought I frostbit my buns." He sat on

the end of a bale then lay back with her astride him.

She was nude, deliciously bursting with her personal brand of wholesome vigor. He wanted to match his lust to hers and revel in it for hours. Annie could drain him, then stir him into a second blaze with a peak of desire that seemed just unattainable. No matter how exciting a diversion seemed to be, he always crawled back to Annie, like a drunk to a bar. And, as long as he could crawl to the bar, Annie served him.

David knew it would be a quick, stimulating shot now, no more than an appetizer for tonight. He also knew that, even if he had to sneak out and meet her somewhere, he would find a way to be with her tonight. One taste of the peach created a ravishing desire for more.

"Annie, girl, you're part siren, part demon, and all crazy."

"Fun, isn't it?" She kissed him and nipped at the moustache that was starting to look serious. "It's prickly. Like I'm kissing a bottle brush."

"Mom kind of hoped it would go with the haircut, but she lost out. I think it gives me that Burt Reynolds image."

Annie laughed at him. "That and about forty years might do it." She tilted her head to give him an appraising look. "You're on the right track, but I don't think it's the moustache."

"David?"

He stiffened at his mother's voice outside the trailer and rolled Annie down beside him so she was facing him, snuggled up against his chest. "Be very quiet."

"What should we do?"

"Nothing." David whispered in her ear. "If she tries to come in, I'll tell her I was taking a nap and need to get dressed."

"David?" Sharon stopped next to Casey and looked around. "David, are you here?"

When silence answered her, she shrugged and walked to Colin, who was righting the water bucket Casey had tipped over. "I guess he went to get lunch. I don't think anything can keep David away from food."

Colin's hand caught her wrist. He drew her to him and then

backed her against the side of the trailer until only the painted steel wall separated her from the tack room. "Don't dash off. It's quiet here and we can be alone for a few minutes." His arm circled her waist and held her in front of him while he reached for the handle to the dressing room. He twisted, but the handle refused to move. "Is it locked?"

"I'm sure David locked it before he left." Sharon relaxed when he dropped his hand from the handle. He had been hovering around her all morning and it made her uncomfortable.

"Do you have a key?"

"Not with me. It's in my coat and I left it with Hugh."

"Oh drat." Colin scowled.

Sharon looked around and noticed they were quite secluded, being the last trailer in the line beside a fence row thick with brush and flowering thorn apple. It unnerved her and she wanted to move away. But she would have to push him, which would be awkward.

"Sharon, I really must talk to you." His manner was urgent, too agitated for Colin. "Your plight last week has been on my mind constantly. You're undergoing ghastly stresses, but I haven't been able to break away to meet with you. I was disturbed when you said you had no one to turn to. Yet, at the same time, it lifted my feelings tenfold."

"It's not so bad now. I do have David. We seem to have rediscovered the ability to communicate with each other. David's years wiser than I was at seventeen. He's wiser than I was when he was born. He's on the edge of manhood, and I was seeing him as a child."

She sensed a change in Colin, a wariness, but she was too intent on what she was piecing together in her mind to put any significance to it. "Alexander the Great was king of Macedonia when he was twenty years old. By the time he was thirty-three, he'd built an empire and was dead. George Armstrong Custer was a general at nineteen."

"David's a smart boy — a little too smart."

"He's his father all over again, but with a sense of purpose Marc didn't have. There's some of the Collingwood drive to hang onto and build with what he achieves, not throw it to the winds with no thought for where it lands or what it seeds." She could sense that Colin was uninterested in, even jealous of, her views of David. "I'm sorry if I used you last week. I thrust you into an unpleasant situation. It wasn't a kind thing for me to do."

"But I was glad to do it. I want to be the one you turn to." There was earnest desire in the tone of his voice. It reminded her of the way he had been in England when she had allowed him to see how much Marc's wandering hurt her. "I want to win you back, Sharon. It was so hard to give you up last time, I almost failed on my promise to end it when Marc came home."

"You were most gracious about it, Colin. I thought I sensed relief."

"I knew there was no chance against Marc. I was no more than an interlude seized when you were angry with him and he was far away." His hands rubbed on her back, moving her closer to him with relaxing motions. "But Hugh isn't Marc."

"Hugh is my husband. I have no intention of having an affair with you while he is my husband. I thought you understood that."

"Hugh is paralyzed. He can't satisfy—"

"Hugh can, a lot better than you think. It's only his legs that don't work. He is neither helpless, nor impotent. It angers him when people think that way, and it's beginning to anger me. People give me looks that say, 'You're so enduring, such a wonderful martyr to stick by your half a man.' Well, he's no half a man. If any of those woman ever got in bed with him, they'd stop pitying me and go back to envying me in their catty little ways."

"Is my only appeal the truth that I've loved you for eight years and see those few months we had together as the best in my life?"

"It was fun, Colin, but it was a long time ago."

Sharon was startled by his confession of love. She hadn't read him that way when they had spent those few months dashing from bed to bed like children on a school holiday. There had been affection and enjoyment, but she hadn't sensed anything as deep as love in Colin. Of course, he had been married then, and she had been in love with Marc in spite of her flight into rebellious adultery.

The caress of his hand on her face made her shiver with a

pleasure she wanted to deny. Colin had a tenderness Hugh rarely offered. His touch was gentle when he caressed her throat and guided her mouth to his. The kiss grew with a warm stirring she found disquieting. It was more sentimental nostalgia than desire, but she was moved, even when she didn't want to be.

"Please, Colin, don't bring it back."

"I thought it was something I could forget. When I learned you were in Michigan, I had to come here. I didn't even know what Michigan was. But when I met the Harringtons from Michigan, who knew a boy named David Breton with a mother named Sharon, I about fell over myself accepting their offer."

"You said you didn't know I was here." She gave him a sharp look. "You were startled when we met."

"I didn't know how you would accept me. I felt I couldn't just pop back into your life and botch it up. Meeting Hugh was a dash of cold water. I was expecting a rich old bloke who was keeping you in horses and out of bed. I had a marvelous mental picture of a doddering old bastard with an aged and flaccid member, not six feet two inches of macho and dash."

"Why did you expect that?" She laughed at his puckered face.

"Marion Harrington said you were married to the owner of Jamison Aircraft. I looked into him. Hugh Arthur Jamison: West Point 1936; Army Air Corps in World War II; Air Force officer, who founded Jamison Aircraft in 1958 when he retired from the Air Force as a brigadier general. He was over seventy."

"He was also dead. That was Hugh's father. He was killed when a car full of teenagers pulled out of a stop sign on a rainy night. He tried to swerve, lost control, spun across the road, and wrapped around a tree." Sharon gave him a wry, almost caustic look. "Somehow it wasn't proper to mention he was doing over eighty and the inexperienced teenager may have tried to pull out even if he hadn't had a few beers. Colin, Hugh is still six feet two inches of macho and dash. He's just sitting down most of the time."

"Another Marc?"

"Hugh is not another Marc. They are vastly different men. Marc had compassion, sentimentality, and emotional inconsistencies. Hugh has propriety, duty, and control of his emotions. He staggered under his tragedy, but he's conquering it. There's no way in the world I could feel anything but rotten if I cheated on Hugh, who sees fidelity in marriage as essential, even sacred."

"You cheated on Marc."

"Marc cheated on me all the time."

"Marc was continental. He saw a man's roaming as expected."

"And I was an American, who said, `Stuff it in your ear. I'm as free as you are.' Marc's boneheaded double standard was a big factor in my walking out on him — that and the constant fear that someone was going to break in again and kill us all, or just soak the house with gasoline and throw a match at it. It may be his choice to take chances with his life, but not his child's life."

"That's why you left him, isn't it? He wanted to train David, so he could work with him, the way Marc had with his father. You wouldn't let him. He told David more than he told you about what he did, and you knew where it was leading. You may think you took David away before Marc taught him too much. I think it was too late. He'd already taught him to think the way he did."

"I was afraid of what could happen. He had no right to expose David to dangers like that. No, it wasn't the women. I was used to that."

"Marc's infidelity was casual without involvement."

"It still infuriated me. I took it, but I never took it well." Anger put a bit in her voice and heated her neck and cheeks. "He was like a kid with a sweet tooth. When a woman dangled sex in front of him, he had a paralytic mental block against the word no. Most of his lays had no more meaning than a candy bar, which galled me. He acted as if it would insult his manhood to say, `No, thank you, I'll go home to the one I love.'"

"You're still in love with that man." He set his hands on either side of her head, fencing her against the trailer while he studied her face.

"If I am, it's with someone who used to be and has no relevance to me now."

"But what if he did? Would you go back to Marc if he asked?"

"I don't know." Her twisted face reflected the anxiety in her mind. "David says I would, but David wants to go back to him.

He sees me through his eyes. I love Hugh. I'm married to Hugh. I plan to be faithful to Hugh as long as we are married."

"What if that accident had been fatal? What if there was no Hugh? Could Marc step in and pull you back into his world?" He paused, staring into her. "Could I?"

They were questions Sharon had considered several times since November. She had never let herself answer them. At least not the ones about Marc. She had always thrust the possibility from her mind before she allowed it to trap her.

"Colin, there is Hugh. There will be Hugh. That has little bearing on the question. I didn't run to Hugh. I ran from Marc. The answer depends on Marc and how I would relate to him now. I really don't think he's changed much." She looked up at a calm, inquisitive face that waited for her to finish sorting her thoughts.

That's the way Colin had always been. He had never forced her decisions, just quietly waited until she made her choice. He had always accepted it with dignity and a patience that waited until he was needed, in one way or another.

"Colin, right now the answer is no to running off with Marc. And it's no to you. There will be no more jaunts to fun places, no surreptitious meetings in hidden places, no jokes on hotel registers like Mr. and Mrs. *L'esprit d'Amour*." She ducked under his arm and moved away from the trailer. "I gave a horse that name. He lacked boldness. I sold him and he's done well as a pampered show ring hunter."

"Is that intended as an insult, or did I just take it that way?" Colin stepped up to her and caught her wrist, turning her to face him.

"It's a true statement. I didn't mean it to be anything." His indignation surprised her and made her wonder if there had been a facetious motive behind her comment. Since her talk with David, she found herself pitying Colin. He always seemed to come up just short of winning.

"I was never sure whether you were laughing at me or not. Now it's important. I don't want you laughing at me. Too many people have laughed at me, as if I'm of no consequence. My last wife laughed at me. She saw me as a ludicrous misfit in her aristocratic world. She felt my inferior breeding was a mockery and made me peripheral. Your son laughs at me as if I'm insignificant."

"If I ever laughed at you, it was with affection. I'm insensitive to blue-blood. Remember, I'm the product of rebellious backwoods colonials, to use Sybil's wording. Sybil was a bitch who tried to degrade you to puff herself up. I'm surprised you ever let it penetrate."

When his moustache twitched, she teased him with a smile. "I enjoyed my affair with you, but it has no place now. I didn't marry Hugh so he could keep me in horses. There was and still is a lot of man in Hugh, and I'll keep him."

"You've left me with no recourse but retreat. Forgive my persistence, but it's hard to bow out gallantly when it hurts so deeply."

"I forgive you, Colin. You've always been a gentleman. You're still a gentleman when you have every right to be rude and irrational. Don't you ever get angry, Colin? Don't you ever demean yourself with an action that is ungallant, unchivalrous, ungracious, or just plain nasty?"

"I have my dignity, Sharon. No, I could never demean myself with rude behavior. You have been honest with me and you've tried to be kind. Gracious defeat is far more dignified than a display of uncivilized conduct."

Inside the dressing room, David sat up and peered through the slats of the door window. They were walking away from the trailer toward the secretary's stand. He watched them for a moment before he said, "Remember the Avon bard, Colin, 'The prince of darkness is a gentleman.'" He laughed and lay back down next to Annie.

"You don't like Colin much, do you?"

"I like him less now that I know he seduced my mother."

"Maybe your mother seduced him. It's been known to happen." She rolled onto her back. "I'm glad they left. The silent, slow-motion petting was driving me crazy."

"Driving you crazy? If I don't get some action, I'm going to split open like a micro-waved kielbasa."

Soft thighs gripped his when he slid into her. She started to move under him and he moaned at the warm, receptive clutch of her body. His hips thrust forward with long, slow motions that were torturously tantalizing. It was powerful and building, reaching for a fantastic blast of final effort that was—

"Oh shit." His knee slipped between the hay bales that had been steadily moving apart, and he collapsed with a deflating grunt. He tried to pull his knee out, but he had forced the horse blanket between the bales and it was tangled around his foot. In frustration, he shoved his hip against the bale behind him. When it slid across the steel floor, he rolled off the bale Annie was on. He sat spraddle-legged on the floor and stared up at her for a blank moment.

"I have to hand it to you, David. You often strive for originality. This time you truly mastered the surprise ending — the, shall we say, shot in the void." Her words dissolved in laughter.

"By God, the earth does move," David said. "Papa Hemingway was right all along."

"What?"

"It jumped right out from under me. We're fantastic, Annie. We control cosmic forces. Think of our power." He gave her a sudden, sober look. "We better keep the hell out of California."

"Do you know you're insane, Breton?"

"Certainly. It's part of my heritage."

"So are lays as meaningless as candy bars." She gave him a sideways look that said a lot more than her words.

"Yeah, well, she also said I had a better sense of purpose." He bounced to his feet and glanced at his watch. "Good grief! I only have forty minutes. I have to tack Casey, and I don't remember where his splint boots are." He looked around in alarm. "I can't even find my damn underwear."

Dismayed, David surveyed the mess in the small, steel room that had been an example of meticulous Matt Stone efficiency before he had arrived. His coat was hung up. Nothing else was. He had spilled two boxes of leg wraps when he pulled Casey's blanket off the first aid box, and his white breeches had landed square on top of a messy can of Koppertox. He snatched them up, gaping at the bright-green stain that resembled a map of Australia on the left thigh.

"That blows using Mom as an alibi tonight. She's going to be trying to strangle me with a pair of hundred dollar breeches." He bent over and plucked his shirt off the floor. "How in hell do I do it? I'm instant chaos. *C'est un ensorcellement!*"

"Your shorts are under the blanket. I'll go get some chicken." Annie finished dressing and zipped out the door, leaving David, totally nude, with the mess and his frustrated ranting.

When David led Casey out to the warm-up field with the practice jumps, several people smiled and nodded or winked at him. Some people tossed him friendly encouragement. A few glowered at him. He was somewhat puzzled, even embarrassed because he had no idea why.

Sharon trotted toward him on Limerick, wearing a bright yellow pinny with a black number 31 on it over a knit shirt the same bright blue as David's. Her safety helmet cover was striped with the blue and orange of Eminence Farm. Her breeches, like David's, were steel grey — boots and gloves black.

"When do you start?" David asked when she halted beside him.

"Two-O-six. How do you feel about that score?"

"What score?" Her question startled him.

"David, you scored 74% on your dressage test. It was fantastic."

"I did?" His stunned expression broke into a wide grin. "That's why all the notice. I was beginning to wonder what people were wise to."

"Didn't you look at the board?"

"I didn't get a chance." He vaulted on Casey and slid his toes into the stirrups.

"David, you rode dressage almost two hours ago. Where were you? It puts you in first place. You can win if you and Casey keep thinking together like that."

"I plan to win, but hold back on the prediction. I haven't jumped the first fence yet."

"Casey usually makes up for dressage penalties by a clean

cross-country."

David reached out and gave her hand a squeeze. "Relax. You're all keyed up. Where did you place?"

"Sixth."

"That's good. Has Colin finished cross-country yet? He was riding fourth."

"I don't know. He was second to you by nine points after dressage. The first cross-country ride had sixty jumping penalties — bad riding not the fault of the course. Second was clean — a horse from Ohio. I only have ten minutes. I better get over to the starter."

"I'd watch some of it, but I'm only thirty-three minutes behind you. I want to keep him moving. Good luck." He gave her shoulder a squeeze then watched her trot toward the starter for roads and tracks, six kilometers at 240 meters per minute, an energetic, ground-covering trot. There was a vet check and a ten minute rest between roads and tracks and cross-country.

David stretched and straightened his pinny. He was number 42, which only had significance in that it was his father's age. It was one of David's games to relate numbers to something important in his life. This one had taken some thinking. He thought it odd that until he found an answer, the game would plague him with amazing persistence.

David saw Colin by the fence and rode up to him. "Are you giving out any secrets?"

"About the course?"

"What else?" David crossed his leg over the pommel of the saddle and dug a cigarette out of the pack in the pocket under his pinny. "I know all your other secrets."

"Somehow that doesn't surprise me. You've always known too much for your own good. It's quite straightforward really. Stay to the left on the bullfinch. Something's catching at feet on the right — no mishaps, but startling. In the ravine, I suggest you go straight into the drop. Come clean over the center and you'll be right for the turn. I angled a little from right to left in an attempt to use the upside slope to control momentum because he tends to come down too heavy on his forehand. Too much scrambling. The fence is designed right and jumps well. Dead over the center is the way to do it."

"Were you clean?"

"Two point eight time penalties. I lost it on that wrong move at the drop, and he came into the hay rick snorting and back pedaling. I thought he was going to quit on me, but at the last instant, he responded to the bat and squat jumped." Colin made a comically pained face. "I think I joined up with him somewhere near the apex of the bloody leap and left the zone plastered to his neck with the reins flapping. I lost time uncrossing my eyes and sighting in on the next fence."

"Ouch." David winced in empathy. "You going to watch Mom? She's off in eight minutes."

"I thought I'd get my photo equipment and wander around catching what shots I can. Go for it, David. You've got twelve points on me."

"You really mean that?"

"Of course. The sport's the thing — may the best man win and all that sort of shit."

David burst out laughing. "I can never tell whether you're Anglicizing the American or Americanizing the British."

"Rot and bother went out with *bully* and *by Jove* and *keep your pecker up*. Dreadful loss of tradition, old chap. I'm deucedly corrupted by you American curs. You, too, are losing your delightful, European omnium-gatherum to a Midwesterner's nasal *A* and, `where's it at?'" Colin finished with a mockingly accurate imitation of David's voice. "Cheerio, Davy-lad."

David laughed when Colin walked away from the fence with his purposeful stride, just short of stiff but in no way undignified. He saw Sharon's last three fences and was waiting to start roads and track when she led Limerick past him, carrying her hat and grinning like a Cheshire cat. The horse was dark with sweat, foamy with lather, breathing hard, but not heaving, tired but not dragging.

"Well?"

"Clean, David, only four seconds below optimum."

"How was the scenery?"

"There was scenery out there?" She widened her eyes in mock surprise. "I thought it was all a blur between O-my-Gods!" She wrinkled her nose then looked serious. "Take the drop left of center, but straight on."

"Colin said to take the center."

"Maybe when he rode. It's getting dug up in the center." She nodded to the starter, who was beckoning to David.

While he was in the start box for cross-country, listening to starting instructions he had heard so many times he could recite them, David looked at the field where the course started and ended. He especially looked at the first jump. It was an excellent first jump, a twenty feet wide arc of big logs, three high, gently sloped away with a clean gallop approach and a flat landing with space to settle into a good pace before the second fence, a rustic zig-zag of stacked utility poles.

"You have one minute. I'll warn you at ten second intervals and count the last ten seconds. You may leave the box any time after I say go. Time will start at the word go. One minute — now."

David cocked his head when he heard a siren on the paved county road below the ravine. He paid little attention. There were often sirens on the pavement. Speeders and accidents were too common on the curving, hilly roads of Wellington Township. Most Michigan drivers weren't used to roads making sudden changes and usually drove too fast.

"Fifty seconds —"

There were two sirens now. It seemed to be more than a speeder, maybe a hurry-up accident.

"Forty seconds —"

On the blacktop highway, two police cars were gaining on the slower, sand-colored Jeep, but they were still a good quarter mile behind it. The vehicle hugged the white line on the inside of a curve. Its tires squealed in protest when it swung into the reverse curve of the S.

"Thirty seconds —"

When the reverse curve put the Jeep well out of sight of the leading police car, the tan vehicle crossed the center line and slowed. The man driving grabbed a green nylon day pack and stood up. He yanked down on the hand throttle just before he leapt from the vehicle. Clearing the low guard rail, he hit, feet first, gave with his knees, and rolled down the embankment with the pack clutched in his arms.

"Twenty seconds —"

The Jeep gained speed at an alarming rate. It stayed on the road for a good fifty yards before it smashed through the opposite guard rail. After a nose dive, it flipped end for end, tumbling toward the stream below the embankment. It's engine roared, its wheels spun while it continued to accelerate with a wide open throttle.

"Ten seconds, nine — eight —"

A sheriff's patrol car squealed to a stop near the smashed guard rail. A police car swung off the road behind the deputy sheriff. Detective Reed stepped out of the driver's door while Detective Stanwyck opened the passenger door.

"Seven — six — five —"

A bearded man with a pack on his back vaulted a fallen tree and scrambled up the rocky stream bed into the ravine. He was unseen by the policemen, who were across the road, staring down at the dead Jeep.

"Four — three —"

David settled into the saddle just enough to prepare Casey and push his energy into his hands.

"Two — one — Go!"

Casey left the starting box at a powerful trot. He was galloping evenly by the third stride. The pull was there, but it was impulsion not perversity. David could hold it, control it with the movement of his back, the use of his weight. The horse was with him, right with him, an extension of his own nerves and muscles. They were in harmony with David setting the pace.

Casey took each fence the way David wanted — high or long, straight or angled, with no resistance or hesitation. They were still communicating as if their minds and bodies were linked. A horse couldn't actually read a rider's mind, but if the rider was able to translate his thoughts into physical expression, no matter how subtle, a sensitive horse could learn to interpret that body language and respond to it as if he were mind reading.

While they rode the course, Casey flipped his ears back to listen to David's voice or eagerly pointed them forward when he approached each fence. With his attention on the fence, Casey was using the binocular vision that was the best a horse could do to judge an obstacle he approached. Unlike man, a horse had no stereo vision, no true depth perception. In order to clear complex fences, a horse relied on experience, memory of similar obstacles, and the way his rider prepared him in his approach. A horse had to learn to see his fences through a long, slow process of trial and error. If pushed too far, too fast, errors could result in injuries and loss of courage. Overfencing a green horse by failing to give it time to learn to see a fence for what it was, not what it looked like in its vision, was probably the greatest contributor to accidents in jumping.

Casey was the result of an extremely athletic and terrain-wise horse, that had received careful gymnastic schooling, coupled with a bold spirit and a genuine enjoyment of the run, the contest, the challenge. David was just like him. Today, everything was right, except the four pieces of fried chicken David had eaten too fast and too recently. He would never have allowed his horse to stuff himself with grain so close to a ride, but he never thought to curb his own eating. Fortunately, man had a will to push himself beyond bodily discomforts that an animal only exhibited in moments of stress, such as fear or rut.

David forced the discomfort out of his mind and concentrated on riding.

On the smooth, clear, ridge trail, he let Casey open up in a long, reaching run until he neared the marker for the ravine turn. He had paced it off several times yesterday, knew exactly when to start easing him into more collection so it was gradual with no pulling, no abrupt movements to break the rhythm. Casey left the trail smoothly. He was put together enough to negotiate the stepped banks with metronome precision and land with his haunches under him on the short slide.

David looked between the horse's pointed ears at the logs of the Coffin Drop. His mother was right. The center was overused. He came out of the slide just left of center and drove Casey forward into the three powerful strides he knew would fit just right. David's eyes were centered beyond the jump at a point in space that would drop him well clear of the logs onto the sloping floor of the ravine.

A flicker, an almost subliminal disruption of the air, jolted David's concentration. He felt Casey falter on his last stride, felt something horribly wrong when the driving hindquarters came into stride for the surge of suspension that would take him over the fence. In reflex, David vaulted out of the saddle and shoved off the neck, propelling himself away from the horse. Casey's forelegs buckled the instant he tried to jump. The strength of his hindquarters sent him forward and over the coffin toward the jump. He crashed, chest-first, into the top log while his head and neck reached beyond it. For an interminable second, all twelve-hundred pounds of horse seemed to be balanced on its chest like an acrobat. Momentum won. Casey flipped over the solid structure and thudded onto the shadowed ground below the jump.

David saw it happen in wavering surrealism while he rolled toward the logs. The scene was upside down and right side up and spinning in surges of grey brightness. He thumped into the logs lining the coffin, first his hip then his shoulder. He forced himself to his feet, swayed for a moment while a sharp scream rang in his ears. Images faded, dimmed, and went out like a turned-off monitor. He fell, face down, in the churned up dirt in front of the jump.

With the scream still in her throat, Sharon tore away from hands that tried to hold her. She charged past a knot of spectators and half-ran, half-slid down the steep dropoff with one of the fence observers. The other observer called for assistance on the C.B. radio in her hand. The girl was calm when she told them to stop the next horse. She asked for an ambulance and veterinarian to come by the road below the jump. She made everyone get back and take the trail to the road below, explaining that the man with Sharon was a fireman. He was trained in first aid and could handle it.

Sharon dropped to one knee beside David and stared at the big, freckled hand that was carefully touching David's face and neck. "What happened?"

"The horse just went down." The man felt David's warmth, his strong pulse. When David started to lift his head, the fireman held his hand on the back of his neck, restraining him. "If anything hurts in your neck or back, don't move."

David moved his head slowly before he carefully rolled onto his back and blinked up at his mother and the beefy, freckle-spattered man beside her. "I'm all right. Casey? What about Casey?"

"I don't know. He went over the jump." Bewildered, Sharon looked up and saw Harold Babcock hustling toward her from below the jump. He was with Colin Trombley, who was sweating from running, looking more distraught than she had ever seen him.

"I heard a horse was down on the C.B. I knew it had to be Casey. I ran through the woods, then Harold picked me up." Colin stopped beside her, disheveled, his boots scuffed and muddy, missing a spur. "Is David all right?"

"I'm all right. How's Casey?" David stared up at Colin.

Colin glanced at Harold, who was standing beside the logs, looking down at the immobile horse. When he looked back at David, he pulled himself together and answered with more than his usual helping of dignity, "Casey's dead."

David didn't hear the words. He felt them slam into him with a force he thought was going to crush his chest. He rolled onto his side, buried his face in his bent arm, drew his knees up until he was a tight ball with all his vulnerability wrapped up inside him. He was numb and silent while he tried to grasp a why, or a how. There was no reason Casey should have fallen. It hadn't even felt like a fall. There had been no trip, no dropping into his hands. Casey had shuddered. That's what it had felt like, a sudden, jerking shudder, almost a spasm.

David felt his mother's hand slip into his and grip it. When she pressed her face against his shoulder, he said quietly, "I want to know what killed my horse. He didn't fall."

David refused to leave. He was there when the vet came. He helped when they removed a partition from one of Babcock's trailers and hauled Casey into it with a tractor. Hugh thought he might send him to Michigan State for a necropsy, but it was a weekend, which made it awkward, so he shrugged and said he would bury him at home. David did not accept it well. Something in his mind refused to see it as an accident, or natural. He was adamant about wanting to learn the actual cause of death.

When Hugh, in a cold, practical manner, told Dr. Acheson to say it was an accident — death from trauma or injuries — and leave it at that, David lost it. When he should have been thinking, he lost control and shouted, "You can't do that. I'll pay for the goddamn thing myself, but I want to know why that horse died."

"It doesn't matter." Hugh pivoted the wheel chair to face David with a hard glare of authority.

"Hugh, he was dead before he went down."

"You don't know that."

"Yes, I do. I felt it, but you don't want to believe me."

"It isn't important."

"Something killed my horse, almost killed me. Am I crazy to want to know what?"

"The why won't change what happened. Damn it, David, it was an act of God. Now let it rest."

"I want the truth, even if you don't."

"Face the truth, David, no necropsy will change the fact that one of the best horses I ever bred is dead because you dropped him on his nose in front of a fence."

The accusation snapped through David. He acted out of blind fury when he drew back his right fist, ready smash it into Hugh's face. "You son of a bitch."

David finished his swing, but Hugh blocked it and it glanced off a hard forearm. When David lunged within reach of his stepfather's strong right hand, Hugh grabbed a wad of shirt. He gave David a startling shake and held him close in front of him. "Think, David." His voice was low, his jaw rigid. Only David could hear him. "I have to do it this way."

Hugh's words were confusing, but David started to understand what he was trying to say. Hugh had to bury the horse or alert the killer by showing suspicion. He started to relax, but the hand tightened suddenly and thumped against his chest. "Play it out. You have no choice." With his barely audible advice, Hugh thrust David backwards into the solid body of Leon, who wrapped strong arms around his torso. "Take him home, Leon. He's too distraught to accept what happened."

David saw Hugh's eyes shift beyond the rope put up to keep back the growing crowd. He caught a glimpse of a man with thick sunglasses and a black beard. Then the man was gone, melting through the crowd toward the other side of Babcock's trailer and van.

"I didn't drop him." David yanked Hugh's attention back to him.

"Please, no more arguing. The horse is dead. I'll bury him at home where he belongs."

"He's your horse, but I don't think you're right." When Leon let him go, David turned from Hugh and started toward the van. He hesitated when he saw the police car crossing the bridge and recognized the two officers in it as Reed and Stanwyck. Leon's hand closed around his arm. "I want to talk to them, Leon."

"Not now, David. There's too much at stake to make waves. Let Hugh handle it." He opened the van door for David. "We're not as blind as you think."

"I want to learn what killed Casey."

"Perhaps you will."

When David looked across the van at Leon's ageless, dark face, he realized there was nothing he could do but accept Hugh's decision, even if he disagreed with it.

At home, David took a shower. In a silent mood that was resigned, but not convinced, he fixed pizzas for himself and Leon. He heard the trailer rattle by the house. A few minutes later, the back hoe started and chugged toward the sloping hillside behind the hay barn, where several other Eminence Farm horses were buried. David sat in the television den staring at a sports show, without knowing what was going on, until the back hoe shut down.

With a surge, David shot from the chair and stormed past Leon. Outside, he saw the trailer turning toward the road. He ran until he was beyond the barns in a hilltop pine grove, where he could look down at the farm and see it all from the outside. He pulled his knees up in front of him and folded his arms on top of them while he stared down at the patch of brown dirt that interrupted the lush green of the gentle hillside.

"What do I do now? What would you do, Dad? What would

you have taught me if she hadn't taken me away?" His voice was throaty, and he tightened his arms around his knees. "Was I wrong to let Hugh win again? He's right, but he's not all right. I can't defeat him, and I can't get close to the man with the answers. I need your help. Why aren't you here? Something's killing what I love, and I can't do anything about it." He buried his face in his arms and cried with the same helpless grief he had felt for Liz.

David was aware of her presence, but he stayed wrapped up in his grief. When she sat beside him and slid her arm around him, he toppled over and lay with his head in her lap. Her fingers teased the curl in his hair while she rubbed a gentle hand on his shoulder.

"I didn't do it, Mom. I didn't drop Casey."

"I know, David. Hugh does, too. It hurt him. I know it did."

"I don't want to talk about Hugh."

"No, I guess you don't. Casey was fantastic today. I'd never seen him show as much elegance as he did in that dressage test."

"His swan song." Pain clogged his voice. "I wish he'd jumped out of the dressage ring the way he did in our first event. It would have eliminated him, and he'd still be alive."

"Wishes and if-onlies can never change an instant that's already flown."

Sharon squeezed her son's shoulder and thought, *Not even the romance of a Breton can do that. Where are you, Marc? He's your son and he needs you. I was wrong. He believes in you and will follow your ways. I was afraid you would expose him to danger. Now he's found his own and doesn't know enough about it.*

🐎 10

David was not asleep, even if it was almost midnight. He was lying in bed, staring out the window at the black, interlaced branches of the big maple trees in the side yard. Their bud-pregnant twigs twisted and genuflected in front of the bright gleam of the moon, then cringed and shivered away from heavy, storm clouds that devoured the light.

Black clouds grappled with the moon in flashes of turmoil before the storm broke with a violence of thunder and slashing rain, punctuated by lightning so blue-white, so close, David could smell it, even taste it. When the bolt of light hit the tree across the yard, every finger of branch burned into his mind in searing black and white. With a great, wrenching crack, the old tree split down the center, pierced through its heart by the crackling bolt of unleashed energy.

David shuddered and stared at the blackness, knowing the tree was dead, killed in an instant by a weapon that vanished into the ground, leaving only the nose-pinching smell of ozone. It reminded him of Casey — big, strong, vibrant Casey. David still insisted the horse had not fallen. He was positive Casey had been too healthy for a heart attack or other physical failure. Casey had been fit and conditioned and unstressed. David could see no natural reason for what had happened.

While he lay in bed, with rain thrashing against his window, David became more and more convinced he was right. He knew he hadn't dropped Casey. The horse had been balanced and light in his hands until that horrible shudder convulsed him as if he had felt a sudden, unbearable pain.

When the storm moved farther away, its lightning shimmering beyond the ridge, David recalled the instant of flickering disruption when he approached the drop jump. It wedged itself into his mind, refusing to let him believe it was his or Casey's error. A flicker, as if a strobe light had shimmered on a fragment of mirror in front of him. The sun had been dappling through foliage. It could have been a flash of sunlight on glass or metal somewhere on the ravine bank. But somehow, it seemed to be suspended in front of him, a flicker in the air itself. He could be all wrong, but he was unable to convince himself of it. At the same time, he had nothing positive to go on.

Too many people had been poking around that jump lately. Colin, as David himself, made sense. He had to jump it. But why the bearded man in the Jeep, or the man on the motorcycle? Until now, David had been sure it was the same man. But what if it weren't? Could one be the hunter, the other his prey?

David knew Hugh had more reason for avoiding the necropsy than money or spite against him, but there was no other way to find the answer he wanted. The more he thought about it, the more he was convinced Casey had been killed in an attempt to kill him. It would have worked if the unknown disruption had not alerted him and his reflexes had not pushed him away from a foundering horse. If he had stayed on Casey's back, he would have gone over the jump and twelve hundred pounds of horse would have fallen on him. A little late, David realized he should have put more value on Colin's warnings or his mother's fears. Instead, he had continued to barge into a situation he failed to understand. Someone seemed to think he knew more than he did.

Or maybe he already knew enough but hadn't put it together right.

A quick, rapping knock on the door startled him, and he twisted to face it. "Come in." He switched on the lamp beside the bed. The door swung open into his discarded riding boots and stuck.

Hugh angled the wheel chair through the opening before he

thumped the door closed and scowled his disapproval. "How the hell can you live in this disaster area?"

"I manage." David sat on the bed, wearing only a pair of faded blue gym shorts. He tensed when he saw the cold set of Hugh's features. They showed no emotion but were hard with command. Hugh had never stopped being an officer. David guessed he never would.

When he dropped his eyes to Hugh's shadowed lap, David noticed his left hand was wrapped around the end of a shaft that was hidden beside his thigh. His insides puckered with a familiar apprehension. He knew he had angered Hugh, but he hadn't expected retaliation. The apprehension chilled into a fear impossible to quell. What if Hugh believed he had shot him? Hugh may have tried to take his own revenge and it failed. He had lost a horse, but David had survived. Did he want a confession David would never give him?

When he looked up from Hugh's hand, he shuddered deep in his guts. He knew all too well that this man could inflict more pain than he could endure.

"We don't understand each other very well, David, and we should."

"I understand fine. You're going to tell me I let Casey down, and that I have no right to defend myself from what you see as the clear truth. Bullshit. I feel right. There's no way I'll let you say I caused an accident that killed your horse. I know it wasn't an accident."

"You know it wasn't an accident?"

"I tried to tell you that, but you wanted to hurry up and bury the evidence. It made some sense then. Now it makes more sense. It wasn't just Casey who was supposed to die at that jump. You wanted me dead. Casey was a sacrifice, wasn't he? In the turmoil of the tragedy, it was easy to bury the horse and declare it an accident."

Hugh gave no answer. He just hardened. His face became rigid, the tendons in his neck tight, his massive shoulders squared. David felt trapped and tried to plan how he could keep out of Hugh's reach. There was a chance, but not a very good one. With Hugh in front of the door, he would have to tip over the wheel chair or Hugh would get to him before he could open the door. That was not as easy as it seemed. Wheel chairs were amazingly stable, designed to remain upright, especially this one, which was custom made for a very active man.

David prepared himself to put up a fight. He'd had enough of Hugh's demands for confessions. Maybe some of them were deserved, but not this one. This was a lie, even if Hugh believed it was true.

"Where's Mom?" David asked.

"She took two sleeping pills. I can't get a response out of her. But it's you I want to talk to, not your mother."

"I didn't kill your horse, and I didn't shoot you. There's no way I'll say I did, no matter what you do to me."

Hugh stared at him for a long moment before he said, "Are you sure of that?"

"Yes, I'm sure of that."

"Then I doubt if anyone could make you say otherwise."

"You're damn right." He was frightened enough to keep protesting. He knew it sounded like begging and he felt horribly out of control. "I didn't do it, even if someone's trying to make it look that way. You're not going to get what you want out of me."

"What do you think I want? Do you think I see you as my assailant?"

"You want me to confess, but I won't because I didn't do it. I hated your guts, and maybe I wanted you dead, but I couldn't kill you, not like that."

"I have never asked for more than the truth."

"But more truth than I wanted to give."

"It's a matter of viewpoints and priorities. Sometimes it's necessary to have the whole truth and nothing but the truth. It goes with law and justice, which are not concerned with one person's misplaced loyalty."

"That's more bullshit."

"David," Hugh held his gaze with deep-sea eyes that showed no anger. "I know you didn't kill Casey, just as I know you didn't shoot me. I never considered that possibility."

"You do?" He felt disoriented, spinning relief, but the apprehension was there, telling him something was still wrong.

"I have a good idea who shot me, or had me shot, but I can only wait. He has to show himself by making a wrong move, or a right one. If he does that, I hope Leon and I recognize it in time and make the right moves."

"What do you want from me?"

"Something beside enmity, like cooperation."

"Does that mean blind obedience no matter how I feel?"

Hugh shook his head slowly and let a skeptical smile twist his lips. "That is an impossibility."

"If you knew it wasn't my fault Casey's dead, why did you publicly blame me? It was a low blow."

"I know, and I'm sorry. When you get righteous, the only way I can get you to shut up is to get you mad. You lost your temper and forgot the arguments that sounded too convincing. David, I didn't want him to know I believed you."

"Him?" An image of a bearded man slipping behind the trailer flashed through David's mind, along with the quick dart of Hugh's gaze.

"My nemesis. If my guess, which is somewhat researched, is right, he was listening to everything we said. I've been expecting him to try again, but only at me. Liz was a shock, and I never expected him to attack you. It was all wrong and threw my reasoning into a scramble. I really felt the fall was an accident until you started denying it, and I had to keep showing that I didn't believe you. I was on edge, and for the first time I was afraid for someone else. I've never wanted you dead, David. I've occasionally wished you were more like me, but never dead."

"Why are you afraid for me?"

"If my suspicions are right, we're not dealing with a rational man."

"What do you mean?"

"All along I've felt you and your mother were safe because I believed it was your father."

"Never." David recoiled. "There's no way he'd do anything like that."

"I don't really know. I've never met the man. I felt he was capable of shooting me, but I never thought he'd try to kill his own son. I did think I knew that much about him. I'm sorry you hate my guts. I'm sorry we can't understand each other better. I never believed you shot me, even when some other people tried to convince me you did, but I can believe you wanted to be free of me. God knows, I wanted to eliminate my own father a few times when he made me eat my pride or humiliated me in front of my peers."

"I see no reason for either." David sensed that Hugh was uncomfortable and realized it was because he was still edgy. He felt a nagging tension that made him keep glancing at Hugh's hand where he had seen that slim shaft.

"You have a different view of discipline than I do," Hugh said.

"Is that what it is? Discipline?" David shifted toward the edge of the bed, ready to bolt as soon as Hugh made a move. "Is it because I called you a son of a bitch? Is that what brings you up here with that fucking riding whip? Am I too inferior to express an opinion against you?"

"What?" Hugh recoiled. "I didn't come up here with any of the intentions you've tried to give me."

"Oh?" David eyed him warily. "This isn't a punitive visit?"

"I came to show you something and explain where I've been." Hugh lifted a small diameter cardboard tube and carefully fished out a thin, polished, steel shaft that was about ten inches long with a tapered, knife-sharp head at one end, a precision milled notch and fine fins at the other. "Do you know what this is?"

David made a sour face. "It looks like a nasty hunting arrow, only too short, as if isn't all there."

"You're close. It's a specially made bolt from a crossbow. They are illegal for hunting in this state because they are extremely accurate and horribly destructive. This one was designed for total penetration — a silent weapon that conceals itself in its victim."

"Where did you get it? Where have you been?" Replaced by curiosity, David's tension unwound like a released spring.

"I've been at Westridge Veterinary Clinic with Dr. Acheson, and this was in Casey. It entered his chest, tore through his heart and abdominal cavity then lodged itself in his spleen. The wound was unnoticed because his chest was badly lacerated when he fell against the jump."

"But Matt buried Casey."

"Matt buried a horse that had died at the clinic. We buried

Casey on our west forty when we were finished. I'd already agreed to do a necropsy with Dr. Acheson before I made a point of saying I didn't want one. I used you, David. The accusation was cruel but you backed me into a corner and blaming you seemed to be the easiest way out. I tried to let you know I felt you were right. As it turns out, you were absolutely right. He died under you. Only his tremendous impulsion sent him over that fence. If you hadn't acted as fast as you did, you would likely be dead, too."

"Where would anyone get a crossbow?" David gave Hugh a puzzled look and his mind filled with the sensations of a medieval fair with knights and colorful pageantry.

"They aren't hard to buy or make. But you know as well as I who has several crossbows. He competes with them as well as with more standard bows."

"Leon." The images of snapping pennons against green, English hills dissolved when he answered. "He's also good enough to hit whatever he aims at precisely when and where he wants to."

"Exactly what Detective Stanwyck said."

"When?"

"When we found the bolt. The two police officers were insistent about attending Dr. Acheson's late night surgery. They've been on this case since November. They've missed very little."

"Are they the only ones on it?"

"They indicated as much." Hugh gave a huffing laugh. "I'm not worth all that much to our law enforcers. And it isn't the only case they've been on. Actually, I wasn't aware anyone was assigned to it until today. They arrested Leon on suspicion of attempted homicide, which I don't like. Leon didn't do it and I don't like being without him."

"They don't believe you?"

"They say they don't. I'd sent Leon to the farm before Casey was killed, so I couldn't swear I knew where he was. I think they believe, as you did, that I think you shot me, even though I told them I don't. They suspect you shot me and that Leon tried to kill you for me. It's a shaky theory at best, and I don't know why they're using it, except that someone seems to be very interested in blaming it on you. It is a neat solution. Blame you for shooting me, then get rid of you and blame it on Leon. Neat, tidy, logical, but wrong."

"The first part is. I'm willing to believe the second part is, too."

"Could it have anything to do with a tan Jeep the police ran off Ridgeway Road this afternoon?"

"The driver?" David felt his nerves tightened.

"He was no where to be found. He never seems to be anywhere. Everyone has seen him somewhere, but no one can say anything about him. He has a beard, wears thick, dark glasses. Otherwise, he appears to be totally normal, so normal no one remembers anything about him."

"He had coffee with Liz and Pam. Pam said he was just a normal man." David shrugged at Hugh's frustrated expression. "They thought he was a cop. So did I."

"The police don't. They want him badly. I would guess Leon's arrest is to draw him out, but it makes me feel naked."

"I don't think he's the killer, but he's important."

"Why don't you think he's the killer?" Hugh asked.

"He's a stranger with nothing to gain."

"He could have been hired to kill me."

"Then he'd have disappeared after he failed. The killer is someone we know. He can't disappear, and he's guilty." David let his thoughts open up. Hugh was receptive and agreeing. "Or else he's some kind of psycho with a guilty compulsion to wipe out anyone too suspicious. If it's the bearded man, he's a nut. Maybe he hates your planes. Maybe he's a fired employee, or has some other grievance. He could have hated you in Nam."

"Any of that is possible."

"But I don't feel that way about him."

"Did you notice anything about him that was unusual?"

"Only the thick, tinted glasses." He could see that his answer was not what Hugh wanted to hear. "I've seen him at a distance. Hell, I damn near ran into him at school. He's plain and normal, as everyone said. Sort of a Columbo figure. After you see him, you don't remember him." He smiled. "If it wasn't for the beard and funky glasses, he'd probably be invisible."

"Reed and Stanwyck only found out about him from your

mother last week. He disappeared until today."

"I think he may have been on a motorcycle Thursday, but I'm not sure."

"They've been looking for the Jeep all week. It turns out it had stolen plates from a totaled Bronco belonging to a man in Plymouth, who's been in the hospital since his accident on Thanksgiving weekend. The Bronco was towed to a field and left with a collection of other junked vehicles. No one knew the plates were missing. They can't find anything on the Jeep itself."

"I know less than you do, but something tells me I only need one insight and it will all fit together. Liz saw a man with a gun the day she came to meet me at the cabin."

"That's where Liz fit in."

"Yeah, but the meeting wasn't only to make a little grass transaction. It would have torqued me if you'd busted in on us."

"Maybe I'd have waited until she left."

David's laugh was sarcastic. "Ha! Not you, Captain America, legal avenger and protector of American moral myths."

"I have respect for the privacy of some liaisons. I wanted to prove you'd been lying to me. Now you seem willing to admit it."

"I quit peddling it a long time ago. It's not safe to stay in that game. You get known too well and are expendable. It served its purpose. When I got a free ticket to Liz, I stopped using her for business and tried to get her off drugs."

"Are you saying Liz could identify the man?"

"I don't know if she could or not. Nothing she told me was helpful. She didn't really get a good look at him. She had no reason to and was more worried about the rough trail. Maybe he thought she could. Over the winter, she remembered less and less about everything."

David looked into green eyes that were calmly judging with the unabashed direct stare that often made him squirm with guilty discomfort. He no longer felt guilty, but he did feel uncomfortable. He had never tried to see things from Hugh's view. "I can't help you, Hugh, but I can sure as hell sense some of what you've been living with. How do you cope with the cold, clawing feeling that someone may be out to kill you?"

"I look over my shoulder a lot. I like having Leon nearby." His

face relaxed when David softened the intensity of his stare. "I
lived with it in Nam a lot. I wasn't always sure which side the fire
would come from. When you take away the rules and force men to
be killers, you can't always be sure whom they see as the enemy.
I understand resentment. Cowards, assassins, or nuts shoot men
in the back. Your kind meets a son of a bitch head on. If you lose,
you lick your wounds, pick yourself up, and try again when you're
stronger. I'm not sure which we're up against, but I wouldn't out
rule any of the motives you mentioned. I'm not without enemies.
I do know it isn't Leon Williams, and without him, we're
vulnerable."

"Hugh, we still don't see the world through the same lenses,
but if it makes any difference, I no longer see you as a complete
son of a bitch."

"It makes a difference." Hugh smiled with a warmth he had
not shown around David for a long time. "You're not always an
arrogant brat either. Sometimes, you're downright charming.
However, I would like to give you one item of practical advise."
Hugh cleared his throat and looked serious. "Run the wheel down
on the jack."

"Huh?" It made absolutely no sense to David.

"It stabilizes the trailer and minimizes sway."

"I can't pull a trailer with the wheel down. It—" With a jolt
of revelation, he knew what Hugh was talking about. David rarely
showed embarrassment, but, when the first jolt of realization
flashed into a hot blush, he felt mortified. "Oh Christ!" He
flopped back against the pillows with his hands over his face for a
moment, then rolled onto his elbow. "How obvious was it?"

"It was obvious that the trailer was active. I happened to see
her walking over there earlier when I was looking for your mother.
I forgot it until Bruce started chuckling over it. When Harold
noticed us, I told Bruce to go stop Casey from rubbing on the other
side of the trailer." His grin was slow. "Babcock was too busy
running an event to worry about anything else. There were a lot
of things I could distract him with."

"I'm glad of that." David gave him a grateful look.

"I am concerned with your welfare, which is why I have some
personal advice, too. Keep away from that girl. You're playing

with a loaded pistol. Harold thinks that piece is still hermetically sealed in purity. I wouldn't want to be around if he learned otherwise. I sure wouldn't want to be the one he put the blame on."

"That bad, huh?"

"That man would kick your ass so hard and for so long you wouldn't sit a horse for a month. And her three older brothers would help him. They see her as a perfect bauble of pristine virtue."

"She sure is." David gave him a look of exaggerated assurance. "And I'm the Easter Bunny."

When David left the house and jogged to the equipment shed, the grass was wet from the storm and a bright moon flashed on and off behind fleeing dark clouds. He took the newest pickup because it was the quietest and waited until he reached the road to switch on the lights. He had no explanation for why he felt he had to go there, and when he thought about it, he realized it was probably a foolish move. He also knew it was the only way he was going to get any sleep.

After Hugh left, David had tried to sleep, but every time he was almost asleep, or maybe just after he fell asleep, the fear would return in a terrifying replay. The flicker of disruption before the jump was as cataclysmic as the lightning bolt that had split the tree across the yard and he woke up shaking and afraid, with an image of the coffin drop looming like a death trap in front of him. He disliked being afraid and knew that next to riding another horse over the jump, which he planned to do tomorrow, the only thing that would help was to go back to the coffin drop and see it for what it was. He had to reface the obstacle and stop seeing it as a horror magnified beyond reality. He was reluctant to face it tomorrow when there would be people there — people morbidly curious, people mildly curious, and curious people showing other curious people.

David drove beyond the bridge below the jump, backed to the end of the road, and parked the truck in the cul de sac. When he shut off the engine, he glanced at the steel box bolted to the floor beside his right leg. He had no solid reason, but an intuitive apprehension made him find the key under the dash and open the box. He drew Hugh's gun out of its case and stared at the three-fifty-seven magnum revolver for a moment while he thought about what it meant and why he felt a need for it. Had he lost his self-assurance? Or was it because he realized he was no longer playing a game? An unsettling sixth sense told him he was not the only person interested in the coffin drop tonight. Was it right? Or was it an outgrowth of his knowledge that someone had tried to kill him here?

Whatever the reason, real or imagined, he decided he would feel better with the gun than without it. He was familiar with it and, thanks to Hugh, more than a competent marksman. His stepfather had first taught him to shoot with shotguns, then rifles, and finally, hand guns. David snapped open the cylinder and filled it from the box of shells beside its case. As an afterthought, he slipped the remaining shells into the pocket of his nylon jacket. When he stepped from the truck, he thrust the gun under his belt and swung the door closed.

David avoided the road and hiked up the steep ravine to the trail so he could approach the jump from the top, the way he had on Casey. He jumped down the Three Steps and stopped to stare at the coffin drop. The terror faded and he relaxed. It was a jump, a little amplified in the shadows from the low moon that floated just above the trees on the western rim of the ravine, but just a jump.

David felt no terror anywhere. It was a gentle night with no wind. The occasional sound of water dripping from trees and the steady background rush of the stream below him were the only reminders of the storm that had crashed through the area a few hours ago. He started to smile and walked forward, casually relaxed, wondering why he had let his imagination build to such a peak of anxiety. He had a habit of doing that, the way he had with Hugh tonight. It made him feel a little foolish. He should have known Hugh would never try to strong-arm him over something as horrendous as murder.

He even chided himself for seeing killers in everyone, finding motives by obscure thinking. It was all telling on him, and today it had peaked. He lost his cool by fighting with Hugh instead of stopping to think. And later, he let his imagination create fear when there was no reason for it. Coming here helped put it into proper perspective and made him see that the worse fear was fear of his own making. Things could be faced when taken as they were. He would not make the same mistake again. He felt too foolish.

With his mind drifting to the possibility of tempting another kind of danger by trying to wake Annie, David started down the hill to the logs of the jump. He had forgotten about his promise to meet Annie while he had been on edge about how Casey had been killed. Now that he knew and had faced down his fear, he was tired of being alone. He wanted to talk to someone about it and, he had to admit, he wanted some sympathy, a little coddling, a shoulder to cry on. Annie had nice shoulders and would make him feel he could still give love.

Before he reached the jump, David saw movement in the darkness ahead of him. Someone was crouched in the shadows on his side of the jump. The form was barely discernible, but it was beckoning to him. It had a stage whisper voice, "David, get down and come here."

Any hope that it was Annie crashed when he recognized Colin's voice. He was disappointed and irritated. It seemed Colin popped up like an unwanted weed at all the wrong times. He ducked forward and hurried to him. "Colin, what the hell are you doing here?"

"I could ask you the same."

"I had to face it again."

"David, I was no more satisfied with Hugh dismissing it as an act of God than you were. It seemed to me you knew what you were talking about."

"That's not what you said Thursday."

"Yes, it is. I saw you heading for trouble then, which is why I tried to warn you away from looking too hard. Tonight, the whole thing kept niggling at me until I had to come here and put it together."

"Why? What's it to you?" David had resented Colin's prying before. Now it irritated him. It even made him uneasy enough to doubt Colin's answers.

"Your mother pulled me into it. I found I couldn't turn my back any more than you could. When I came to set things straight, I ran into a problem. Someone was already here, someone claiming a weapon he'd left earlier. Casey didn't fall, David. He was shot."

"I know. With a crossbow. The cops arrested Leon. Hugh's hopping mad. He swears it wasn't Leon and losing Leon leaves him without a bodyguard."

"How do you know?" Colin grabbed his arm and twisted him to face him.

David looked at the face that was an indistinct form in the darkness. "Hugh made a lot of noise about burying Casey without a necropsy, but it was all a lie. Dr. Acheson did it at the clinic. They found a crossbow bolt in Casey."

"What's in that grave?" Colin sounded confused. "I saw it when I took Limerick home for your mother."

"A little out of your way, wasn't it?"

"I was curious. And," Colin looked grim. "I suppose I wanted to pay a last private respect to a valiant horse."

"It's a horse from the clinic. Casey's buried in the orchard on the west forty. Hugh feels he knows who did it. He didn't want him to know he was suspicious."

"Hugh's smarter than I thought."

"Yeah, I had to accept that myself. He's been doing a lot of research on the whole thing, but he and Leon have kept it to themselves. The truck's down there with the keys in it." David pointed down the brush-covered slope beyond the end of the jump. "Why don't we get the hell out of here?"

"Because that bastard is down there with his crossbow. I caught him trying to stash it in his pack. I knew better than to stay in the open, but I only got this far before he had it ready to shoot."

"I don't think there's anyone else here." David slipped his hand under his jacket and fingered the shape of the gun's handgrip, found the loop of the trigger guard. "Why hasn't he come after you? Are you armed?"

"No. He was coming after me until you drove over the bridge.

That's when he ducked into the brush."

"Maybe he left."

"He won't leave while I'm alive. I saw him too well and know the truth."

"Who the hell is it?"

"That bastard with the beard."

"Maybe you aren't armed, but I am. That son of a bitch has given me the slip once too often." David pulled the gun out from under his belt and held it cradled in his right hand.

"Can you shoot it well enough to hit anything?" Colin gave the gun a skeptical look when he crouched beside David.

"I did all right with it on cans and bottles. I've popped off a lot of rats in the barns with a .22 pistol. People are a lot bigger, and he isn't more than sixty meters from us. It was only thirty to the course turn. If he knows he's facing a gun like this, I think he'll let us go. I want some answers from him."

"David, don't be an ass." Colin snapped at him. "He's a killer. He won't let us go. If we show, he'll kill us. He has the bow. He may have a gun, too. Do you think you can pick him off if he shows himself? He knows I don't have a gun. He has no reason to believe you do."

"Do you want to shoot him?" David asked while he studied the heavy brush through a gap between the butt ends of two of the logs in the jump. He had thought of the gun as a device of threat, not a weapon of death. He was still confused about Colin, but the man was beginning to make sense, especially when he thought about how Hugh had been shot in the back, Liz held under water until she drowned, and Tim pushed into a suicide attempt by a threat to expose his homosexuality. "I'll bait him if you want to shoot him."

"I'm afraid I'm not very good with a gun." Colin cleared his throat. His voice was rough with embarrassment. "I always thought guns were rather nasty things. I'm bloody awful with a gun."

While David listened to his apologetic tone, misgiving clouded his thoughts. Things in his mind were unsettled. He wanted answers. "Why did you sleep with my mother?" he asked what had been annoying him since he overheard the conversation outside the trailer.

Colin looked stunned, then recovered and shrugged. "She thought it was a good idea at the time."

"Didn't you have a wife?" David was perplexed. "You've been here almost a year. Until today, I never remembered you had a wife in England."

"She died. Very nasty car crash. Hit a lorry head on. She'd been drinking. Sybil did a lot of drinking. Port. Sickly sweet stuff. Always made me gag." When David made no response, Colin continued to talk, but he was nervous and kept looking around like a trapped rodent. "I never regretted my affairs. She was a consummate bitch. I say, David, wouldn't it be better if I catch his attention by making a dash for the brambles right of the jump? From there, I can slither on down the hill and draw him toward the road."

"You'd have to be fast." David jerked his mind back to the immediate problem, letting his misgivings dissolve into the back of his mind. Colin was an ass, but he could use him.

"Precisely my thought." Confidence crept into Colin's tone. "I feel fairly safe with you covering me. After all, we have to do something. By splitting up, we'll force him into making a move. I trust you to protect me if he tries to kill me. Remember, it takes several seconds to reload that bloody bow. He can't get us both unless he also has a gun. If I were you, I wouldn't take that chance."

"I won't let him kill you."

Colin let out a slow breath before he said, "If I make it over the edge, I'll be out of his sight. He'll have to move toward the bridge to locate me when I reach the road. Watch that opening where they dozered through for the maintenance road. He'll have to cross it or the stream. It's running deep there and the rain spread it enough to muck up the banks." He grasped David's free hand and shook it. "Make sure you drill him a few times if he shows. I don't want one of those barbarous things in me."

"Don't worry about that, Colin. At that range, it would go clean through you almost anywhere it hit."

"Thanks for the kind thought."

"Any time." When he looked at Colin, David realized he could see him more clearly. He wasn't sure he wanted him for an ally, but he was the only one available. "You better do it. It's getting light."

"You've a damn cool head on you, lad. I'm glad I'm not the one facing your gun."

"He killed my girl. He killed my horse. He tried to kill my stepfather, my best friend, and me. I'm cool enough to blow the mother-fucker to hell if I have to. Now split, will you?" He gave Colin a sharp, tense look just before he moved away.

David may have been cool and hard on the outside. Inside, he was a tight wad of agitation that refused to relax. It was Colin who was cool, and that calm bravery amazed David. He had always seen Colin as a bungling wimp. Now he was forced to reconsider. He could see that Colin was low-key, proper rather than macho, blasé on the surface, flint hard underneath.

David felt the tension, hard and tight in the back of his neck, while he waited with his eyes steady on the tangle of swamp maples where he knew his target was waiting with a weapon that had torn the life out of a half ton horse in full gallop. He was tense, but he was sharp, steady, ready to destroy any threat to the man he had promised to protect. He knew he couldn't kill for no reason, but he felt he could do it in defense of himself or a friend.

Out of the corner of his eye, David saw Colin reach the end of the jump and crouch for the leap that would send him out into the open. He would have two strides without cover before he could dive into the scrubby brush and scramble down the other side of the cleared area around the jump.

David pressed his back against an anchoring post and, keeping another post in front of him, inched himself up until he was standing with the gun gripped in his hand. He could lift it and shoot in an instant. When he saw Colin spring from behind the logs, he drew in a breath and held it, counting off slow seconds. He felt suspended in a time vacuum where nothing was happening. He waited, frozen in brittle tension, watching for a movement that would spring him into action.

It was faint at first, an unconscious awareness of something totally incongruous. He shook his head with a quick jerk, but it refused to go away, only became more obvious. He tried to tell himself it was something in the sound of the stream, but it was too persistent. He insisted it was his imagination playing tricks on him, an unconscious need for courage. It was a melody, his melody, low, but clear, filling him with gnawing indecision, cutting away at his confidence, breaking down courage, not supporting it.

Colin was gone, safely over the hill. David saw movement and raised the gun. It was too far to the left, away from the bridge, not closer to it, as if the man were ignoring Colin and coming for him. He braced his back against the hard cedar post, holding the gun in front of him with straight, but unlocked arms. His left hand closed around his right wrist. The gun butt was hard against the heel of his right hand and he sighted along the top of the barrel at the brush that was showing too much motion in the windless dawn. The gun was steady, right on target. If he shot now, he would hit the man before he could do anything. He held his position while he remembered Hugh's words, "You don't shoot what moves. You shoot what threatens. You can't take back a bullet. It's the final word."

It was louder, in a clear whistle. It came from directly in front of him. The man grew out of the brush, empty-handed, casual. He was whistling the haunting, catchy French melody from David's past, the melody that was a part of him and could lift his spirits, remind him of the man who had taught it to him. While the man walked toward him with an assurance that projected authority, not normality, David felt weak, shaky. This was a man with a sure bearing, a man who was remembered. He pressed his lips together and felt his eyes burn with tears. He told himself to do something, make a decision. The walk was right. The gait had catlike balance and spring. Very slowly, with a heavy, numb sensation, he lowered the gun until it pointed at the ground. He stared down the slope in a trance. Uncontrolled tears ran down his face.

The man continued to walk toward him and lifted his right hand. He pointed his index finger at the brush he had left and pantomimed shooting a gun. He did it three times, clearly and distinctly. David hesitated, then understood. When the man stepped toward the rise of the ravine wall, David aimed at the brush and squeezed the trigger, once, twice, a third time.

While the sound of the last shot echoed in the ravine, David looked at the man standing beside the churned, rain-eroded ground below the jump. He was a wide-shouldered man in dark jeans, dark turtleneck shirt, with a square-trimmed black beard. Black hair showed touches of grey and the brightening day erased shadows from strong-boned features and brightened violet-blue eyes. The unobtrusive, easily forgotten man had evaporated. He had been an act, a dull cloak to conceal a vibrant man, who had never seemed normal or insignificant.

Thrusting the gun under his belt, David vaulted the jump and landed crouched. As if a spring released in his chest, uncertainty vanished, and he lunged forward. Hard arms wrapped around him, crushing him against a strong chest that was heaving with emotion. It was an embrace that felt good, familiar, and right. There were no doubts or misgivings. This was Marc Breton, and David knew he would have the right answers.

"Dad, I almost shot you."

"He was betting on it." Marc's voice was low and thick. A flood of intense feeling emanated from him, engulfing David with its power.

When the arms relaxed and the lump of emotion released his voice, David gaped at his father. "Colin?" He reeled with stunned disbelief. "It was Colin?"

"Yes. Colin." The answer was a flat statement of fact.

"I saw him as a harmless ass."

"You're reading emotions and using them for motives. Colin doesn't have any. He only does what's good for Colin with no regrets when someone gets hurt."

After what seemed too short a time, Marc released his embrace and held David in front of him with strong hands gripping his shoulders. "I want you to keep that gun ready to use when you go toward where I'm supposed to be and don't for an instant take your eyes off Colin. I want to catch him alive, but I don't want anyone else hurt. I've screwed it up enough already."

"Colin doesn't have a gun."

"The hell he doesn't."

"He says he's a poor shot." David's mind was still a muddle of confusion.

"He was piss poor with a shotgun. I'll give you that. Don't believe him. Colin can shoot. Now yell for him. Tell him you got me. Make a scene about it. You're upset because you just killed a man. Get a little hysterical, but don't overdo it or loose your edge on him."

David nodded, then shouted in a strained voice, "Colin, I hit him. Help me with him." He paused and heard nothing, so he started yelling with more hysteria in his voice. "Oh God, I think he's dead. Colin, where are you?"

When David stopped in the road below the jump, the door slammed on the pickup truck. He turned to his father, who watched him with a perplexed expression.

When the truck started, Marc stepped next to David and turned him with a firm hand on his shoulder. "Did you leave the keys in the truck?"

"Yeah, I did." His blush engulfed him. "It was a damn fool thing to do, right?"

"Right. I hope you're agile and can haul ass at a run."

When the truck skittered around the turn to the bridge, Marc dropped his hands and ran to where he had been hiding in the brush. He picked up the crossbow he had thrust under a bush, disassembled it, and slipped it, in pieces, into his nylon pack. "Let's move it, David. It's a hairy trip down that stream bed. We'll have to burn it at a run to beat Colin to his own car."

"We're going to run down that stream? It's a fucking waterfall." David gaped at him.

"Not quite. I've been up it twice. Do you have another idea? It looks as if we missed the last tram." Marc paused and lifted a hand to hush David. "Did you hear the truck jouncing over the rutted part of the road?" When David shook his head, Marc said, "Give me that gun and scream no in the loudest, most horrible way you can."

Marc took the revolver and, when David threw back his head and let out a bellow of pain and horror, pointed it at the ground. He fired one shot that shattered the woods with its rudeness.

"Let's get the hell out of here." He thrust the gun into his pack and, swinging it onto his back, ran toward the stream.

11

David was sure he was following a mountain goat when he descended the stream bed behind Marc, who never seemed to waste a motion or miss a step and was there to catch his son's arm a few times when he missed a step. When they started, David was sure they would never make it down the steep, rocky cut that was a torrent of spraying water. While they were going down, he was concentrating so hard on following his father's moves as exactly as he could that he was aware of nothing else. At last, he was standing at the bottom, soaking wet, with his arm held out in front of him while Marc wrapped a handkerchief around a bleeding gash on his forearm. Seconds later they scaled the embankment to the road and were off at a run down the gravel shoulder.

By the time David reached the white Triumph, Marc was in it with the engine running. David jerked open the passenger door and flopped into the seat, slamming the door. The car leapt toward the road, fishtailing and spraying gravel before its tires bit on the pavement. Rubber squealed and the car shot forward.

For the first few minutes, David sat with his arms wrapped around his ribs, sucking air into his heaving lungs.

"Some people sure are out of shape." David blushed when he heard the rolling chuckle that had teased him for most of his life.

"Did we really do that?"

"I know I did."

"Did Colin leave his keys in the car, too?"

191

"I have my own set. When I know I might need sudden transportation, I make it a point to have keys that fit cars belonging to people I'm going to be near. I have keys for this, Hugh's Buick, your mother's Mustang, and both your pickups, as well as Liz's car and Honda."

"That wasn't Liz's Honda you had Thursday." David gave him a sideways glance.

"I bought that baby. It's the old, 'Be prepared' Boy Scout in me."

"You were a Boy Scout?"

"For a while in Washington. I tried to join the Girl Scouts, but they were kind of shitty about that then. I kept pushing for camping in small co-ed tents."

David turned to look at his father and pulled in a sharp breath. He grabbed the bar on the dash when the car rounded a curve in a four-wheel drift. Marc casually corrected it with a slip of the wheel and a quick acceleration when it came out of the curve.

"You've forgotten the Alps already?"

"I forgot your driving." David jerked out his seat belt and fastened it. "I spent most of my childhood wondering why my mother always looked like a ghost in the car."

"This is a nice handling car. Colin has changed his image from the carriage class to the jet set, from Bentley's to TR-7's. But if he wants your mother, he's paddling in the wrong channel."

"She already told him that."

"Good for her. She wasn't so smart last time."

"You knew about that?" David dug a crumpled pack of cigarettes out of his shirt pocket and found that after the first few deteriorated in soggy ruin, there were some dry ones farther in the pack. "She thinks you didn't know."

"Your mother doesn't sin very well, even when she thinks she has a right to."

"But you do?"

"Sinning is in the mind of the sinner. I never felt I was sinning." When David started to light the cigarette, Marc reached across the car, plucked it out of his mouth, and flipped it out the open window. "Don't get another one."

"What the hell is with you?" David fired up like a splashed cat. "I don't happen to feel I'm sinning by smoking."

"But I feel I am by letting you."

"Well, that's too bad. It's my choice, not yours." David snapped. "I don't need someone telling me how to take care of myself."

"That's what you think."

"It sure is." With a huff of defiance, he jerked the cigarette pack out of his pocket. The fist that thudded onto his chest didn't hurt much, but it knocked the wind out of him and made him cough. He was powerless against the hard fingers that twisted the pack out of his hand and crushed it into a wad of useless trash that dropped into his lap.

"Put it in your pocket. I don't want it left in the car." Marc stared ahead at the road while David glared at him with hot anger. "I see you're still stubborn enough to get your ass kicked."

"I'm not a damn kid any more."

"I certainly hope not. I don't want a kid. I want a partner I can rely on."

"For what?" David lost his anger when his father's words jolted him.

"Right now to corner this rat and serve him up with giblets and gravy."

"You really think Colin shot Hugh? Colin is such a nothing." He was still trying to sort out the truth. Marc's appearance had jumbled things up so much he lost the thread of credibility.

"I know Colin shot Hugh, but the law needs more than my word for it," Marc answered. "He could throw it on me even better than on you. I wanted to stop him, but I got here too late."

"How did you know before it happened?"

"I didn't know. I took a highly educated guess. Colin likes to brag. It's his weakest link. I guess he felt safe in telling an old friend in Devon about a scheme to go to America and take up with an old flame, who had conveniently married a rich old codger he didn't think would last long."

"He had the wrong Hugh Jamison. I heard him tell Mom about that."

"Which is why I didn't connect it then. I knew which one she married. You see, the old friend also knows me and loves to gossip about Colin, whom he sees as a local scandal. Colin is the illegitimate son of a housemaid, who committed suicide two days after he was born, and the local vicar. The vicar's rich, horsy sister took Colin in and raised him with *beaucoup des riches*. She was a sour-faced hag, who kept telling him she only did it for the honor of her brother, the vicar, who'd been bewitched by Colin's demented mother — a fifteen year old cottage girl, who was reported to be a touch retarded and terrified of the vicar when she worked for him. The vicar's sister spent a lot of time exorcising Colin in her own ways. At an opportune time, the poor lady fell down her front stairs and broke her neck. Colin came out of it with a comfortable fortune at twenty-two. Shortly after her death, the vicar's fishing boat capsized off the coast. His body washed up on the rocks a few days later. Colin's first wife was kicked in the head by an unreceptive mare in season when a stallion dragged the frail woman up behind the mare. No one, Colin included, knew why the mare was cross tied in the aisle. That wife was an heiress. Colin got the fortune. The second wife, Sybil—"

"Hit a lorry head on while drunk on port." David finished the sentence.

"Very good. A lawyer she'd been running around with was in the car with her. There had been talk of a divorce before the accident. She had money, too."

"And I told Mom he was a clinger, but not dangerous."

"You underestimate the workings of a devious mind. He's the most dangerous kind of scoundrel — one with no passions, only greed."

"Hugh said cowards, assassins, and nuts shoot in the back."

"Colin's a little nuts, a lot of coward." Marc nodded his agreement. "When I realized what Colin was up to, I didn't want your mother to be number three wife. I didn't even want her to be an eligible widow à la Colin Trombley. I didn't feel it would be smart to let her husband know about her previous relationship with Colin, so I tried to get to her father when he was in Zurich. I thought he could tell her to keep her guard up around Colin and let him know she wanted no part of him. Old C.C. not only slammed the door in my face, he threatened to torpedo my chances for an acquittal that had become very important to me. My first reaction was, `Fuck-off, Charlie-baby, it's not my life any more.'"

"But you didn't give up."

"I tried, but it wasn't so simple. It was still my life. I knew that people who could help or hurt Colin somehow ended up dead. It wasn't only that my ex-wife was a likely victim, my son was, too. Colin doesn't like to share his wealth. If your mother thinks I'm good at spending money, she should see what Colin can do with a fortune. Once you start pouring it into those four-legged haybags, you can't damn up the outflow. I supported your mother's and your habit long enough to know, and she wasn't trying to breed the ultimate English race horse the way Colin is. He has a breeding farm in Devon that would bankrupt an earl."

"But how did you figure it was Mom? You said you knew she wasn't married to an old codger."

"Colin wrote to his friend to say that even though the husband wasn't the old bugger he expected, he had a feeling things would work out. When I saw the Wellington, Michigan postmark, things started to click. That's when I tried to send a warning."

"Why didn't you just write Mom or me?" David's question was a short, indignant scoff.

"I wasn't sure she would believe me." Marc's face twisted with discomfort, his eyes deepened. "She often accused me of seeing too much evil in people. Colin was one of those people. She saw him as unfortunate and wronged because of the situation of his birth. The way people kept dying when it was convenient for him was merely coincidence to her. Like you, she saw him as a harmless hanger-on, a pleasant, well-mannered person of little consequence — an image Colin takes great effort to preserve. I tried your grandfather again in October and had no more success. Since I'd become a pariah to him, I suspected I may have gained the same status with your mother. She may have rebelled against him at one point, but she always respected him and loved him as a father."

"But he sent you to prison." David twisted to face Marc. His chest was tight with the bitterness he had felt toward his grandfather since he had overheard the conversation with Hugh last summer.

"Where did you get that idea?" Marc swept a startled glance at David, then back to the road. "I went to prison because I was arrested at the airport with two kilos of heroin in my possession."

"You really had it?"

"Of course I really had it. They couldn't arrest and convict me without evidence. I had it, but I didn't know I had it. The other woman wasn't happy with my decision to run to my wife." A sly smile grew from his twisted frown. "Fortunately, I had enough information that another agent could take up where I left off and expose her as a link in the drug trade."

"She went to prison?"

"Shot herself to avoid arrest."

"But what did Granfather do? He told Hugh he could keep you away from Mom."

"It was not so much what your grandfather did that harmed me. It was what he stopped doing." He paused to give David a thoughtful look. "I'm telling you this because I don't want you to continue to condemn your grandfather. If it became known to some people, he could be ruined. Your grandfather supplies, services, and programs a network of computers used by Interpol. All information concerning me was put into a computer file. Your grandfather coded the file so it would only release information he flagged for release. There were times when I became involved in illegal matters. Charles Collingwood protected me by making certain information unavailable. When I was arrested, he had no choice. He had to make my total file available. Some of it helped convict me."

"But how was he keeping you from Mom?"

"By keeping my name prominent as an undesirable alien. Charles risked a great deal to protect me because he loved his daughter, who loved me. I don't condemn him for anything he did."

"But he pulled it away when you most needed it."

"He didn't love me, or do it for me. He did it for your mother. He pulled away when he risked discovery and believed I was guilty."

"But you were an Interpol agent."

"*Au contraire.* I was always an independent agent. Interpol keeps records. It has no power and no agents. I never gave your grandfather any reason to believe I was a narcotics agent for anyone. Your mother didn't even know how involved I was."

"Why did they let you go to jail?"

"Interference would have endangered other agents. When it was no longer a danger, they helped. David, it isn't glory. Most of it is hell. I preferred to keep that part of my life to myself."

"Why are you telling me?"

"I'm no longer a narcotics agent. It's in the past. Let's consider the present. When I got no where with your grandfather, I tried to forget it. Then I heard, in a round about way, about Hugh's accident. I decided to nail the bastard, not just scare him onto someone else. The only way to do that was to go to Michigan myself. I was here for a while last fall learning what I could and getting familiar with the area, but I couldn't stay. Colin was laying low after covering his tracks too well with the only trail pointing at you."

"You could have looked me up." David cut at him.

"Not then. I checked you out and didn't like all that I learned." He looked sideways fast enough to catch David's wince. "You seem to have shaped up and set your feet on solid ground this spring. I had to leave because I'd slipped into Florida on a pleasure boat belonging to some people who thought they'd picked up the victim of a swamped sailboat. My acquittal was still in chambers, and I didn't want to blow it. I came back a month ago, with a clean record, after a stop in Mexico for some plastic surgery and to regrow the beard I'd shaved off after leaving here in December."

"Why the beard?"

"The left side of my face looks as if I lost a slapping contest with a barbed wire fence. The beard was a good disguise, since I'd never had one before. I'm even fond of it now."

"What happened to you?" David watched Marc's expression harden, and for the first time, he saw signs of age in the strong face. He regretted the question when the silence grew and he saw pain tighten his father's features.

With his son's question echoing through his mind, Marc turned to see a troubled face that was like a haunting image in a mirror from the past. He tried to remember how it had felt to be like David — young, sure that his efforts would make the world a better place, ready to strike a crippling blow against corruption. There was little of the ideal left. Twenty years later, he saw it all on a reduced scale of realism, where the victories were small inroads and did little more than hold the line and maintain a balance of power. There was no less crime, no elimination of corruption. It grew back like scum in a sewer, leeches in a swamp. He saw an innocence in David that was not ready to accept it.

"I will only tell you to keep out of French prisons, or any other prison for that matter." His answer was low, but firm, making it clear that he would say nothing more about it.

"I'll do that." David watched the tension leave his father's face when he accepted the answer. He was unconcerned about Marc serving time. He saw it as a dreadful mistake that had finally been righted. He looked forward for a moment, then asked, "Why the sunglasses?"

"You should know the answer to that. People remember my eyes. I can change my posture, my facial expression, even my gait and voice. I can't change my eyes any more than you can."

"They did more than hide your eyes." David wrinkled his nose. "They made you look dorky."

"Exactly dorky enough that no one paid attention to much else." Marc started to laugh. "And you didn't recognize me because you wouldn't admit you had a dorky father."

"Why didn't you want me to know you were here?"

"I liked it that way."

"Why was Liz killed?"

"She saw him."

"She saw him in November. He killed her in May."

"He was trying to do it slowly, or at least make her useless. When he saw her at the dance, he thought she recognized him. He was afraid she would remember it and mention it to you. After you left Liz, he called her in a fair imitation of you. I'll buy that. Colin's a good mimic. He told her to meet him by the pool —

something about the spring stars bringing on a case of the hards."

"Damn him!"

"She certainly had a hunger for it."

"You, too, huh?" David wasn't sure how that grabbed him, but it didn't surprise him.

"There are a few happenings in life that are jolting and drive home the fact that age is not just a word. One of them is when you're making love to woman and she calls you by your son's name."

David laughed with a needling chuckle. "Especially when she says, 'You're usually better.'"

"I thought she said I was improving."

"It's wine that improves with age, old man." David laughed and gave his father a puzzled look. "How do you know all this?"

"I had a long talk with Colin before you showed up. I asked him most of the questions you asked me."

"He told me he surprised you trying to pack up your bow."

"Right story, but twisted. A good liar uses the truth but makes it fit his story. Speaking of the bow," Marc nodded toward the boot behind the seats, "take it out of my pack and put it back in Colin's camera bag and tripod case. It fits. That's how he got it there."

When David started to open his seat belt so he could turn, he looked at the road, then at Marc. "Are you going to do anything crazy? I'd kind of like to stay with the car so the ambulance medics can find me."

"I'll be very cautious." He laughed when David gave him a skeptical look.

"So you caught Colin with the crossbow?"

"No. I took the crossbow yesterday afternoon. I've been tailing him a lot and suspected he was going to pull something at that jump. He planned it out, even rehearsed it before you showed up Thursday."

"He told me he was taking pictures."

"He took a lot of pictures."

"He also told me I didn't know half of it and to be careful."

"That's about the closest to a warning Colin ever gave out. I knew your time slot and planned to be in the cut long before you

started, but the police had the area under close watch. They'd
been giving me trouble all week, which is why I switched to the
cycle for a while. Yesterday, they were thicker than flies on horse
turds. I got desperate and ran a barricade with two of them after
me. Cost me a good Jeep."

"You paid for it?"

"Certainly. It's all right to scrounge plates or a few needed
extras." He winked. "Or borrow cars in emergency situations, but
I'm strictly petty. I don't get into grand larceny, unless its against
a bigger thief. I bought the Jeep in Texas last month. When I got
to St. Louis, I put on the Michigan plates I'd swiped last fall. The
sticker says they're good until June."

"That's the guy's birthday. They're due on the owner's
birthday."

"Sounds reasonable. Colin had stashed the bow after he shot
your horse—"

"Casey," David said in a quiet, husky voice.

"What?" Marc gave him a quizzical look.

"Casey. My horse's name was Casey Jones. He didn't just
shoot a horse. He shot Casey."

"Oh." He seemed to digest what David was saying. "I'm sorry.
I sometimes forget that losing your horse is not like losing my
Jeep."

"It's like losing a best friend, maybe more than that. But he
wasn't just a horse. He was Casey."

"I understand. After he shot Casey, he cut across the stream
and through the woods, so it looked as if he had come from
somewhere else on the course. He had his camera and tripod
cases with him. I knew he'd come back for the bow, so I waited for
him. He parked on Ridgeway Road and hiked over the ridge
because he suspected someone might be watching the farm roads."

"I didn't see anyone."

"Even if no one saw you, the gunshots will attract someone, so
Colin doesn't have much time to get out with your truck."

"Why didn't you nab him yesterday afternoon when he was
hiding the bow?"

"As I said before, he could pin it on me easier than I could pin
it on him. It would have been a damn fool thing to do. I couldn't

stop it, so I backed off. I confronted him last night, right after he discovered his weapon was gone. He wasn't happy to see me because I know his past too well, but he had guessed that I might be the mysterious stranger in the Jeep. We never did get along after he tried to ride me down on a `runaway' horse. It left me with an ass full of gorse bush and a bad feeling about Colin Trombley."

"Why'd he do that?"

"I told him I'd restructure his face if he didn't keep away from my wife."

"You were never married."

"It wasn't registered, but I always thought I was married."

"How did Colin get by that jump?"

"I made a mistake. I didn't expect him to have a gun. Colin has a bungling way of appearing to be unprepared and unwary. He's not. I should have known it. After he turned the tables and held a gun on me, he was not only willing to tell me the whole thing, he was excited about having an audience. He planned to kill me so he had no qualms about bragging on how cleverly he could kill me, then blame it all on me. Since I was in no hurry to die, I asked a lot of questions. I figured an opening would present itself if I waited long enough. Although, it may have been his intention to bore me to death."

"How did you get away?" David chuckled at the sense of humor that had always been a part of his father. No situation had ever seemed too serious for a joke when Marc was involved.

"We heard the truck. He turned just far enough I was able to kick him in the gut and roll away from him, taking the crossbow with me. Since he couldn't shoot while vomiting, I made it behind some rocks. Colin knew I had the bow and took off up the hill to the jump while I was getting it ready to shoot. He also knew I only had two bolts and wouldn't waste them, while he had a full magazine, maybe more, for his gun. Neither of us wanted to let the other get away. We had too much on each other. Then you came down the hill. He was trapped."

Mark paused, giving David a thoughtful look before he continued, "I guess you believed his story, which told him you didn't know who I was. I'm sure he felt he lucked into the ideal situation. He'd get you to shoot me. If I'd tried to say anything, he would have shot you right then. His bravery was a sham. He knew I didn't want to kill him. Dead men can't confess, and there's more evidence against me than him. A situation I hope to remedy as soon as possible."

"The son of a bitch knew he was setting me up to kill my own father."

"Certainly. Colin doesn't care about things like that. It's a sure bet he killed his own father. I thought he'd come back to be sure I was dead. He probably planned to kill you in a way that looked like suicide, which isn't untenable. You killed a man you thought was your enemy. When you found out it was your father, you killed yourself. A psychiatrist could go along with that by declaring you unstable at the time. Your best friend tried to kill himself, your girl was killed, your horse was killed under you, almost killing you, and you shot your father. Your strong emotions are no secret. It's not far-fetched."

"Is that why you fired the gun again?"

"I'm sure Colin left you alone so you would fall apart and then waited down the road, hoping you would do just that. I'm hoping the time factor keeps him from going back and finding we're not dead but gone. It's not in his pattern to check, and I'm sure he doesn't want to tangle with you angry while you have that gun."

"I can tell the truth. Isn't that enough evidence?"

"You can tell what I told you was the truth. He can find a way to turn it on me, so it doesn't much matter to him, especially if he thinks I'm dead. Colin has usually assumed his plans worked or didn't and waited for someone else to find the victim. He didn't check on Hugh. I'm sure he thought he was dead."

"But he did on Liz."

"Only because he wanted to give your mother a report and wanted it to be accurate."

"Why did he want to kill me?"

"You're too nosy. Your mother told him you knew too much, and you acted as if you knew too much, especially when you told him you knew all his secrets."

"I was referring to his affair with Mom."

"He didn't know that. He'd already planned how to do it.

When you said that, and your mother told him she could turn to you instead of him, he made it a positive. At that point, you became a man and a threat, not a boy to be reckoned with later. Colin can kill easily when he sees a reason, but he does feel guilt and fears discovery. When a person is guilty, he sees everything in relation to that guilt."

"That's for sure." David nodded.

"Hugh, Tim, and Liz were Colin's prime secrets and you said you knew them. He felt you were testing him the way your old man would have." Marc winked when David chuckled. "Colin is losing control and running scared. He had a simple plan when it all started. He found out about your grass racket and saw an opportunity. When it came, he acted in a way that would throw all suspicion on you or the people you were dealing with. If Hugh had died, Leon would have told the police why Hugh went after you. But Hugh didn't die and both he and Leon refused to tell the police the truth."

"Why?" David asked the question that had been agitating him for months.

Marc looked startled. "I imagine they did it to protect you."

"Why would Hugh want to protect me?"

"Because he isn't the bastard you think he is."

"Okay, I admit I was an asshole about that, but he pissed me off." David felt his face flush with humiliation. "It surprised me because if I'd been him, I would have thought I did it."

"The outcome was it left no trail and baffled the police because the shooting looked like the accident Hugh said it was."

"Why didn't Colin just let it go then?"

"He tried to, but this spring, you started getting nosy and Tim said a few things that unnerved Colin. Last Saturday Liz stared him right in the face. It made him paranoid. He's not too rational right now and is out to eliminate anyone who knows too much. But that's a never-ending spiral. The more people he kills, or tries to kill, the nosier people will get. He was ready to crack when he was with me and I think I pushed him over the edge. To Colin, I mean trouble. I know too much about him. And, like Dudley Do-Right, I have a reputation for getting my man."

"I told him Hugh felt he knew who did it."

"That's bad."

"But Hugh thinks it's 'the man in the Jeep.' He was almost sure it was you until yesterday. That blew his mind because he didn't believe you would try to kill your own son unless you were a psycho case."

"That's kind of him." Marc made wry face. "Colin will be very willing to help him believe that scenario. As long as Hugh doesn't suspect Colin, he should be all right. Beside, Hugh keeps Leon right near him. In view of all I've heard about Leon, Hugh should be safe. I wouldn't want to try to get past Leon, certainly not past both of them. They're sort of a two-man S.W.A.T. team."

"Leon is in jail."

"Of all the damn fool things, that has to be the stupidest." Marc's burst of anger startled David. "The damn asses left Hugh with shaky defenses."

"I suppose they're watching Hugh."

"But they're looking for me, not Colin Trombley."

"The police arrested Leon because he's an ace archer."

"So is Colin, but his acclaim is in England. Don't you remember the medieval fairs and contests he took your mother to? He even took you."

"Oh shit." David felt like an idiot. Of course he remembered. As a nine year old, he had found them exciting but had never put any importance on the fact that his mother returned to their room late at night. It was an adult matter that tired little boys paid no attention to. "That simple memory would have put it together. He was an excellent archer, especially with a crossbow. When Hugh told me it was a crossbow, I had a flashing memory of pageantry and knights. When he reminded me of Leon, I lost it. Leon's contests seemed more relevant and real. The other was a part of my imagination."

"Don't sell your imagination short. It's filled with insights and mind openers. Does Colin know Leon was arrested?"

"I told him that, too."

"It may throw things into overtime. He may be willing to take on Hugh without Leon around."

"Where are you going?" David was puzzled when Marc turned in the back driveway to Harrington's stable.

"We're going to put Colin's car in his garage where it belongs. I had a simple plan, which may still work. You are going to call one of those detectives and tell him you're sure it was Colin who shot your — shot Casey," Marc corrected himself. "If they're worth their pay when they search in the daylight, they'll find Colin's missing spur wedged between two rocks where he crossed the stream yesterday. They'll find the crossbow in his car. It's only circumstantial evidence, but it does amazing things to a guilty person. You can also tell them you confronted him and he stole your truck to get away."

"What about you?"

"I prefer to stay backstage, in the way of all stage managers."

"Why didn't Colin retrieve his spur?"

"He didn't lose it there. He lost it on purpose over by jump seventeen before he went to shoot Casey. That was to show that he'd run from that direction. I saw him formulate the idea in his rehearsal Thursday. I had a much better place for it, so I moved it."

"I thought you were watching me all the time."

"So did Colin. I made a lot out of tailing you, even your mother, to convince anyone I could that I was some kind of detective on your scent."

"It worked, except for Mom, who thought you were out to kill me."

"She always was paranoid about you." Marc gestured for David to open the door of the single garage under the porch of Colin's cottage that overlooked a small lake on Harrington's property. Inside the garage, he handed David a key and one of Detective Reed's cards. "Go up to the kitchen and call. You'll get the station. They'll find him fast enough when you tell your story. Put a little urgency into it and say you're at home. Make it quick. I want to get there as fast as we can."

"How?"

"You should have your wind back by now."

"We're going to run? It's twelve miles."

"By the roads, not through the trails."

"That's five tough ones. I can't do that."

"You could make it easily if you'd stop smoking those goddamn cigarettes."

"What pisses you, doesn't it?" David bickered.

"More than you can believe, but this is no time to fight over it, unless you want to get caught here and blow the scheme."

"Isn't he going to be suspicious when he finds his car in the garage?"

"He probably won't even look. Just do what I tell you. If I'm going to train you and take you on as my partner, you have to believe I know my trade. If he finds his car, he'll shit, but it won't matter. I'm betting he won't look in the garage unless you leave muddy tracks on the kitchen floor. Take off your shoes at the door then wipe up when you leave. Don't touch anything but the phone and do that delicately with this." He threw him a towel from the peg board over the workbench. "Colin's neat and meticulous. He always has been." He nodded toward the stairway to the kitchen and rummaged through the workbench drawers. "He should be damn surprised when the police find his car, with crossbow, in his garage."

"What are you going to do?"

"Fix his car so he can't move it if he does see it. Sometimes the name of the game is to delay all you can." He found a flat headed roofing nail, rolled a front tire over it, and smiled smugly at the slow hiss of released air. It only took a few seconds to remove the valve stem from the spare.

12

Sharon sat at the kitchen table with a coffee mug in her hands and stared out the window. She watched the new barn and arena grow out of the darkness as if they were being painted by an unseen brush against a background of morning mist. The farm was quiet, holding its breath for a moment of balance between night and day. She tried to believe in the magic of dawn the way she had as a child.

She remembered rising in the dark and racing to a hilltop behind her house so she could watch morning creep across the land. She had believed that if the fairies saw her in the first light of dawn they would listen to her wishes and make them come true. One whole summer she had asked the fairies to give her a new mother or make the one she had well again. Of course, there had been no fairies and her mother had been the same until she died. But sometimes, when she watched a new day begin, Sharon felt a moment of hope and was once again a child who looked for fairies dancing in the morning mist.

There were a lot of things Sharon wished the fairies could change today, but she was unable to glimpse a single fairy before the mist burned away and the buildings were substantial structures.

The sleeping pills had worn off a while ago, and she had been unable to go back to sleep. Rather than disturb Hugh with her restlessness, she got up and showered before coming downstairs for coffee. Hugh had been out when Sharon went to bed, and she had been dozy from the pills when he came to bed. She remembered him pulling himself from the wheel chair on the heavy bar above the bed. She had turned the covers aside for him, then snuggled her back against his chest while his arms held her tightly. He kissed her neck in the way that usually made her wiggle inside, even caressed her with hands that knew where to touch. She was unable to stay awake to make love or even talk to him. He sighed and told her he wished she wouldn't take sleeping pills. She had drifted back to sleep, cradled in his arms with her head on his chest.

The door to the dining room swung open, startling Sharon. She turned to see Hugh zip through the door and roll to the counter, where he poured himself a mug of coffee. When he parked beside her chair, she looked at him with guarded scrutiny to see if he was brooding. He seemed at ease, almost cheerful, more like he had been before the accident.

"I'm sorry about last night," she said. "I was too zonked to move."

"You needed the sleep. I just have this unpopular discomfort with drugs."

Sharon fought a scowl, but said nothing.

"I know my solution of drinking myself into a stupor wasn't a better answer, but it was something I was familiar with." When she gave him a curious look, he said, "A buzz of scotch-glow every night used to keep me from smacking the mouth off my first wife, who could find fault with everything from her treatment at the beauty parlor to how the carpet was cleaned."

"Maybe you should have." Sharon chuckled deep in her chest. "I would love to see Midge spitting blood with her perfectly straightened teeth knocked askew. A big, black eye would top it off just right."

"You're a vindictive thing, aren't you?" He gave her an awesome look. "Why does mention of Midge bring out the bitch in you?"

"Because I grew up with her. She always found fault with me, too. Midge Paxton shamed me every chance she had by blabbing about how everyone talked about my mother behind our backs.

Even after my mother was dead, Midge would find ways to bring it up, so everyone would know my mother was a shameless lush."

"Sounds like Midge all right. Sharon, after Nam, she came at me like she had honey on her tits. Since Papa Paxton was willing to buy our planes for his executive charter service, it all made sense. Four years later there was no sense left, but a few things to be ashamed of." His jaw tightened and he turned away from her to drop an English muffin into the toaster.

"What's wrong? All of a sudden you're uptight." Sharon usually ignored him when he looked that way. He would rarely give an open answer and bugging him turned him stiff-necked and cold — what David called hard-assed. "What could possibly matter about Midge?"

"It's not about Midge, really. It's about me."

"Why don't you tell me about it? Why don't you let some of these things out if they bother you? I don't expect you to be perfect. You act as if I'm not supposed to know you have misgivings or flaws. I love you. Tell *me* what bothers you instead of Leon."

He stiffened and met her questioning gaze. "There are some things I don't even tell Leon. I keep him near me as a bodyguard, not a confidant. We don't discuss my sins."

"Well, I need to, Hugh. Your awareness of them keeps coming between us."

He squared his shoulders for a moment and then let out a breath and slumped into the chair. "I did hit her. I didn't fight with her or slap her in a burst of temper. I was tired of her refusing to talk about a divorce. I pinned her to the bed and smacked her ass until she agreed to talk divorce on my terms."

"And she didn't try to crucify you with it? How unlike Midge."

"Nothing was ever said about it. She was docile and let me push through everything I wanted, regardless of what her lawyer said. It's probably the only thing in her life she ever kept her mouth shut about."

Sharon smirked. "It couldn't have happened to a more deserving ass."

"Sharon, it isn't funny." He snapped.

"Funny humorous, no. Funny satisfying, yes," she answered

firmly, then gave him a sympathetic look. "I'm sorry, Hugh. It's the thought that pleases me, not the reality. I don't mean to mock your feelings. You're right. It's wrong to do that."

"It's my own sort of rage. I can't stand defiance. When I forget to think, I do things like that to people."

"Like David? Is that what you're trying to tell me?"

"Yes, like David." He thumped his hand on the table and looked straight into her eyes, but something in him relaxed at the same time. "Nothing else worked. He just stared at me and shouted `No!' to everything I said. I blew up and used a riding whip on him. Christ, I thought he'd give in after a few whacks, but he wouldn't quit. Then I couldn't let him win. I get so damn wrapped up in the obsession to defeat that I can't pull myself out of it." He dropped his gaze from hers and stared at his coffee.

"He told me." Sharon slid her hand over his and squeezed until he looked at her. "David's compulsion to win is as strong as yours to defeat. It's a bad combination when it meets a no compromise situation. You're the more adult, maybe you could give a little and let him know there's no shame in negotiation, no failure in relenting."

"I keep forgetting that because he can dig into me so well."

"There's no dishonor in apologizing, either. You could have let him save some pride. That's all he needed."

"He upset me last night. He thought I was going to punish him when I had no such intention. I don't understand the kid. He resents me for being hard on him, but when I left him alone, he goaded me as if he was daring me."

"You made him betray himself. That's what he resents. You don't understand David and you don't understand Marc. You have your opinions and won't listen to anyone else. I admit I get bitchy about Midge, but that's because there are things between Midge and me that have nothing to do with you. Any mention of Marc raises your hackles. All you do is condemn him when you've never even met him. If I try to say anything positive, you get jealous and turn hard-ass on me, so I leave it alone. I loved Marc Breton, maybe I still do in one way or another."

The muscles in his face tightened. He jumped when the toaster popped beside him and stared, coldly and silently, into her eyes.

"But there is no way I'll leave you to go back to him. There's a lot more to my life with you than passion and adventure." She pressed his hand. "And there's enough of that, too. Butter your muffin before it gets cold. I'll see if there's any thimbleberry jam left."

Hugh watched her walk to the refrigerator. "Do you mean that, Sharon?"

"Of course I mean it. You're my choice. I made that decision yesterday after Colin Trombley made me think about it."

"Colin?"

"I had an affair with Colin once. He wanted to renew it. When I told him no, I realized it was because I love you. Don't be jealous of Marc. There's no reason for it." She set the jam on the table and nipped at his ear before she sat down. "No sleeping pills tonight. I promise."

"What don't I understand about David and Marc? I understand that David expected to be spoiled, his waywardness ignored. I'm not Marc Breton. I won't let him run around any where, any time he wants, breaking laws and acting like an arrogant brat."

"And you think Marc would?" She frowned when he nodded. "Hugh, that's where you're wrong about Marc."

"David was an arrogant, spoiled brat when he came here."

"No!" She slapped the table with her rebuttal. "He was an angry, misbehaved monster out to punish me for taking him away from his father. He behaved exactly the opposite of what Marc and I expected. Marc didn't spoil him. He loved him too much. He was totally open with David, spent a lot of time and patience on David. When I stole his son, I wronged Marc more than he ever wronged me. It was the cruelest thing anyone ever did to David, probably to Marc, too. I never should have taken David away from his father."

"In other words, you wish you'd stayed with him."

"That's not what I mean. Marc and I had about burned it out. I was selfish and didn't see it from David's view. I'd hoped you could fill his loss. You're like Marc in many ways."

"Not to David."

"No one is like Marc to David." She screwed up her face. "I'm not even sure Marc is. You could understand more if you would open up more often. Who told you it was weak and degrading to cry, or shameful to have good shouting battles and let it out? You pull it all in, so when it does come out, it's rage, and huge, and cruel. I thought you and David were going to let it loose this winter, but you buried it again. He took it as rejection and blame."

Hugh scowled. "I thought he wanted me to leave him alone."

"No, silly. David can't stand to be ignored. He wants his views recognized and a chance to bargain for his rights. He doesn't want to be treated like an unwanted lodger." She leaned over and kissed him. "When it comes to disputes, David's like I am. We'd rather fight than sulk."

"You're asking me to go against generations of proper, in control officers and gentlemen. I don't know if that's possible."

"Sometimes I think the word gentleman is a synonym for cop-out." She sighed, then sank back in the chair. "While we're on the subject of copping out, can I scratch from stadium without getting dirty looks for a week? I don't think I can take it."

"Sharon, we have to face things as if it was no more than a terrible accident. David's all right. We lost a good horse, but it doesn't stop the world."

"It puts a hell of a hole in mine. I'm in no shape to jump a horse."

"How about if I lunge him while you think on it? He needs to be lunged to loosen up whether you ride him or not."

"No stormy looks?"

"No sleeping pills?"

"It's a deal."

David and Marc were crossing Eminence Farm's west pasture when David started to drag behind his father. Stopping, Marc turned to face the boy, who was running awkwardly with slower and slower strides. When David started to weave, Marc ran to him and caught him by the arms before he fell.

"Just let me sit down." David tried to sink away from the

strong hands that held him up. He was dizzy. He weighed a thousand pounds. His chest hurt, his head hurt, everything hurt.

"What do you taste?" Marc's hands tightened on David's arms. "What does it taste like down at the bottom of your lungs? What is it, David?" He gave him a rough shake.

"All right! It's tobacco!" His shout made him cough and gag.

"It builds up. Every time you smoke, you put a little more in there. When you really need those lungs, they'll fail because you've destroyed them. We can walk a little, but I won't let you stop. You wouldn't let a horse stand after a run like that. You aren't any different."

"Do you ever get tired?"

"Certainly. I've been so wiped out I was euphoric — that was just before I passed out. I want you to work with me, but I can't use you if you can't take it. I rarely work with a partner, but I think I could work with you."

"I didn't know you worked." While they walked, David was able to breathe a little easier.

"You bet I work. Sometimes my life depends on it."

"You're no longer an agent. Is running cons work?"

"It can be damn hard work." Marc laughed. "But that isn't all I do now any more than it was then. It's a good cover and explains the lifestyle I need to lead. I work for a variety of causes from corporations to wronged old ladies. Some ask, some don't. Some pay, some don't. I do a lot of the same things I did before, but strictly free-lance. In Europe I worked for several police forces and government agencies, usually in drugs, smuggling, and jewel thefts. But the prison sentence, then the pardon blew any cover I had. I went private, but I'm still too well known where I don't want to be known. I thought I'd try my luck in the states for a while. I choose my jobs by my own criteria and do them my way."

"Sounds exciting." David's eyes were bright with interest.

"Sometimes. It's rarely boring. I hate boring. Prison was hell."

"Why did you quit soccer?"

"It got boring — not the game, the business of it."

"Did you come back for Mom?"

"I don't think she'd go back to me."

"She still loves you, even if she tries not to think about it."

"People change in five years. You can't back up and rerun the same script. It's all wrong."

"She thought you would come for us. She wanted you. I wanted you. Why didn't you come?" He grabbed Marc's arm and jerked him around to face him. "Why didn't you stop her? You let her run away and I hated you for it." The hurt let loose in a rage of tears, and he threw a powerful punch at his father. The blow hit air, then he fell forward, beating closed fists on Marc's hard chest. "Why didn't you help me?"

"I tried, David, but the world fell on me." Hard arms wrapped around David, clasping him to his father's chest. "Then I felt it was too late. I was sure I'd never see either of you again. Sometimes I felt I'd never see anything again."

"Dad, I'm sorry." Shuddering, David broke down and cried.

"Please, don't be sorry. I hate sorry. Almost as much as I hate boring. I like truth. I like love. You just gave me both." His arms tightened, sheltering David, absorbing his sobbing release.

While he lunged Limerick in one end of the new arena, Hugh studied the easy, free-moving trot. The horse showed no stiffness, no sign of unsoundness. The vertically striped hooves fell rhythmically into place with the hind hooves tracking into the prints of the fore hooves. Hugh was pleased, contented, while he listened to the soft, echoing ker-thumps of the even strides in the empty arena. It was a relaxing sound that told his experienced senses almost as much about a horse's condition as its appearance and behavior.

Hugh was in the large wheel chair, holding the long, woven lunge line and whip in gloved hands while the horse trotted around him on a comfortable, twenty meter circle. The chair was lifted off its wheels onto a swivel base that rotated on quiet roller bearings to keep its occupant facing the circling horse. Hugh could adjust the speed and direction of rotation with controls on the right of a swing away console board in front of him. Controls for operating with the wheels down were on the left. Although the whole contraption looked like something out of science fiction, it did the job, and Hugh had become skilled in its operation. He had converted his rider's ability to form a physical bond with a horse to the chair until its mechanism was a part of his involuntary muscle control and responded to his reflexes. He could handle the chair, the coil of lunge line, and the long whip skillfully enough to feel confident, even with young horses with unpredictable natures.

When the door from the stable aisle opened and closed, Hugh looked down the arena at Colin. "Good morning. What brings you here so early?"

"I brought back your truck." Colin ducked under the line when Limerick trotted past him.

"I didn't know you had my truck."

"I took the Ford after I brought Limerick home. I asked that redheaded kid who was painting jumps to tell you."

"That bozo would forget his ass if it wasn't following him around."

"How's David?"

"I don't know. He's still asleep. I doubt if he's in a hurry to go to an event he's out of, especially the way he was eliminated."

Hugh glanced at Colin, then back at the horse. He knew there was no reason for it, but since Sharon had confessed to her affair with Colin, it was impossible to accept him casually. It made him bitter. It even started to make him suspicious about a few unanswered questions concerning Colin.

"You never know what's going to happen, do you, Colin? Who would think a horse as tough, sound, and skilled as Casey would go down like that? It's as big a plug of fate to swallow as some asshole shooting at anything that moves in the hope of hitting a deer on posted land. Too much bad medicine makes a man look for answers. Sometimes the answers don't come until one thing fits into place."

Colin kept his eyes on the horse and walked a slow circle while Hugh snapped the whip and talked the horse into a longer trot. A tense muscle twitched, just above Colin's jawbone, but he nodded with calm agreement.

"A lot of people would have me cast a suspicious eye on David, then give Leon the job of removing David," Hugh said. "But there's no truth in that, is there?"

"I can't see it, but there is merit in it, I suppose."

"Not a hell of a lot. It makes more sense to suspect a man who wants my wife and her wealth. That makes me look for someone who has already had my wife and feels he can re-interest her."

"Then you also feel the nameless man with the beard is Marc Breton?" Colin gave him a judging look and, again, ducked under the sweeping line before Hugh swiveled away from him.

"I can't convince myself he would try to kill his son. It's someone else." Hugh waited until he was again facing Colin before he asked, "Can you tell me who?"

"No." The Englishman shrugged and answered calmly, "I can't imagine Sharon having a lover. She's far too loyal a person."

"Maybe now, but maybe not to a man who was not loyal to her."

"Why the vaulting surcingle?" Colin asked, pulling Hugh away from his line of thinking with a casual disinterest that made Hugh feel he was chasing the wrong rabbit again.

Hugh looked at Limerick, who was wearing a lunging cavesson, fitted with a plain snaffle bit, on his head. The long line Hugh held was attached to a ring on the front of the padded noseband. Limerick was also wearing a vaulting surcingle around his girth instead of a simple lunging surcingle or a saddle. It was wide and heavy with leather-covered steel handles. Riders could vault on from the ground and do the gymnastics on horseback that was called voltige and had evolved into circus bareback riding. Voltige was widely used in Europe to develop balance and suppleness in the rider.

"Sharon's tack is in the trailer. That was available. Do you vault?"

"I used to. How's the horse?"

"David says he's good. Try him."

Colin barely waited for Hugh to finish speaking before he started toward Limerick. While the horse trotted around the circle, the slender Englishman ran up beside him. He matched his speed to the gelding's, then grabbed a handle and vaulted to the broad back. He landed astride, kicked his feet up behind him and touched his heels together. When he dropped back onto the horse, he landed awkwardly and hard enough that his face twisted in pain.

"Not bad, but I think *used to* was the way to put it." The grimace of agony erased Hugh's apprehensions. He decided that if Colin was this rusty at voltige he was going to put on a brief but enjoyable performance.

Balancing himself in a comfortable sitting trot, Colin pointed at the looped reins clipped to the surcingle. "Can I put the side reins on to collect him a bit?"

"It might make it more comfortable. Walk, Limerick."

Colin leaned forward to clip the reins to the bit rings just below the tight, padded noseband. When attached to the surcingle, the side reins would hold the neck arched and round the horse under its rider, keeping it from hollowing its back. After the side reins were attached to the bit in Limerick's mouth, Colin sat up, holding them like riding reins instead of clipping the loose ends to the surcingle. It confused Hugh for a moment, but only for a moment.

A flash of revelation alerted Hugh an instant before Colin turned the horse. With a sudden kick, Colin sent the animal straight toward the wheel chair in a leaping gallop. There was no confusion now. Colin's intention was schematically clear in Hugh's mind. It would be a believable accident. In fact, it was something he had thought about many times since he had lost his mobility. A horse could easily spook and charge into the chair before he could drop its wheels and get out of the way. If the lunge line became entangled in the chair, the horse was likely to trample him in its panic. After such an accident, it would be hard to determine how he had received the coup de grace.

Acting in reflex, Hugh cracked the whip in the horse's face. Limerick slid to a stop and reared in surprise, but Colin clung to the white mane and forced the animal down and forward. The striking forelegs just missed the chair that dropped to its wheels when Hugh released pressure in the hydraulic cylinder beneath the seat.

Hugh swung the whip again, making the horse shy away from him, but the image of the rearing horse's underbelly and shod hooves towering over him hung in his mind like a terrifying premonition. He threw the line away before it could tangle in the chair and slashed the whip at Colin, hoping to unbalance him enough that the horse would throw him in its panic to get away from the zinging, snapping lash that cracked like gunshots. The pinto reared and tried to wheel away from the whip, but Colin clung to his mane and was able to force him forward with strong legs and a driving seat.

Hugh met the Englishman's eyes and saw the starkness of fear and madness distorting the gaunt face. In that instant of contact, he knew Colin had snapped beyond reasoning and would kill him unless he stopped him. The knowledge sharpened Hugh's battle conditioned instincts until he felt an electrifying jolt of danger pump adrenaline into his blood.

At the last instant, when the horse shied away from the chair, Colin caught the lash and wrapped it around a handle on the surcingle. The horse's weight ripped the whip away from Hugh, giving Colin both the whip and control of the horse. Hauling back on the reins, Colin wheeled the big pinto on his haunches and charged toward Hugh. The heavy, butt end of the whip arced away from the horse like a polo mallet while Hugh backed the chair toward the nearest door. The speed of the electric drive was slow and no match for the excited horse.

With retreat impossible, Hugh knew he would have to make a stand. His first weapon was his knowledge of this horse. His second would be his strength, if he could get a hand on his assailant. He also knew he only had to fear the man, not the horse. If he refused to move, Limerick would either jump him or swerve around him, but, even knowing this, he had to force down the fear goading him into reckless flight. Exerting his will against panic, Hugh made himself stop the chair and remain calm while the broad-chested animal bore down on him at a pounding gallop.

Hugh knew Colin was a strong rider, but Colin didn't know Limerick. The horse was a bold jumper. He was also a nasty quitter. When he lost his confidence, or was frightened by an obstacle, he snaked his head down, took control over his rider, and ducked out to the left. His runouts were sudden with no warning. Better riders than Colin had been left in the dirt beside fences Limerick disliked.

At the last instant, Hugh threw up his arms and shouted.

Predictably, the pinto spooked around the narrow chair, but Colin stayed on his back by dropping the reins and grasping the far handle of the surcingle.

"Shit!" Hugh shouted when he saw Colin dive forward, retrieve one of the loose reins, and haul the horse around in a tight circle. "Keep away from me, you crazy son of a bitch."

When Colin charged him again, Hugh grabbed for the whip handle that swooped toward him. If he could get a hold on the whip, he could either jerk Colin off the horse or regain possession of his only hope for a material weapon. He got a hand on it, but Colin kicked out when he passed, catching Hugh in the temple and knocking him sideways in the chair. Hugh's hand closed on air and the horse's haunches crashed into the wheel chair.

The machine skittered sideways before it rocked onto one wheel and toppled over, throwing Hugh onto the arena floor, sprawled out and dizzy. He forced himself to his elbows. Pain exploded in his head with a shimmer of colors. In pulsing vertigo, he saw the fuzzy image of a man race across the arena. He brought him into focus in time to see him dive for Colin in a powerful leap. Everything went brilliantly white, totally black, and he crumpled to the floor.

There was something about the shape of the hill that had brought the sound to Marc. It was clear and loud — a shout of alarm, the thud of uncontrolled hoof beats. He spun from David and bolted toward the arena that was just below him across a fenced lane. He heard David behind him, but there was no time to wait. He sucked in deep breaths, pushing into an all out run. After hurdling two panel fences, he sprinted across the gravel stableyard and skidded into the barn aisle.

When Marc yanked open the walk-in door to the arena, he saw Hugh tumble from his chair and force his upper body to a half-sitting position. A huge brown and white horse charged the fallen man.

Marc's shoulder drove into Colin's side. He knocked him off the horse when his dive took him clean over the animal's back. They landed, locked together, on the deep sand and tanbark floor, where they grappled in a desperate tangle. Colin's knee found Marc's groin and dug into it when he rolled over him. Marc jerked from pain that weakened him long enough for Colin to scramble away and snatch up the whip he had lost when he had fallen from the horse. The lash snaked out and cracked on Marc's back. It bit into him while he rolled with the groin pain that was surging through him in waves of nausea. The sharper pain of the whip arched him but cleared his head with a flash of adrenaline spurred rage.

In spite of the cutting snaps, Marc willed himself to his knees, then his feet, and lurched toward Colin. The whip cracked on the side of his neck, arms, and chest while his assailant backed away. Colin was frantically trying to keep Marc at bay with the whip in his right hand while his left hand fumbled at his waist.

Marc never faltered in his advance toward Colin. "I'll get you, Trombley. I came too far for this. You won't stop me."

"You're dead, Breton. Get away from me. Christ, don't you ever die?"

When Marc shook away the weakness and gained speed, Colin flailed the whip at him and turned to run, still jerking at the closed holster strapped inside his belt. It was well concealed, but awkward, not meant for an emergency draw. Just before Marc's hand could close on the whip arm, Colin dove sideways. He worked the small automatic pistol free while he rolled and fired as soon as he was on his feet.

The gunshot echoed in the steel-sheathed arena. Marc staggered, but refused to go down. His right arm knocked Colin's hand up and the next shot tore a hole in a fiber glass skylight under the eaves. Marc's left arm hung useless. Blood dripped off his hand, but he clenched his jaw against the pain that wrenched at his stomach. He spun and kicked, smashing a running shoe up under Colin's chin, sending him reeling away from him. The effort weakened him, and he staggered in a spinning, black and white world.

The whip cracks, the commotion, the gunshots added to Limericks's fright. He continued to tear around the arena with the long lunge line trailing behind him until he spotted the open door and ran for it. When David burst into the arena in front of him, the horse slid to a stop and stood tensed with his forelegs spread, his head thrown high.

David grabbed the lunge line and gathered it in large loops. He was confused when he saw Colin backing toward him away from Marc. He saw the gun when Colin raised his arm, aiming at Marc's face.

David leapt forward. He threw the coils of line over Colin's head like a lariat and spiraled the loose end around him like a shroud. His motions spooked the horse and it bolted forward with scrambling strides.

The lunge line snapped taut with the loops around Colin's neck and one shoulder, staggering him sideways. For an instant, while the coils tightened, the raised arm and the discharging gun lingered behind the stumbling man with disembodied surrealism. The line yanked Colin off his feet, dragging him behind the terrified horse, whose instinct was to run from danger, run for his life with the panic of the hunted.

Colin grasped for the line, but it was beyond his reach. In desperation, he tried to shoot the running horse, but he was bouncing and jerking. He careened off the wooden kick boards and somersaulted in the churned sand while the horse tore around a corner. The gunshots were wild and frightened the horse into a faster, more terrified run. The lunge line made its last slip — off the shoulder, around the neck. Colin jerked and thrashed for a few seconds, then was a motionless burden to the bolting horse.

A louder shot from across the arena severed the cotton line and freed the horse, leaving what looked like a bundle of bloody, sand-crusted rags in a heap on the arena floor.

Leon lowered the police revolver and handed it to Detective Reed before he ran to Hugh, who had dragged himself to where Marc had collapsed. Hugh was holding Marc across his lap while his strong fingers stopped the flow of blood that pulsed out of a bullet track on the inside of Marc's upper arm.

David ran to Limerick, grabbed the surcingle, and vaulted to his back. He let him run down the boards before he eased him down to a nervous walk. When he slid off, the horse was drenched with sweat, wild-eyed, and trembling. The animal blew harshly through red-lined nostrils when David handed the truncated line to Matt Stone, who had arrived with Sharon.

David saw his mother standing in the doorway. Her face was blanched, her dark eyes as round and terrified as the horse's. He ran to her, sliding his arm around her waist. When he felt his legs buckle, he tightened his arm and they steadied each other.

"It's all over, Mom. He said we'd get him, and we did."

"Who?" Sharon asked while she walked beside David. Her eyes met Hugh's, then shifted to the bearded face with smears of blood, dirt, and sweat. She saw the slightly off center jog of nose and thick-lashed, violet-blue eyes. "Marc? What are you doing here?"

"Bleeding to death. He can't hold it forever. Would someone get something clean and put a pressure bandage on the damn thing?" His clear, sure order broke the static trance.

David ran for clean bandages while Sharon ripped Marc's sleeve open. Leon helped Hugh into the wheel chair when Detective Reed replaced Hugh's hold on the pressure point above the torn artery. Detective Stanwyck hunkered beside Colin.

"Who are you?" Reed asked Marc.

"I'm David's father. Marc Breton."

"We have a list of offenses against you — stolen plates, running a police blockade—"

"Detective," Hugh's powerful voice filled the arena, "he caught your killer and saved my life. I wouldn't be pleased if it caused him any more inconvenience than he's going to have with that arm."

"That man is dead." Detective Stanwyck stopped beside his partner. "We can't be sure he was the one we wanted."

"I can," Hugh answered with the tone of command that was final and meant, "Don't argue with me because I can make you regret it."

"Yes, Mr. Jamison." The policemen gave him an awed look before they hurried to their car to radio for an ambulance.

When David hunkered beside his mother with clean bandages, he winked at Hugh. "I never thought I'd be glad you're such a hard-ass."

"You'll probably start thanking him for a lot more when you start playing my games." Marc winced when Leon twisted a tourniquet tight above the wound.

"What does that mean?" Sharon eyed Marc suspiciously while she pressed a wad of sterile gauze in the wound. She held it while David wrapped a clean bandage around it.

"I want my son back. I'd like to see some of the American West and hike in the Rockies. I thought I'd take him off your hands for the summer."

"Not yet. He isn't out of school until June tenth. And if he doesn't quit cutting classes, he'll have to go to summer school."

"Oh shit." The jolt of mundane reality made David gape at his parents.

"I'll be here on June eleventh." Marc glared at David, his expression set with no-argue firmness. "You better be free with a decent grade report. And if you're still smoking those damn cigarettes, you may learn where the concept of hell came from."

Smiling smugly, Sharon sat back on her heels. "Haven't changed a bit, have you?"

"Oh, a bit here and there. I just hope you didn't run around with anyone else. Your old lovers are hard to get even with."

"That should be my line." Hugh set his hand on Sharon's hair and tousled it affectionately. "It's extremely hard when he plays hero and saves my life."

"There's nothing to get even with. You have her." Marc gave Sharon a long, penetrating look before he added. "And that's the way she wants it."

Hugh cupped a hand on his wife's shoulder in a protecting, yet possessive, gesture. "She's right. You're a charming son of a bitch."

Marc laughed with a deep, rolling chuckle. "She's half right, as usual."